The
Widow's
Walk

The Widow's Walk

Robert Barclay

An Imprint of HarperCollins*Publishers*

HarperCollins books may be purchased for educational, business, or sales promotional use. For information, please e-mail the Special Markets Department at SPsales@harpercollins.com.

FIRST HARPERLUXE EDITION

HarperLuxe™ is a trademark of HarperCollins Publishers

Library of Congress Cataloging-in-Publication Data is available upon request.

ISBN: 978-0-06-227866-1

14 ID/RRD 10 9 8 7 6 5 4 3 2 1

The long, unmeasured pulse of time moves everything.
There is nothing hidden that it cannot bring to light,
nothing once unknown that may not become known.
Nothing is impossible.
—SOPHOCLES

The Widow's Walk

Prologue

New Bedford, Massachusetts
September 1840

Her name was Constance Elizabeth Canfield, and for as long as she could remember, she loved gazing at the ocean.

No matter the weather, Constance found the froth-topped waves reassuring and filled with promise. In her world she could rely upon few things, but the waves were always there. She loved their consistency of purpose, and their constant determination to assault the rocky shoreline that lay so near her house. She also found them exciting, because they would one day bring her husband back to her. So she patiently watched and waited as they worked their welcome magic on her lonely soul.

She had invented an enticing fantasy in which she sometimes indulged while watching those never-ending waves. She liked to imagine that one of them had actually touched the hull of her husband's ship, no matter on which of the earth's four corners the vessel had been venturing. And, like some God-sent message in a bottle, that same wave had somehow reached her shoreline to confirm that her husband remained alive and well. Sometimes she would even pick out one such wave, thus pretending so, and watch it closely until it destroyed itself against the rocks.

These imaginings were pure foolishness, of course. But she had not received a letter from Adam for a long time, and such dreams—silly as they might seem to others—were important to her. One had to be the wife of a whaling captain to understand.

Now, she stood on the porch of Seaside, her home on the ocean. She had put her blond hair up, but the strengthening wind had caused several errant strands to caress her face. The weather was threatening, so she had donned a comforting shawl because sometimes the seawater would splash against the rocks so forcefully as to mist her porch. This was not yet one of those days, but her instincts said that it soon would be.

Just then she heard a pair of gulls cry out, and she looked up to see their feathered underbellies as they soared high above the coastline. They seemed to ride the air currents effortlessly. *If only those ocean winds could make Adam's return to me so simple as well,* Constance thought.

Given the worsening weather, she had known that she would become damp and windblown. Even so, she would not be dissuaded from this twice-daily ritual, these interludes with which she always fortified herself, just before climbing the stairs to the widow's walk that graced the roof of her beloved home. She realized without looking that the sun had nearly set, and as the wife of a sea captain she always knew the time of day without the need of a clock. Before she lost the light, she would take up her husband's old brass spyglass and make yet another hope-filled pilgrimage; the same journey she had made each morning and evening, every day, for the last two years.

Constance lovingly touched the scrimshaw locket that hung about her neck on a gold chain. Adam had made it himself during his previous voyage. She opened it, and for the thousandth time since Adam's latest departure, Constance looked at the small portrait that lay inside. He was a handsome man, with a dark beard and welcoming brown eyes.

Adam had been first mate aboard her father Benjamin Monroe's ship. Benjamin, also a whaling captain, had taken an immediate liking to Adam. Their marriage was arranged by their parents, and it had not been love at first sight for the nervous bride. Adam was thirty, she had been twenty-four. But to her surprise and delight she soon came to love him deeply. He was strong and kind, and he treated her well; qualities that her unmarried woman friends had long searched for in men, but never found. Constance's lone heartache was that she was thirty-two now, and still childless.

She closed her eyes for a time while remembering her wedding night. She had possessed no illusions about whether Adam had been with other women before. He was a roguishly handsome sea captain who had sailed much of the world, and she would have been very much surprised to learn otherwise. As for her, she had come to the marriage untouched, and to this day Adam was the only man she had ever known. That first night, he had shown her the jagged scar that lay upon his left upper arm, the product of a fellow crew member's mishandled harpoon. To his pleasant surprise, Constance had immediately found it endearing. Because it was a part of him, she had said, it would also be a part of her love for him.

With help from his father, John, she and Adam had purchased their large house by the sea, just outside the town of New Bedford. They had thought long and hard about what to call it, and at last they decided on a name that was simplicity itself. "Seaside." Very soon after moving in, Seaside and Adam became Constance's entire world.

Before her marriage, Constance had been a very successful midwife, a valuable skill taught to her by her late mother. Several times a year, women of Bedford would still call upon her talent, and it was a service that she loved doing. She never charged a fee because she always considered it to be a privilege seeing a new child brought into the world. She was very good at what she did, but occasionally a child would be lost despite her best efforts. And although that broke her heart, she had no choice but to accept it.

Even so, Constance had few regrets in life. She lived in a beautiful home, and she and Adam lacked for little, provided she judiciously handled the funds he always left in her care. She had many friends in town. Nonetheless, she mourned her lack of children, for they would have fulfilled her and greatly assuaged her loneliness.

She worried what would become of Seaside should she and Adam die childless. If that occurred, the house might one day fall into disrepair, because it needed constant attention due to its nearness to the sea. She smiled slightly as she thought about Adam forever scraping and painting every time he was home. In a way, Seaside had become their child, their mutual object of love and attention. The house had been neglected when they bought it, and returning Seaside to its former glory was hard and expensive work. Nevertheless, Adam had toiled diligently, sometimes hiring idle whalers to help him. Now Seaside was a beautiful, comfortable home, and Constance loved living here.

As the daylight waned, the oil lamps hanging on the back wall of the porch seemed to glow brighter because of it, their comforting radiances causing her to smile. Those burned whale oil, harvested by Adam and brought to Seaside for their personal use. Whenever Constance filled the many house lamps she again thought of him, the emotions coursing through her heart always bittersweet. So far he had always returned. Even so, entire crews were sometimes lost during their hunts for the great whales, and every time Adam put to sea she feared that she might never see him again.

She then thought of the guesthouse that lay on their property some fifty yards west of the house proper and of Eli, Emily, and James Jackson, the three Negroes living there. Eli and Emily were husband and wife; James their young son of eight years. Adam's father had been a southern tobacco farmer who freed his slaves and came north to New England to find a more honorable way of life. Although emancipated, Eli and Emily chose to come with John and his wife, Clarice.

With the passing of Adam's parents, Adam had offered the Jacksons continued employment and lodging in the guesthouse. Eli and James maintained Seaside and her grounds, while Emily helped Constance with the cleaning and cooking. But even though the Jacksons provided a constant presence in Constance's life, her deep loneliness for Adam continued unabated.

Just then Constance remembered the huge, bright red pennant she had made for Adam before he departed on his current voyage. She spent many nights sitting by the fire, hand sewing that piece of fabric, all the while teasing Adam slightly by refusing to tell him why. Only upon finishing her work did she allow him a proper look at it, telling him that on his return to the harbor, she wanted him to fly it from the very top of the mainmast. She could then charge her carriage straight for the wharves without a second to lose. Even so, for more than two years there had come no ship bearing such a pennant. Her loneliness had become so acute that she had begun wondering whether it had all been a dream—the making of the pennant, her giving it to Adam, and even his promise that he would indeed fly it when he returned to her.

Suddenly feeling foolish, Constance shook her head. *No,* she realized. *I did make that pennant. I also know in my heart that one day I will see it flying from my love's mainmast, announcing his long-awaited return . . .*

As the wind rose and the sky darkened, she took a moment to look down at her dress. The pink leg-of-mutton sleeves and broad skirt accentuated her narrow waist, which lay imprisoned by stiff, whale-bone corseting. On her feet she wore low, square-toed slippers made of fabric. She always dressed formally, though her friends would tease her about it. Constance would only smile and tell them it was because she enjoyed dressing this way, but in truth there was a secret reason for it. When Adam's ship finally appeared, she wanted to waste no time preparing.

At last she picked up the brass spyglass that lay on the neighboring chair. *It is time,* she thought.

After taking another wistful look at the waves, she finally left the porch and went into the house, where she lit each of the first-floor lanterns. With her spy-glass and a lantern in hand, she climbed the set of stairs leading to the widow's walk. Putting her items down on an old table that stood there, she cast her hope-filled gaze across the restless sea.

By now, the sky had darkened, and it had begun raining. The waves were stronger, striking the rocky

shore with even greater intensity and literally exploding into infinite numbers of salty droplets. After again
gathering her woolen shawl closer, she pulled open the
old telescoping spyglass and put it to one eye.

Although protected from the rain by a shingled roof,
Constance knew that the worsening weather would
make searching the harbor difficult. The rain was
coming nearly sideways, stinging her face and soaking
her dress. Even so, she would not be dissuaded from
her task. Hoping to improve her view, she stepped
closer to the railing, but the darkness and the raindrops
collecting upon the lens of her spyglass conspired to
make searching the harbor increasingly difficult.

Some moments later, Constance caught her breath
when she saw a tall ship nearing, her great bulk being
cast up and down at the waves' behest as if she were
some child's bath toy. Nevertheless, as Constance
searched further she saw no bright red pennant flying
at the mainmast, and her heart sank. Deciding to search
another area of the harbor, she leaned against the railing while still holding the spyglass in place.

What Constance did not know was that over the
years, this particular section of her widow's walk railing had grown rotten and weak from the constant
assaults by the salty sea air. As she leaned against it,
the railing suddenly gave way, giving her no chance to

catch herself. Screaming, she tumbled end over end as she fell, first striking the roof of the porch she had just left and then crashing headlong onto the jagged shoreline rocks.

As the light left her eyes, her final thoughts were of Adam.

His name was Adam James Canfield, and for as long as he could remember, he had always loved being on the ocean.

Half a world away, Adam rubbed his weary eyes and leaned back against his desk chair. He had been writing a letter to Constance and because he could not be sure about when they might next put in, he knew that there was a good chance he would arrive home before the letter did. After staring down at the written page for a few moments more, he decided to finish it later. He never wrote well when he was tired, and he always wanted to properly convey not only his great love for his wife, but also his reassurances that he was remaining true.

This had been a long voyage and he was tired right down to his bones. His fatigue was not entirely the sort that one earned from honest labor. Rather, it was an insidious anxiety that had plagued him for nearly two years now; a strange ennui that even he could not properly describe. It would end only when he at last walked back down the gangplank in New Bedford and took Constance into his arms. He desperately needed to be home, as did every other man aboard this whaler.

Adam was captain of the American whale ship *Intrepid,* a 299-ton vessel out of New Bedford, Massachusetts. Owned by the Simon Pettigrew & Sons Whaling Company, she had set sail in June of 1838 and headed straight for the South Atlantic, where the hunting had been poor. With the *Intrepid's* hold still empty and her crew grumbling about their lack of success, Adam had decided to round Cape Horn and then sail on into the Pacific Ocean. Navigating the Cape was always a treacherous business, and it had taken the *Intrepid* a full ten days to cross as she braced the infamous winds. And the return leg, Adam knew, was even more dangerous.

From there they had gone on to ply the waters off Australia, where the hunting had been much better. Now some two years later, and with her hold filled with barrels of sperm oil and whalebone, the *Intrepid* was at last on her way home. By Adam's reckoning, the dreaded Cape was less than one day's sail from their current position.

On replacing the quill into its inkpot, he walked across his small stateroom where he lay down upon the narrow bed, thinking. It was late evening and he watched the glowing whale oil lanterns hanging from the ceiling as they swayed in time with the rocking ship.

Despite its profitability, this expedition had not been an easy one. Given the initially poor hunting in the Atlantic, some of the crew had grown dangerously restless, forcing Adam and his first mate to take up arms and return order to the ship. Mutinies were rare on whaling ships, but not unheard of. Even so, Adam had known that had they not successfully rounded the Cape and soon found good hunting, the situation would have worsened. But now each man would fare well in the take. Adam was glad for that, because he knew how hard they had worked, and the kind of joyous pride he would see in their eyes when the *Intrepid* finally reentered New Bedford Harbor.

On some of his previous voyages the crew members had not been so lucky. Because they often bought their clothing, tools, and sundries on credit, many of the poor devils were already in debt even before their ship set sail. If the voyage was unsuccessful, it was conceivable that some might return home without enough share of the take to set accounts right. Because of that, most of those same men were forced to immediately sign onto yet another risky voyage, leaving them barely enough time to kiss their wives and sweethearts "hello" and then "good-bye."

Given the terrible living conditions on board a whaling vessel, Adam had always thought it a wonder that so many men remained willing to risk their lives chasing and killing the great beasts. He ate well, but the crew's rations ranged from unpleasant to outright revolting. Worse, life aboard a whaling ship was largely repulsive. Rats, cockroaches, bedbugs, and fleas were facts of life, their continual presences owing to the residual whale offal and blood. Injuries and illnesses were commonplace, and it was usually the captain who tended to the men, using his limited knowledge and whatever supplies were available at the time. He did his best, but the results were often far from favorable.

There was also the terrible nature of the job at hand—the chasing and killing of the whales, the stripping of their flesh, the boiling of it to create whale oil, and the grisly harvesting of their bones for the making of such seeming trivialities as women's corsets and children's toys. And although as captain he did not participate directly, the overseeing of it was horrible enough. Accidents abounded, as was evidenced by the jagged scar on Adam's left arm.

As if those hardships were not torture enough, there was yet another deprivation that many of the men considered the worst of all. For two long years they had been without the comforts of their wives, mistresses, and lovers. There were always whores in the ports, but their lurid services were expensive, short-lived, and often dangerous. Adam had indulged during earlier days, but since their wedding day he had been ever faithful to Constance.

Constance, he thought, . . . *my beloved Constance . . .*

Reaching under his shirt, he produced the scrimshaw locket that was the exact duplicate of the one Constance wore, and he opened it to admire her likeness. She was a beautiful woman, with long blond hair and a lush body that caused a deep hunger within him every time he thought of her. After staring at her portrait for a time, he at last slipped the precious locket back under his shirt.

He then left his bed and walked across the cabin, where he produced a ring of keys from his trousers. After unlocking his sea chest, he removed the great red pennant that Constance had fashioned for him just before he left on this voyage. Holding the pennant against his face, Adam tried to smell the last traces of the perfume with which Constance had laden it the night before his departure. He could barely sense it now. But even this faintest of scents helped make it seem as if she were really there; her firm body pressed against his, her soft cheek lying gently on his shoulder. With great reluctance he finally refolded the precious pennant and locked it back in the chest.

Soon, now, my love, he thought. *Soon the* Intrepid *will enter the harbor, and from our widow's walk you will at last see your bright red pennant flying proudly from my mainmast. Even so, there is something that you do not know. When I return home I will tell you that this is my last whaling voyage, for I can bear this life no longer. It is not just my terrible loneliness for you that fostered this decision, but also my ever-increasing loathing for the awful things we do aboard these ships. I remain unsure about how we will live, but I will find a way. All I know for now is that I will never again leave your side.*

In truth, Adam's disgust for his occupation had been growing for years. So much so that the grisly realities of whaling now seemed nothing more to him than a grotesque tragedy designed to slaughter God's greatest of beasts with an arrogance that only mankind could muster. His mind made up, he would do no more of this. He believed that Constance would be overjoyed to hear of his decision, however that was small comfort, because his worries about their financial future haunted him day and night. *But first,* he thought glumly, *we must again survive the rounding of Cape Horn.* Just then Adam knew that something was amiss. Like any sea captain worth his salt, he sensed the impending danger well before being told about it.

Perhaps it had been the oil lamps in his cabin swaying excessively, or the extraordinarily loud and sudden moaning of the mast timbers. Or it could have been the unusually swift rise and fall of the ship's bow. In the end the reasons mattered not, because just as he realized the arrival of the impending gale, he heard the first mate shout out: "All hands on deck! Batten down the hatches!"

After frantically donning his rain gear, Adam tore from the cabin and hurried topsides. The sky was pitch-black, and his crew was already scurrying about the deck and up the masts. His helmsman, a man he had known for some twenty years, was doing his best to hold the ship's wheel steady against the growing storm. The sea was quickly turning into a black maw of ferocious power, its rising waves rivaled only by the terrible wind and stinging rain that now mercilessly pounded the ship. Without warning the masts shuddered horrifically again, and the *Intrepid*, her sails straining to their utmost, heeled dangerously to port as a huge sidelong wave nearly engulfed her. With her heavily laden hull groaning torturously against the pressure, she finally righted again.

Mere moments later, the storm unleashed her full intensity and the *Intrepid* became totally ensnared in her power. Adam went to help the helmsman hold fast the wheel, but even then it was all the two of them could do to keep it from spinning out of their hands. Adam knew that there was but one prudent course of action during a storm of such ferocious strength. He immediately lashed down the rain-soaked wheel amidships with heavy rope. The only way to survive such a maelstrom was to keep the rudder neutral then haul in the sails and let her go where she will, hoping that she could ride out the storm.

"Reef the sails, lads!" he screamed, trying his best to be heard above the raging storm. "And restrain all the booms, if you wish to survive!"

Suddenly terrified that his navigation had been imperfect, Adam now feared that they were uncontrollably nearing the dreaded Cape. Holding fast to the gunwale as he made his way along, he struggled inch by torturous inch toward the bow so that he might survey the churning ocean lying ahead. Once there he grasped a line in each hand and then spread wide his legs, trying to peer through the gale-force winds and rain. The bow was now rising and falling so violently that it was all Adam could do to keep from being swept overboard. The Cape was known for spawning terrible storms, but this fatherless nightmare had seemingly sprung out of nowhere, and he had been totally unprepared for it.

"Goddamn you!" he shouted defiantly into the violent darkness. *"From which corner of Satan's Hell were you spawned?"*

As Adam had hoped, with her sails reefed and her wheel tied off, the *Intrepid* nosed directly into the wind. However even this tactic was not without its dangers, as the now directly oncoming waves made the ship rise and fall with even greater ferocity, literally dumping wave after wave of seawater onto the bow deck. His position becoming ever more perilous, Adam nonetheless stayed his post, doing all he could to hold on while peering dead ahead. Without warning a halyard suddenly gave way, its block and tackle swinging dangerously past his head and nearly killing him outright. Then he heard a man scream.

As he turned around to look, he saw that his bosun mate had slipped down onto the rain-soaked deck. Mere moments later, a rushing wave clambered its way up the starboard hull and burst aboard, the angry seawater exploding everywhere. The ferocious wall of water slammed into the poor man and suddenly propelled him overboard, his plaintive screaming fading away as he tumbled into the dark sea. Then the terrible ocean assaulted the decks yet again, this time also from starboard and taking another precious man with it.

The rain was lashing Adam's face so hard that he had to squint through the pain, and he could barely see ahead. The only respites from the blackness were the abrupt lightning flashes that came crackling out of the night sky like fiery bolts hurled by angry gods. As he stood holding on to the lines for dear life, Adam quickly realized that he had never before experienced a storm of such ferocity, and that only a miracle could save them from this ruthless tempest. While the lightning flashed and the thunder roared, he did his best to stand his ground atop the pitching deck and peer out into the fathomless blackness, hoping to see nothing lying before them but the open sea.

And then, incredibly, he thought he heard a woman's voice. It was as if someone, he knew not who, was screaming at him, trying to warn him of his ship's impending doom. Then the woman's voice was again lost to the raging storm, its tremolo fading as quickly as were the *Intrepid's* chances for survival.

But such a thing cannot be! Adam realized as he again focused his gaze upon the churning sea ahead. *I have heard tales of the sea winds blowing through a ship's rigging and sounding like a woman's plaintive voice, and now I have heard it for myself!*

After a time the woman's voice came to his ears yet again, her warnings now even more strident, and for a split second he could have sworn he was hearing his beloved Constance, warning him of the rocks that lay dead ahead.

Like brave Ulysses, I too am being seduced! But unlike Ulysses's temptresses, mine is not real, nor am I tied to the ship's mainmast to keep me from joining with her! Ignore what you are hearing, for she does not exist!

No sooner had the woman's voice faded away again than did Adam spy the one thing that every seaman fears the most—a rogue wave. The Cape was a breeding ground for such monsters, which seemed to come out of nowhere. They could tower as high as thirty or even forty feet, easily reducing the strongest of ships to matchsticks.

Before Adam could shout out a warning to the others, the great wave slammed into the *Intrepid*'s port bow, washing Adam overboard and directly into the churning sea. Screaming wildly and gasping for breath, he tried his best to ride the waves but then a broken mast spar and some of the *Intrepid*'s torn sailcloth were driven his way, entangling him and sending him under. At first all he could think about was how cold it was. Unbelievably cold, and with an all-encompassing darkness that he never knew existed.

As the churning seawater at last invaded his lungs, Adam's final thoughts were of his beloved Constance.

Chapter 1

New Bedford, Massachusetts
Present Day

His name was Garrett Richmond, and he had always wanted to live alongside the ocean.

Garrett pulled his black Jeep Wrangler to a stop then turned off the engine. For a time he ignored his passenger and looked lovingly out the window at the ramshackle old house he had just bought.

"You've really lost it this time," his friend and business partner Trent Birch said. "Do you know that? I can't understand why you want some dump that's going to take *years* to put right! You've gone crazy!"

Garrett realized that everyone thought he was nuts. But in his heart he knew better. He had expertise in classic American antebellum architecture that few others of his profession could claim, and he'd easily seen the promise in this house. But Trent was right about one thing. Without question, the impending restoration would be both difficult and costly.

He turned and smiled.

"Crazy?" he asked. "Maybe . . . but it's my funeral, right?"

Garrett got out of the Jeep then reached behind the driver's seat and opened a cooler. He pulled out two bottles of cold champagne, a couple of Styrofoam cups, and a small box. He next produced the two folding chairs he had also packed. When Trent saw the cold champagne, he smirked.

"Don't tell me, let me guess!" Trent exclaimed. "You're going to christen this dump, aren't you? But why two bottles? It seems like one would be plenty."

After handing the box and chairs to Trent, Garrett smiled and carried the bottles toward the front porch of the house.

"Simple," he replied, with Trent in tow. "One bottle to christen the house and the other one to drink. What's the matter, anyway? You like champagne, right?"

"Sure," Trent answered as he followed Garrett. "That's not what's bothering me."

"So . . . ?" Garrett asked.

"The champagne is worth more than the damned house is. Not to mention that the entire place might collapse!"

Garrett snorted out a short laugh. "Truth is you could be right on both counts."

Pausing in his walk, Garrett stopped to admire his recent purchase. For once, Trent knew when to be quiet and let his friend enjoy the moment.

Built in 1835, the large home had had many owners on its long and convoluted journey to Garrett Richmond. He'd closed the transaction only yesterday, but while growing up in New Bedford he had always loved this property. So much so, that he'd often pass by to both admire it and to mourn its condition. Something about this old house by the sea had fostered an irresistible attraction within him. And it was that very enticement, he had long known, that had led him to a career in architecture.

The two-story directly faced the Atlantic. Garrett had always thought that the original builder put it a bit too close to the ocean, but so be it. It rested on an elevated, scrubby clump of land that ended where the rocky shore began sloping down toward the ocean. As a result, the continual sea air and wave spray were constant enemies, and even once Seaside was restored, Garrett knew that he would have his hands full keeping it that way.

Despite its distressed condition, one could tell that it had once been an impressive and stately residence. Four high, Doric columns graced the front and supported the overhanging roof, which extended forward from the second floor. A long, open veranda shaded by the roof stretched all the way across the face and extended down along each side of the house. The side verandas also had columns that supported two more side balconies with railings, and doors that allowed entry into each of the first-floor side rooms. Another large, elegantly curved balcony extended from the front of the house at the second floor, providing an open sitting area off the master bedroom.

An ornate railing ran along the entire roof edge. The roof itself was flat, with a raised area toward the front that supported an extremely weathered widow's walk, its roof and railings warped with the passage of time. Twin chimneys in bad disrepair exited the roof, one at the far left-hand side where the parlor had once presumably been, and the other one on the right, in the dining room. The front of the house had been sided with bricks. The sides were covered with clapboards that had once been painted a bright white but that had long since faded to a dull and tired gray.

Despite all the obvious damage, Garrett smiled. To his way of thinking, every problem was a welcome challenge, its completion bringing him one step closer to his goal. His eyes saw a diamond in the rough that he couldn't wait to polish. But for Trent, each of those flaws only reaffirmed that Garrett had made the mistake of his life. Like Garrett, Trent was an architect, but he lacked the vision and the wonderful eye for detail that were Garrett's trademarks.

"Let me guess, professor," Trent said. "Once upon a time, this shack was an antebellum, Greek Revival style. It's been a while since school, but I'm correct, right?"

Garrett laughed a little. "Not completely," he answered. "It's really Gothic Revival, with some Romantic style embellishments that someone slapped on her, somewhere along the line. And do you see the widow's walk? That's called Italianate, as you should know."

"If that's the case then I'm even more surprised you bought it," Trent replied, "especially since you're always lecturing your students about 'Frankentechture.' So why did you make an exception?"

Garrett began walking toward the front porch again.

"To be honest, I don't know," he replied quietly. "And you're right—I do hate the mixing of respected architectural types. It's like wearing sneakers with a tuxedo, but as for this particular house—well, I'm not sure why I like it so much. There's just always been something about it that . . ."

As Garrett's words trailed off, he realized that there was no concrete answer to Trent's question. Many had been the time when he asked himself the same thing. Although he had purchased this foreclosed house on a short sale from the bank, most still thought that he paid too much. But for him, this was not a question of money. Rather it was about restoring what to his discerning eye had once been a magnificent place where people lived and loved during quieter, more genteel times.

Moreover, the chain of title had also intrigued Garrett. Coupled with some research he had done on his own, an interesting early history of the house had emerged. It had been built for a well-respected New Bedford lawyer. Soon after its completion, the lawyer lost his wife to what was then called "consumption." His despair was so great that he decided to sell the house and leave, never to be heard from again.

The next owners were Adam and Constance Canfield, and it seemed that their circumstances were no less tragic. Adam had been a whaling captain lost at sea. Strangely, his wife, Constance, seemed to have also disappeared around that same time, never to return. As a result, the bank had foreclosed and sold the property at public auction. In those days the house was called "Seaside," a name that had supposedly been bestowed upon it by the Canfields. Garrett liked the name, and from the moment he signed the papers he had resolved to call it that.

"Seaside . . ." he said quietly to himself as he again began walking toward the house.

"What did you just say?" Trent asked as he followed along. He never could keep up with Garrett's long legs.

"Seaside," Garrett repeated. "That's the name given to it by one of the previous owners. I like it, and I'm going to call it that."

Quickening his pace, Trent caught up to Garrett again while still juggling the chairs and the small box.

"Seaside, huh?" Trent asked. "Wow . . . how original."

Garrett laughed again as they neared the porch. "Go ahead," he replied. "Criticize all you want. But when this place is done, you're going to be amazed."

They climbed the rickety steps, walked across the porch, and put down their things. Garrett set up the chairs, and the two old friends sat down beside one another and quietly looked out at the ocean.

"I've never really doubted you before, Garrett," Trent said, after a time. "But now you've got me scratching my head. You do realize that this place is so rough you might not finish it until you're an old man, right?"

Garrett smiled. "Maybe," he answered. "But there's so much promise here. Even Tara once needed a complete overhaul, you know."

Trent leaned back and gingerly put his feet up on the porch rail, as if the entire thing might collapse at any moment. "True," he answered. "But you don't have Rhett Butler's money."

"Can't you find one good thing about this place?" Garrett asked jokingly.

"The view," Trent answered.

When Garrett didn't respond, Trent turned to look at his best friend. They had known each other since they were roommates during their first semester at architecture school. Garrett had been born and raised in New Bedford; Trent was originally from Boston. Although they were diametric opposites in some ways, their strong and enduring friendship was something upon which each could always rely.

While Garrett was tall and lean, Trent was darker, shorter, and broader. Garrett's hair was a sort of dirty blond, parted on one side and always seeming to fall down into an irrepressible wave on his forehead. But the first thing anyone noticed was his penetrating, crystal blue eyes, which upon studying anything that particularly intrigued him somehow became even more intense. Upon first meeting him, there were few people who did not mention those eyes, and they had long since become a standing joke between him and Trent. Dressed today in tan cargo pants, a black polo shirt, and a pair of deck shoes, he exuded a calm sense of purpose that Trent had always envied. Both Garrett and Trent were still single.

After graduation from architecture school, the two friends had scraped together all the money they could and formed Richmond & Birch, LLC, a New Bedford architectural firm specializing in the design of houses. Garrett was the majority shareholder and thus technically Trent's boss, although neither of them looked at it that way. Their business had struggled mightily at first and nearly gone bankrupt twice before finally gaining some traction. Despite the recent economic downturn, Richmond & Birch had now become prosperous enough to allow Garrett to secure a mortgage for Seaside.

During that time Garrett had also gone to night school and acquired his Ph.D. in architectural history, specializing in historic American schools of the nineteenth century. As much for the love of doing it as his need for the extra money, he now taught night classes in architectural history at Boston College.

"I'm staying here tonight, by the way," Garrett said, finally breaking the quiet.

"Huh?" Trent asked.

Before answering, Garrett also put his feet up on the porch rail. "Yep . . . first night, and all that . . ."

"So how am I supposed to get home?"

"You'll take my Jeep, and then come back for me in the morning."

"But there's no furniture, you said," Trent protested. "Where will you sleep?"

Garrett leaned back a bit more in his chair. "On the floor," he answered. "I brought along a sleeping bag."

"Okay," Trent said. "But dear God, how you must love this place! It's got to be dirty as all hell in there."

"Oh, it's worse than dirty," Garrett answered. "When the bank foreclosed, the owners took it out on the house. They smashed in some of the walls, ripped up the carpets, tore out the appliances—that sort of thing."

Trent nodded knowingly. Much of that had gone on in New England during the downturn. When the banks were forced to foreclose, many angry owners partially destroyed their properties as a form of unwarranted revenge.

"And knowing all that, you still wanted the place," Trent mused.

"Sure," Garrett answered. "They did some of the work for me, because the appliances were all junk, and they had to go, anyway."

"What about the electric and water?"

"It's got both, and the oil furnace works, but it's bone dry. If I get cold tonight, there's a pile of leftover firewood out back. And there's some more in the barn."

"There's a barn?" Trent asked.

Garrett nodded. "Yeah, but it's in pretty bad shape. There was also a guest cottage at one time, but somewhere along the line it was demolished."

"I had no idea that college professors were so adventurous," Trent chided him.

Garrett laughed. "Want to go inside and see just how much?" he asked.

Trent shook his head. "No offense, but I'll pass for right now. I already think that you've made a big enough blunder. If I step inside and see it, I may be forced to have you committed. Oh, and by the way," he added almost lazily, "this place is haunted, you know."

Garrett turned and looked at Trent with a sense of amusement.

"And just how do you know that?" he asked.

"A guy I know is friends with the previous owners," Trent answered. "To hear him tell it, they were always complaining about things that supposedly went bump in the night."

"Oh yeah? Like what?"

Trent shrugged his shoulders.

"Sometimes things were found in different places, the owners would hear strange noises, plus various other kinds of disturbances. You know," Trent added with a smile, "the usual sort of spooky stuff. No offense, but before you finish the renovation, you might want to think about calling Ghostbusters and having this place slimed."

Garrett laughed a little and stood up.

"No offense taken," he answered. "But now it's time for the champagne."

Garrett picked up one of the glistening bottles. After taking its neck in a firm grip, he strode over to the nearest porch column.

"Ready?" he asked Trent.

"I am if you are. But don't blame me if the whole damned place comes tumbling down, just like when Samson destroyed the temple."

Garrett raised the champagne bottle high over his right shoulder.

"I hereby christen thee 'Seaside,' " he said loudly.

He then smashed it against the column, champagne and bits of glass flying everywhere. Happy with his success, Garrett unceremoniously dropped the broken bottleneck and went back to his lawn chair.

"*Thee* . . . ?" Trent asked. "I hereby christen *thee* . . . ? I know that you love the early eighteen hundreds, but are you sure you haven't gone around the bend?"

Garrett leaned back in his chair and smiled.

"Yeah, I'm sure."

He popped the cork on the second champagne bottle and filled the two Styrofoam cups. He handed one to Trent, and the two friends raised them high.

"Here's to lunacy in all its forms," Garrett said, knowing that Trent would agree.

Trent smiled back at him.

"Hear, hear!" he answered.

While sipping their champagne, the two friends settled back into their chairs. Garrett then reached down and opened the small box that Trent had brought to the porch, from which he produced two cigars, a cigar cutter, and a lighter. Among the many opinions and tastes that they shared, a good cigar rated near the top of the list. Garrett cut them both, handed one to Trent, then lit Trent's cigar followed by his own.

Knowing that this was a time to be savored, the men remained quiet. Between sips of champagne and puffs of cigar smoke, they watched the Atlantic Ocean send her countless waves only to destroy themselves against the rocky shoreline. It was one of those New England evenings when the sky becomes a lovely sort of purple, just before night descends in full. Now more than ever, Garrett knew that he was home.

After a time, Trent looked at his watch.

"I should be going," he said. "Are you still sure that you want me to take your Jeep?"

"It's either that or you can stay with me, here among the ruins."

"Not on your life! But you do have your cell phone in case you need anything?"

Garrett nodded.

"In that case, I'll be going."

"Let me walk you down to the car," Garrett said. "There's something I want you to take back."

Garrett walked over to the FOR SALE BY FORECLO-SURE sign embedded in the grass, pulled it from the ground, and dumped it in the back of the Jeep.

"Take that with you," he told Trent. "I'll drop it off at the Realtor's office tomorrow."

"Okay, boss," Trent answered as he climbed into the Jeep and started the motor. "What time tomorrow?" he asked.

"Six A.M. sharp," he said as he reached into the back of the Jeep, this time retrieving his sleeping bag, a small cooler, and an electric lantern. "And don't be late. I need time at my condo to get ready for work, and we've got the Morris presentation at ten o'clock."

Trent smiled and gunned the engine a bit.

"Wouldn't miss it for the world," he answered. "See you tomorrow at six."

While the black Jeep bounced jauntily down the long driveway, Garrett smiled slightly as he watched it eventually disappear from view.

After again looking at the ocean for a time, Garrett began the walk back to the porch. There was some champagne left, and he had no intention of wasting it.

Chapter 2

G arrett settled back into one of the folding chairs and again gazed out over the moonlit Atlantic. Night had fallen in earnest, so he switched on the electric lantern and placed it on the porch rail. As he watched the sea Garrett knew that this view would be forever changing, yet always the same. So too would be the wonderful and ever present sound of the waves, crashing against the shoreline. He couldn't wait to settle into the master bedroom on this side of the house, so he could fall asleep each night and awake each morning to the sounds of the sea. Even as a young boy he had loved watching the ocean, its endless horizons and countless waves always mesmerizing him. He had long wanted an oceanside home, and now he had it.

Restoring Seaside would be an ambitious project, and had he not been "of the trades," the task might have appeared far too daunting. But given his expertise, he was eager to get started. He had selected Jay Morgan, Inc., a local contractor he trusted, for the restoration job. He had used Jay many times when building homes for clients. Garrett knew that with enough time and money he could properly restore this old house and all its furnishings to as near the original as possible.

Although he had designed many homes, this personal project would be uniquely liberating. Leaving no stone unturned, he would make Seaside his masterwork, and the hallmark of his career. Best of all, this time each decision would be his. There would be neither the catering to the dubious tastes of clients, nor any of the last-minute changes that drive architects to the brink of madness. He alone would dictate the work, and pour every bit of his knowledge into it to ensure its authenticity. Even more important, he was confident that when he was done he would own a thing of rare beauty.

His biggest challenge was finding the money to pay the contractor and buy the antique furnishings. He had already used much of his savings as a down payment on Seaside. But by selling his condo in New Bedford he should have enough to do the job. Even so, the timing would be tricky. Because New Bedford was a seaside town, her real estate market was seasonal. It was already October, and he had priced it a bit below market value to help get a quick sale.

Once the condo sold, Seaside would become his only home and need buttoning up before the coming winter. He wasn't too concerned, however. The same Realtor who had helped him purchase Seaside was also the listing agent on his condo, and she had already shown it twice in the last three weeks. With a little luck it was a workable plan, but he was itching to get started on Seaside, and being forced to await his working capital grated on his nerves.

Realizing that he had become hungry, Garrett lifted the cooler to his lap and opened it. A stick of pepperoni, a good-size chunk of aged cheddar, and two sourdough rolls lay wrapped inside. He sliced off a few pieces of each and began eating, occasionally washing them down with what remained of the lukewarm champagne. While enjoying his makeshift dinner and watching the moonlight dance over the incoming waves, he took a moment to think about how he had gotten to this place by the sea.

Garrett was the son of a retired thoracic surgeon and a registered nurse, who met and fell in love while serving together in a MASH unit in Vietnam. After their discharge, Dale and Virginia Richmond settled in New Bedford. Garrett arrived one year later, and his sister, Christine, two years after that.

Every summer during the long march toward his master's degree, he'd worked in the trades of carpentry, electrical, masonry, plumbing, or landscaping. Although he never became a true master of any, he nonetheless acquired the practical knowledge that contractors appreciate in an architect. He and Trent had been in business for ten years now, and during that time each had adjusted to the other's peccadilloes. They had also learned how to produce a united front to prospective clients, though they often disagreed. Even so, Richmond & Birch was reputed for delivering some of the most beautiful and best-designed homes in all of Massachusetts.

Given his great devotion to his work, Garrett hadn't much of a social life. Instead, building the business with Trent had always taken precedence. Several interesting women had drifted in and out of his sphere, but so far none of them had been "the one." His last long-term relationship was five years ago, and it ended badly when the girl finally gave up on competing with his career.

Even so, Garrett remained a romantic. He still hoped that when the time was right, "she" would appear, but as he become older, he was beginning to wonder if she was really out there. His standards were high, and he knew that this was one of the things keeping him alone. Even so, he refused to settle, choosing instead to believe that someday that one special woman would enter his life, and when she did, he would know her.

Perhaps the fact that I'm sitting alone on the front porch of this old house is proof enough of where my priorities lie, he thought. *I don't know . . . The only thing I know for sure right now is that I must complete this project, although I do not fully understand why I feel so compelled to do it. I know that this restoration will require all of my talent, all of my money, and much of my time. Even so, for the time being at least, my path is set.*

Deciding to shelve his thoughts, Garrett stood and stretched. He then gathered up his possessions and let himself in the house.

This was the first time he had been inside at night, and he soon realized that the house seemed different. The shadows created by the moonlight coming through the broken windows added a surreal touch that he had not expected, and the sound of the waves crashing against the shore was muted, helping to preserve the relative quiet. Remembering Trent's quip about the place being haunted, he smiled.

As he explored the first floor, carrying his lantern, even in the relative darkness his excellent eye for antebellum architecture allowed him to identify each room's original use. As best he could tell when he had examined Seaside in the daylight, it seemed that no rooms had been added and that none of the original walls had been torn down. Those were good signs, and they bode well for the impending restoration.

Garrett carefully walked down a dark hallway past a room on the left-hand side that would have been the parlor. Across the hall was a lady's sewing room and farther along a rather majestic curved staircase. Walking onward he came upon two more rooms, the larger dining room, and the smaller on the left, the library.

Moving farther on to the back of the house, he entered what would have been the serving room. On the left was a doorway that opened onto a stairway leading to the basement, followed by the butler's pantry, and beyond that the kitchen.

Everywhere he looked, Garrett saw signs of the vandalism he had described to Trent earlier this evening, and it angered him. The previous owners had spray painted vulgarities on the walls, torn up the carpets, and ripped out the appliances. The walls and staircase had been damaged by sledgehammers. When he had examined the second floor, there too he had seen much of the same kind of destruction. While letting go a distraught sigh, Garrett shook his head at the sheer stupidity of it all.

There were few things in this world that Garrett could not abide, but damaging a work of art angered him to his very core. Clearly the previous owners had no conception of what it took to build a house, even a modest one. And all homes, Garrett had always believed, had souls all their own and should be respected.

Retracing his steps to where he had left his things, Garrett picked them up and brought them to the dining room. To his mild surprise he felt a shiver go through him, so he decided to light a fire. There were two fireplaces on the first floor; one was in the parlor, and the other in the dining room, which he'd inspected earlier.

Taking up his lantern, he went out to get firewood and kindling. Using some old newspaper that he had also brought along, he lit a fire in the dining room fireplace that soon supplied a warm, welcome glow.

Unrolling the sleeping bag before the fireplace, he settled down onto it. It was good to be here, he thought, now that the house was officially his. There was so much to be done! But each finished step in the restoration would be a labor of love, and only reinforce that he was at last where he truly belonged.

Very tired now, he watched the dancing flames for a time with the same sort of fascination that possessed him whenever he stared at the ocean. He could barely hear the waves striking the rocks over the crackling fire.

But just as he was about to cross over into sleep he heard something that was loud enough to wake him. He listened intently for a few moments, but heard nothing more. It had sounded for the world like a woman sobbing, but because he was alone here tonight, that was impossible.

Garrett lay back down. Before entering the long, dark tunnel of sleep, his tired mind reassured him that it had simply been Seaside's way of welcoming home her new owner, and his heart accepted that premise.

His subsequent dream was unlike any he'd had before—so clear and sharp that after awakening he could recall every color, every detail of what he had just experienced. He dreamed of a woman, very different from any he had known before. So different that he immediately felt drawn to her like no other.

He wasn't there with her. Rather, he was watching her from afar. Even so, he could easily tell that she was quite possibly the most beautiful woman he had ever seen. Her long, blond hair was artfully arranged atop her head; her eyes were deep blue. She was wearing clothing that belonged to a different time. Her dress was pink, with large leg-of-mutton sleeves and a broad conical skirt that harshly imprisoned her narrow waist.

On her feet she wore low, square-toed slippers, and around her neck there lay a locket, tan in color, which appeared to be made from some type of bone, perhaps.

The woman was crying uncontrollably. She was all alone and sitting in a dilapidated chair. It was the dead of night, and the room that imprisoned her was dark, and without character of any kind. As the moonlight streaming through the lone window highlighted her form, she soon buried her face in her hands while she wept. She seemed so alone, so helpless, and so much in need of companionship that his heart silently cried out for her.

To Garrett's surprise, she soon removed her hands from her face, then turned and stared straight into his eyes. Her expression, both searching and pleading, was the most desperate he had ever seen. She then raised both arms and stretched them out in his direction, as if she were begging him to come to her.

"Please . . ." he heard her say to him. "Please help me . . ."

And then, as quickly as Garrett's dream had appeared, it ended, the sad beauty that was its subject dissolving into nothingness with it.

With his body covered in a cold sweat, Garrett suddenly awakened.

Chapter 3

It was almost six o'clock the following evening, and Dr. Garrett Richmond, Professor of Architecture, was finishing another lecture of his class, American Antebellum Architecture 101.

As a professor, Garrett was a tough taskmaster. Even so, he never lacked for students. He was young, outspoken, and known for pulling no punches regarding his purist opinions about architecture.

"Consider this final thought," he said as he wrapped things up. "Painting, sculpture, architecture, and literature all seem to spring from one's personal fountainhead, compelling its owner to produce work in a certain medium. Admittedly I am no different in that regard, for it is only an appreciation of the architectural which I am trying to instill within your minds."

As the class filed out, he stuffed his papers into a leather satchel and made the short walk down the hall to his office. Upon closing his office door he relaxed in his desk chair, enjoying the blessed quiet. When this course ended, he would teach one more night class next spring.

He was pleased with a decision he had made earlier in the day. Other than the capital still locked up in his condo, he had some eighteen thousand dollars in cash. He was feeling more confident about things now, enough so that he was planning to give his contractor a check for ten thousand dollars so that the restoration could get under way. By the time that money was used up, Garrett hoped he would have the additional funds from the sale of his condo. But that remained only a possibility, rather than a certainty.

During the process of buying the house he had momentarily toyed with the idea of bending some of his principles, and ordering the restoration to be something more akin to the modern. But in the end he decided that he could not do that. This was to be his personal masterwork, not a project of compromise. He was taking a huge risk, and he could only hope that he would succeed in creating something very special.

By the time he was eighteen, it was a foregone conclusion that he would become an architect. With his SAT scores nearly off the charts, he was readily accepted into college. It was while attaining his master's degree in architecture that his uncanny ability to recognize architectural works and the people who had designed them really came to the forefront. Once he had studied the work of an architect, it was easy for him to identify buildings that had been created by the same hand. He minored in art history, and in this discipline too he possessed an unerring eye for artistic authorship that was truly remarkable.

And then, for what must have been the one hundredth time that day, Garrett thought about last night's dream. He had tried to get it out of his mind but found it impossible. The dream had been so vivid, so lifelike in its colors, intensity, and detail that in many ways it had not seemed like a dream at all. It was as if he had truly been there with that mysterious woman who had begged for his help. Although her beauty had been mesmerizing, her sadness was the most desperate he had ever witnessed. And the unexpected attraction he felt for her at that moment had carried over into his waking hours, her lovely image reappearing in his mind's eye seemingly at will, yet only to vanish again.

Who was she? he wondered. Could she have been someone from his past who lay deeply buried in his memories, only to now reemerge and create that amazing dream? No, he realized. Had he ever met a woman as lovely as she, he would have certainly remembered. Whether this woman really existed or whether she was simply a figment of his imagination, she was unknown to him. He also hoped that he might see her again sometime, be it in a dream or real life. And that if he did, he would not find her to be in such terrible distress.

One hour later, Garrett was happily astride his Harley Low Rider as he headed south from Boston along a lovely coastal road. He had ridden a motorcycle in one form or another ever since his college days, and he still loved it. His parents had stern objections, but expecting him to give it up was an exercise in futility. He was on his way to Seaside to give his contractor the ten-thousand-dollar check.

As he approached Seaside he saw that Jay Morgan's pickup was already parked out front and that some lights had been turned on inside the house, presumably a few lanterns that Jay had brought along with him. After shutting down the Harley and leaning it onto its kickstand, Garrett untied a sturdy leather tube from the bike's rear fender and began walking toward the house. As he went along, he picked up several small stones and put them into one pocket. Jay was sitting in one of Garrett's folding chairs on the front porch, waiting for him, shaking his head in mock disdain.

"It's about time you got here," he said. "There are few clients in the world that I would consider meeting at this time of night. And although you're one of them, Dr. Richmond, it wouldn't do to take me for granted."

Garrett laughed a little as he plopped down in the other chair.

"Yeah," he answered. "But we both know that given the size of this job, you'll be willing to put up with just about anything from me."

"Fair enough," Jay replied. "But even the money won't make up for you being such a royal pain."

Garrett turned and cast his gaze out over the restless Atlantic. Although he had been here for less than two minutes, he already felt at home again.

Jay Morgan was more than just the contractor whom Garrett tried to use the most; he was also one of his best friends. Not only did he trust Jay implicitly, but by now they also had worked together enough to respect each other's artistic differences. Clearly Jay's parents had a sense of humor. His full name was Jay Peter Morgan, sometimes also known as J. P. Morgan. About Garrett's age, he was a great ox of a man. He had been losing his hair for some time now and was mostly bald. Perhaps as some form of hirsute compensation, three years ago he had grown a full, reddish-brown beard.

Best of all, Jay had a wonderful sense of humor. Although Garrett guessed that Jay had always been impressed with his credentials he had never shown it, preferring instead to continually harass him about being a nerdy professor. But Jay knew full well how competent Garrett was—not only as an architect but also as someone with a good working knowledge of everything needed to take on a job of this size.

Jay pointed at the leather tube Garrett had brought along. "Are those the floor plans?" he asked.

Garrett nodded. "Yeah, but they're rough. I paced off each of the rooms and then slap-dashed these together, back at the office. They'll do for a while."

"Good," Jay answered. "Then let's get to it. I'd like to get home before I'm an old man."

When Jay stood up and put on his hard hat, Garrett laughed again.

"It's not that bad!" he said.

Jay smirked at him. "You *have* been in there, right?" he asked rhetorically.

Without further ado, the two men went inside. The stark, artificial light served to hauntingly accentuate the damage that had been done to Seaside. Jay looked around and shook his head. Like Garrett, he had long believed that a home—no matter how grand or how humble—deserved to be treated with respect.

"God," he said while still looking around. "How can people do this to a house? It's almost a sacrilege."

"Stupid as it might be," Garrett answered, "they're angry as hell, and this is their only way to get back at the banks. I certainly don't agree with it, but in an odd way I can almost understand."

Jay had also brought along a folding table, which he had erected in the center of what would presumably become Seaside's renovated parlor. Garrett removed the stones from his pocket then slid the plans free of the leather tube. After unrolling the plans on the table, he used the stones to keep the corners from curling up.

"High-tech," Jay said.

"Works every time," Garrett answered.

Jay looked around again. "This will be the parlor, right?" he asked Garrett.

Garrett nodded. "I'm pretty sure I already know the answer to this, but what's the first step?"

"Well," Jay answered, "luckily the basement and foundation are still in good shape. Before we tackle anything else I'm going to get my electrician and plumber in here. I don't think we'll find anything monumental, but don't drink the well water until I've had it tested. After that, my crew will begin working on the outside of the house. The first exterior thing to tackle should be . . ."

While Garrett listened, Jay did an excellent job of outlining the entire project. Despite Garrett's legendary fussiness, only twice did he comment. When Jay finished, Garrett fished his wallet out of his back pocket and handed over the ten-thousand-dollar check.

"Normally in a situation like this, I'd say: *'Don't spend it all in one place!'*" he said. "But in this case, you have no other choice."

"Yeah," Jay said. "And now, professor, I'm going to blow this pop stand. I should be able to get my electrician and plumber in here during the next couple of days. And am I correct in assuming that you will be out here ad nauseam, constantly adding in your overly educated two cents?"

Garrett nodded. "You bet. After all, somebody's got to keep an eye on you and your band of misfits."

Jay laughed. "How true," he answered. This time when he glanced around the shabby room, the look on his face sobered.

"A lot of people think you're nuts for buying this place," Jay said. "But I want you to know that I'm not among them. Given your expertise, I have absolutely no doubt that once Seaside is finished, she will be spectacular. You're going to silence all the naysayers, Garrett, you really are."

"I hope so," Garrett answered. "And even if this turns out to be a huge mistake, I'll always be glad that it was you who did the job."

"Thanks for that," Jay said. "And now, I'm going home."

Garrett nodded. "Say 'hi' to the wife and kids for me, will you?"

After shaking Garrett's hand, Jay walked out, got into his pickup, and headed for home.

As the sound of Jay's truck engine faded in the distance, silence again overtook the house. As usual Garrett was again struck by the unique sort of stillness inherent in this place. At first he had found it to be rather eerie. But now that he was becoming accustomed to it, he could also faintly hear the reassuring sounds of the sea as it continually assaulted the shoreline.

He picked up one of the lanterns and walked about the first floor for a time, ticking off a mental checklist of tasks that would be done once Jay and his crew turned their attention to the inside of the house. He then went to the central foyer and walked up the battered staircase to the second floor, where he did the same thing. He stood in the master bedroom for a time while trying to imagine the many people who had lived and perhaps died in this house—who they had been, what they had done with their lives, and whether the fates had been cruel or kind. The original parcel of land had been some ten acres, and the plot had retained its size throughout Seaside's many changes of hands. It was then that he got the idea to go up to the roof and inspect the old widow's walk.

Up there the sea air smelled fresh and clean, and before him lay a marvelous view of the harbor. As Garrett neared the widow's walk, he smiled a little bit. The wives of sea captains did use these structures to search for their husbands' ships. But he also knew that widow's walks were in fact a standard decorative feature of Italianate architecture, which was a very popular style during the height of the whaling boom in North America. Also known as Italian cupolas, in most cases they were merely ornate embellishments, and very prone to leaks.

Sometimes these cupolas were built around the chimney, creating access to it. This allowed the residents of the home to pour sand down burning chimneys during a chimney fire, in the hope of preventing the house from burning down. Although Garrett was a stickler for history, he was also something of a romantic and much preferred the stories about whaling captains' wives visiting these structures so as to wistfully search for their returning husbands.

When Garrett neared the dilapidated widow's walk he stopped to examine it. At one time it had surely been lovely. Sitting near the front roofline, it was a two-story affair and had a roof of its own. Supported by columns, the cupola's second-story roof also boasted a full railing. A ladder led from the first floor of the cupola to the second. The reason for it being two stories tall was simple enough, Garrett realized; the taller the widow's walk, the more expansive the view. He was tempted to climb up and look out over the harbor, but given the overall poor condition he wisely decided against it.

What was it like, he wondered, to be a whaler's wife living in this big house? Would she come up here to scan the ships as they entered the harbor? If so, he couldn't imagine her doing it without the aid of a spyglass. It must have been difficult to live by oneself for so long, wondering whether your husband would ever return to you.

Just then he detected an elegant scent, just like a woman's perfume, carried to him on the ocean breeze. And then, as soon as he had sensed it, it was gone. Smiling to himself, he shook his head. It must have been something else, he realized, for he was quite alone up here.

His inspection of the cupola finished, Garrett returned to the first-floor parlor. It was late, and time for him to go. He decided he would leave his rather crude floor plans here for the time being. And then, just as he was about to go from room to room and turn off the lanterns, he heard the noise again.

It sounded exactly like someone crying, just as it had when he had slept here before the fireplace. But this time, he could not dismiss it to his sleepiness. This time he was wide-awake, and hearing it with complete clarity.

Unsure of what to do, he finally began quietly walking down the hall toward the rear of the house. As he went, he looked in turn into the parlor, the sewing room, the library, and the dining room, only to find each of them vacant. Continuing on, he passed through the serving room and then the butler's pantry, also finding nothing. But when he at last approached the open kitchen door and looked in, Garrett saw something that would haunt him for the rest of his life.

He saw *her*—the same woman he had dreamed about only the night before. There could be no mistake, and seeing her so suddenly and unexpectedly like this caused his heart to race, and his breathing to become labored.

But she had yet to see *him*, he quickly realized. Like in his dream, she was sitting all alone in a leftover chair and sobbing uncontrollably. Later on, he would decide that it was because she had been so taken up with her crying that she had not immediately recognized his presence.

Although she was dressed in different clothing than in Garrett's dream, he knew immediately that it was she.

This night she wore modern clothes—a pair of jeans, what appeared to be a man's shirt with its sleeves rolled up, and a pair of sneakers. Her hair was not artfully arranged atop her head but fell down about her shoulders, and like in Garrett's dream she wore the scrimshaw locket around her neck. As she sat there crying, her entire being shook with grief and fear.

Stunned beyond words, Garrett simply stood there in the kitchen doorway for a few moments, watching her. When he at last found his voice, even then he was unsure about what to say.

"Hello . . . ?" he asked softly.

As if with a single motion, the woman dropped her hands from her face, looked at Garrett with terror, and then let go a piercing scream. It was a plaintive shriek that seemed to go right through him, and was one that he would never forget.

Garrett quickly raised his hands in a pleading gesture.

"It's okay!" he said. "I won't hurt you—I only want to know who you are, and why you're here! Do you need help?"

No sooner had the words left Garrett's mouth than the terrified woman sprang from her chair, ran to the kitchen door, and threw it open so hard against the wall that its glass panel shattered. Almost before Garrett knew it, she was running off into the darkness as if her very life depended upon it.

Garrett's first impulse was to catch up to her. But then he realized that he still did not know these grounds well, and that it would be foolish to go chasing after her in the dark. Although it would offer no security, he shut the broken kitchen door and locked it.

He walked over to the chair that the woman had just vacated, and he sat down in it dumbly. In an attempt to calm down he took several deep breaths, letting them out slowly. As his mind began to process what he had just experienced, he started to realize that in his own way, he had been just as shocked as she.

Despite the confusion, one thing was becoming clear. It wasn't his words that had terrified her; rather, it was being seen by him that had rattled her so badly. But why would that be? If she had been in the house for any length of time at all, she would have most assuredly heard him and Jay talking. And if she had been afraid of them, she had had plenty of opportunity to flee without being seen.

But even these realizations were not what shocked Garrett the most. Rather, it was that the woman who had just run away from Seaside was without question the same person he had dreamed of only last night. And then, his mind still flooded with impossible questions, he came to another stark realization.

The crying that I heard last night, just before falling sleep in the dining room . . . that crying was also hers! I cannot say why I'm so sure of it, only that I am. She is also the same woman who I saw in my dream! And now that I have seen her in the flesh, a new sort of pain and yearning is growing in my heart that is far stronger than any I have experienced before . . .

As Seaside's gray shadows and eerie stillness seemed to engulf him, for several moments Garrett began to doubt his sanity. Then he abruptly scrubbed his face with his hands, stood up, and looked back at the kitchen door.

This had really just happened, he realized. The glass had actually been broken, and it now lay everywhere upon the kitchen floor. This had been no dream; nor had been the real, flesh-and-blood woman who caused it. But now that same woman had just vanished, perhaps never to be seen by him again. As he stood there thinking, another unfathomable riddle floated to the surface.

How in God's name could I have dreamed of her, before actually seeing her in the flesh?

Chapter 4

The following morning found Constance sitting like a terrified child on the floor, her arms wrapped around her legs and her forehead resting down atop her knees. A sense of panic had tormented her all night for fear that *he* might come searching for her, but so far she had seen nothing of him.

After running out of the house she had taken refuge in Seaside's barn, in one of the far corners of the second-floor loft. For more than 170 years this had been her secret place; the place where she always came to seek privacy not only from the succession of interlopers who claimed to own her home, but also from an ever-evolving world for which she cared so little. After some more time had passed, the sense of panic finally stopped bedeviling her. At last she lifted her head and looked around.

Perhaps he has gone, she thought, *and I could go back into the house. But what difference would it make? He is Seaside's new master, and because of that he is sure to return.*

Although the barn was old, it remained sounder than it appeared. This corner of hers on the second floor was comforting, and she would come here to be alone with her thoughts and memories. Because of the cold, she did not visit here often in the wintertime. But during the summer she spent many hours here.

Some time ago, when one of Seaside's previous owners had been away, she had used the opportunity to steal a chair from the house and bring it here, to her secret hideaway. Over time she had also absconded with clothing, which she kept locked up in an old chest, along with some perfume she had also taken. When another of the owners had thrown away his old mattress, in the dead of night she had dragged it to the barn and agonizingly hauled it up the stairs.

Finally rising from the floor, she dusted herself off and went to lie down upon the tattered mattress. But she could not sleep just now, for her mind was still too shocked and confused about what had happened. The mere idea of it caused such terror in her heart! That encounter had been no dream. It had been quite real, and totally unlike anything she had ever experienced.

She reached alongside the mattress and looked into a hand mirror that she had also stolen from the house many years ago. Although it was old, its glass remained clear. Seventeen decades had come and gone, yet she hadn't aged a day. She had neither become ill, nor had she ever required food or water. It was as if she were trapped in time, while all the rest of the world had aged. As she continued to regard her likeness in the mirror, another thought struck her.

This is the face he saw; the same face that no one else in the world has beheld during my more than 170 years of this awful imprisonment. But how in God's name had he been able to do so, when in all this time no one else could? Who is he, that he can do such things?

While trying to make some sense of it all, she put down the mirror and closed her eyes. The man named Garrett who stood in the kitchen doorway last night had actually seen her! But how could this be? And perhaps more importantly, what had caused it to happen? Because she had become so startled during the encounter, her spontaneous reactions had been to scream in panic and flee the house. Later on she realized that there must have indeed been some logical reason for what had happened, but to her further dismay, she still had far more questions than answers.

Her strange ability to remain unseen and unheard by others had at first seemed a terrible curse. But as she began to grasp the true nature of her situation, she understood that these qualities were in some ways a blessing. They served as a sort of protection, a way in which she could still operate in the world without being discovered. She had long known that should her existence be revealed, her life would never be the same. She would become an object of investigation, never-ending study, and perhaps even derision. And to Constance, that would become a hell far worse than the one she currently endured.

But now a man named Garrett was able to see and hear her, causing that sense of protection to be vanquished, and it frightened her. Was this the beginning of her salvation, or the start of a new spiral down into some other form of torment?

She would only learn these things through experience, which meant another encounter with Garrett. But did she dare? And if she did, what would become of her? What sort of man was he? Would he treat her kindly and try to help her? Or would he use the nature of her situation to reveal her to the world and perhaps try to make a fortune? Although she was desperate to learn more, she also knew that whatever action she took, she must proceed with caution.

She had of course known that for a second time, Seaside had gone into foreclosure. At first that news had broken her heart. But the last owners had been crude people who never appreciated the house for what it truly was. Worst of all, she was forced to stand by and watch them destroy her beloved home.

Although she knew that it would do no good, she had screamed, wailed, and pleaded with them while they gleefully wrecked Seaside. Each blow from their sledgehammers and every vulgarity they spray painted on the walls had felt like someone was stabbing her. But once her anger had calmed enough to allow some meaningful introspection, she had attributed this violation to the day and age in which she found herself. Despite its many so-called advances, to her the modern world had become a venal and ugly place.

Deciding to take the gamble, Constance left the barn had and began the walk toward Seaside. It was a lovely autumn morning with a bright blue sky and puffy clouds. Before entering the house she crept down along one side and looked out toward the driveway to find that there were no cars present. Emboldened, she went around to the backside of the house and let herself into the kitchen.

For several moments she simply stood there listening, but all she heard were the muffled sounds of the sea crashing against the shoreline. She then walked on down the hall, carefully peering into each room. She also did the same on the second floor, again finding that she was apparently alone. Finally relaxing a little, she went back downstairs and into the parlor where Garrett and the other man, named Jay, had stood talking last night.

She walked over to the table and looked down at Garrett's floor plans. To her amazement he had labeled each room correctly. From her place in the kitchen last night she had only been able to hear bits and pieces of their conversation, but what she had gleaned from it was that Garrett was the new owner, and Jay was the man responsible for the day-to-day activities of renovating Seaside.

Just then a rare smile crossed her lips as she thought about the other part of last night, the part about which Garrett did not fully know. Before Garrett had seen her, he had gone to the roof to view the widow's walk. Summoning up all of her courage, Constance had silently followed him and then hidden in the shadows, watching.

She had been intrigued by the way he had meticulously inspected the widow's walk, almost as if he had been some kind of expert. Then the sea breeze had risen and carried the scent of her perfume his way. She watched, almost mischievously, as he detected the scent then turned this way and that, while trying to determine its source. And when his trip to the roof ended, she had silently followed him back downstairs and gone to sit in the kitchen. But never in her wildest dreams had she ever imagined what might happen next.

As Constance again turned her attention toward the floor plans that Garrett had drawn up, she came to a decision. For better or for worse, next time he was in the house she would confront him. She had no doubt that it would be a cathartic experience for each of them, and that Garrett might well think her mad when she told him her story. But she was at last willing to face her destiny, no matter what it might be. As she thought about it, a chill went through her

When will he return to me? she wondered.

Chapter 5

The following Sunday afternoon Garrett was again aboard his motorcycle, this time roaring toward his parents' house. Whatever troubles he might be suffering always seemed to vanish when he rode, giving him an indescribable sort of freedom that he had never been able to duplicate in any other way.

Earlier this week, his mother had called and asked him to Sunday dinner. Garrett was hoping to speak to his mother in private, but his younger sister, Christine, and her family would be there too.

Garrett's mother was the finest cook that he had ever known, and it was because of her that he could hold his own in the kitchen. He'd packed two bottles of very good wine—one red and one white—inside his motorcycle saddlebags. He smiled as he predicted her horror of transporting wine this way, for she would surely insist that he had bruised it. Downshifting smoothly, he cruised through a yellow light and confidently took the next corner with just the right amount of lean. He then twisted open the throttle and sped up again, the Harley's twin exhausts trumpeting in his ears.

Some ten minutes later, Garrett arrived at his parents' home. This was not the larger house in which he and his sister had grown up. On Garrett's advice his parents had wisely sold that property at the top of the market, then bought a smaller home for cash, pocketing a substantial profit. With the arrival of their twilight years, they were also grateful for the reduced home maintenance. "You don't own a house," his father, Dale, was fond of saying. "The house owns you." Given his huge renovation project that lay ahead, Garrett knew that truer words were never spoken.

Garrett guided his Harley onto the driveway, then unpacked the wine and let himself into the house. At once the unmistakable aroma of prime rib teased his nostrils.

"Garrett, that'd better be you!" his mother called out from the kitchen.

Garrett laughed and went to join her. After putting his wine bottles and sunglasses atop one of the counters, he smiled.

"It's me, Mom," he answered.

Virginia Prescott stopped nurturing a piecrust and crossed the kitchen to embrace her son. Mixing spoon still in hand, she finally released him and stepped back a bit.

"Let me look at you," she said, in that firm but loving way only a mother can master. She smoothed his windblown hair. "You seem a bit thinner. Starving artist syndrome, no doubt. Well, no worries. You'll certainly get your fill today." She then looked disappointingly at the wine. "Oh, God," she said. "Please tell me that you didn't bring those by way of that horrible mechanical beast you ride."

Before answering, Garrett looked at her lovingly. Thanks to her own cooking she was a little rounder than she had been some twenty years ago. Her stylish, rather wayward gray hair was of medium length. Chocolate brown eyes, a full mouth, and a straight, aristocratic nose completed the picture. Garrett had seen earlier photos of his mother, and in her day she had been a knockout.

After her discharge from the army, Virginia had gone on to complete her Ph.D. in psychology, which had been no small feat while also raising two children. The hundreds of patients she helped over the decades had worshiped her, and many became dismayed when she retired last year.

Garrett took a Coke from the refrigerator and opened it. "Where's Dad?" he asked.

"Country club," Virginia answered while getting back to her pie. "His monthly poker game, you know."

Just then Freckles, Dale's black and white spotted English setter came bounding down the hall and skidded recklessly into the kitchen. Whenever she ran she always seemed to have twice as many legs, all of them flailing about madly in her eagerness. Garrett reached down and tousled her ears.

"Hey, girl," he said. "Are they treating you all right?"

Ever in search of food, Freckles relentlessly snuffled every part of Garrett that she could reach. Finally satisfied that he wasn't hiding a porterhouse steak anywhere on his person, she ambled across the kitchen where she made several quick, manic circles before finally lying down on her dog bed.

"Why does she always do that?" Garrett asked absently.

"The snuffling thing or the little circles thing?" his mother asked.

"Both."

"Since they have to do with eating and sleeping, she probably learned them from your father," she answered.

Pausing in her work, Virginia gave Garrett a more serious look.

"So tell me," she said, "how is everything out at the mausoleum? Have you started renovating the place yet? And by the way, have you had any serious bites on your condo?"

From the moment he had first driven his parents out to view Seaside, Virginia had jokingly referred to it as "the mausoleum." But he also suspected that of all the people in his family, it was she who best understood his motives.

"Seaside," Garrett answered.

"What?" Virginia asked.

"Seaside," Garrett repeated. "I discovered that was the name given to the house by its second owners, and I'm going to keep on calling it that."

"Okay," Virginia answered. "So what's going on with Seaside?"

Garrett briefly told her of his meeting with Jay Morgan, and that the restoration was to begin soon. As for his condo, he said that he had heard nothing from his Realtor for several days now, and he made a mental note to give her a call.

"Well," Virginia said, "if the condo doesn't sell and you need some financial help, please tell us. The last thing this family needs is a house-poor architect."

She laughed compassionately at that last thought. "God," she added, "now there's an ironic concept."

Garrett also laughed and then thanked his mother for her kind offer. He loved being here, and it always felt the same—comfortable, forgiving, and safe. Then his expression darkened a bit.

"So we're alone in the house?" he asked.

With precision accuracy, Virginia centered her crust onto a pie dish and carefully trimmed its edges.

"Just you, me, and Freckles," she answered. "And I'm pretty sure that we can count on her discretion. Why do you ask?"

"I need to talk to you," he said.

On sensing Garrett's needful tone, Virginia turned and raised her eyebrows.

"As your mother?" she asked, "or as a shrink?"

"Both, I guess."

"As a family member, it would usually be unethical for me to formally counsel you," she said, "but that doesn't matter much, now that I'm retired."

As Garrett sat down at the kitchen table, his mother poured a cup of coffee and joined him.

"What is it?" she asked.

Virginia had already morphed into psychologist mode, her mood impassive, her mind alert, her facial expression neither condemning nor condoning.

"I had a very strange dream," Garrett said.

"Tell me about it," his mother answered.

For the next ten minutes, Garrett described his dream. He stopped short of telling his mother about actually seeing the woman at Seaside, for fear of sounding crazy.

"So you dreamed of a beautiful woman," Virginia answered. "That in and of itself is not unusual." She took another sip of coffee, thinking. "The part about her begging you to help her is interesting, though. So too is the way that she was dressed."

"What do you think it means?" Garrett asked.

"Easy there, cowboy," Virginia replied. "I haven't heard anywhere near enough yet."

"I'm not sure I understand," Garrett said.

Virginia smiled before taking another sip of coffee.

"Now that your purchase of Seaside is said and done, how do you feel about it?"

Garrett scowled and leaned back in his chair.

"Am I supposed to act guilty?"

"I didn't say that," Virginia countered. "But even if you did feel guilty, you went ahead and bought Seaside anyway. I'm not judging you, son. I'm simply asking."

Virginia got up from the table and went to warm up her coffee. When she returned, she thought to herself for a few moments before continuing.

"I don't know all that much about dream analysis," she said. "But what I can tell you with certainty is that every dream you've ever had, or ever will have, will be a product of your own mind. In most cases, dreams are about subconscious problem solving. In addition, we alone are the actors, the producers, the writers, the directors, and so on. Your mind sensed a problem and tried to solve it."

"What problem?"

"I don't know," Virginia answered. "I wasn't a part of it."

"Okay," Garrett answered. "The woman in my dream was blond, and perhaps the most beautiful I've ever seen. And she was begging me to help her. Help her do what? I wonder. Do you think I'll ever know?"

"Probably not," Virginia answered. "Nor may you need to."

"I don't understand."

"Ah, men," she answered. "I keep forgetting that you're all from Mars, as they say. Clearly, you're searching for your perfect woman." Then Virginia smiled again. "You know," she added, "for a Ph.D., you can be pretty dense sometimes."

Garrett smiled a little bit. "It's indigenous to the gender," he answered.

"No argument there," Virginia replied. "And then there's this business about the way the woman was dressed. What do you suppose that means?"

"I have no idea," Garrett answered.

"Okay, then," his mother said. "I'll spell it out for you. You have a great love for antebellum culture— so much so that I have oftentimes thought you would actually be happier living in the past. There's nothing wrong with that, Garrett. Many perfectly normal people feel that way. As I said before, what your subconscious mind has done is to invent your 'dream woman,' so to speak. Plus the added touch of her being in so much distress and literally begging for your help only made her more attractive to you."

Garrett's expression sobered again.

"It seems that I have some thinking to do."

Virginia nodded without smiling.

"And one more thing about love," she said earnestly. "As you search for it, there's something you really need to watch."

"What's that?"

"Don't let your heart alone dictate your decisions. That's far too dangerous. Although they are often at cross purposes, until your heart and your mind agree, you're still in search of the right woman."

"Thanks, Mom," Garrett said.

She smiled and patted his hand.

"Anytime, kiddo," she answered.

Just then they heard a door open and close.

"Hello the house!" Garrett's father called out.

"We're in the kitchen," Virginia shouted back.

Garrett looked at his mother.

"You'll keep this just between us?" he asked quietly.

Virginia nodded.

"You bet," she answered.

When Dale Richmond entered the kitchen, Freckles bounded up from her languid repose and hurried over to eagerly snuffle every reachable inch of him. After again finding nothing edible, she glumly returned to her bed and expertly performed several more circles before settling down. As if on cue, Garrett and Virginia looked at each other and laughed.

"What's so funny?" Dale asked.

"Nothing, Dad," Garrett answered. "How was your poker game?"

Dale smiled and dropped a wad of bills atop the kitchen table.

"Made two hundred bucks," he said proudly. "Your old man's still got the mojo."

Quick as a wink, Virginia scooped up the money and shoved it into an apron pocket.

"What the hell?" Dale asked. "I was going to use that to buy a new driver."

Virginia shook her head. "It's going into the fund for the new downstairs vanity," she said. "You know— the one you're always carping about because its top is chipped and the doors are hanging askew?"

Garrett looked at his mother and raised his eyebrows. "*Askew,*" he said. "Wow."

Virginia smiled and pointed toward herself. "*P . . . h . . . D,*" she answered. "You should know."

Dale sighed. "OK, Ginnie," he said. Then he looked back at Garrett. "Remember, son," he said. "You don't own a house—"

"*The house owns you!*" Garrett and Virginia chimed in, laughingly.

"God," Dale said. "I've just been mocked by a pair of brainiacs with advanced degrees. You know the types—they can easily tell me how miles it is to the moon, but can't fold a road map. How humiliating . . ."

Virginia turned toward Garrett and rolled her eyes. " 'Brainiacs,' he calls us," she said. "And to think that I gave him the skinniest years of my life."

Dale laughed broadly. His laugh was always the same: a strong, knowing, and uncompromising explosion of happiness that exactly mirrored his nature, and was best suited to the company of other stalwart men.

Garrett looked lovingly at his Dad. Like Virginia, Dale was in his early sixties. He was deeply tanned from his time on the golf course, and he carried a gradually expanding midsection for which he bore no shame. Although short and squat, he was powerfully built. He was balding, but instead of vainly plastering some hair over the top of his head he bore his baldness courageously, like some hard-won badge of honor. Like Garrett's, his crystal blue eyes were mesmerizing.

Dale had been a highly respected thoracic surgeon, whose only real fault as a father was that he always worked too much. When his own father had died unexpectedly from a massive heart attack it had been a great blow to Dale, causing him to seriously examine his life. So he decided to stop and smell the roses for good, he retired early, and he and Virginia sold their big house and bought the current smaller one.

"I see you rode your motorcycle," he said to Garrett.

"Yep," Garrett answered. "I would have brought the Jeep, but I know how much the two of you like seeing me on the bike."

"Very funny," Dale said. He opened the refrigerator and produced a bottle of Heineken. "Want one?" he asked.

Garrett shook his head. "Never when I'm riding," he answered.

Dale opened the beer and sat at the table. After taking an appreciative gulp, he asked, "So how's Trent these days? Is he still chasing girls, twenty-four/seven?"

Garrett nodded. "And how," he said. "In fact, he just—"

Virginia quickly raised a hand. "Too much information," she said.

Dale winked at Garrett. "Not for me," he replied.

"Instead of living vicariously through Trent's escapades, why don't you make yourself useful?" she asked. "Come and take the roast out of the oven for me. It's done and it needs to rest."

Dale looked at Garrett. "Later . . ." he whispered.

As Dale opened the oven door, the wonderful aroma that Garrett had encountered on first entering the house overcame him anew. Just as Dale placed the roasting pan on the counter, Christine's two daughters came bursting in, squealing with delight.

Elizabeth was seven; Allison was five. Like Garrett, they had sandy-blond hair. Virginia loved her two granddaughters more than life, but trying to keep them out of mischief was akin to the impossible. The girls didn't have any pets at home, so whenever they visited, poor Freckles served as their personal pet, third sister, and jungle gym.

As usual, Freckles cowered noticeably when she saw them steamrolling toward her. As Elizabeth pulled on her ears, Allison decided that it would be fun to try riding her. Only after a kindly but firm rebuke from Dale did they finally calm down and leave the poor dog alone.

"Hi, Dad," Christine said as she walked into the room, followed by her husband, Clark.

Christine was a lovely blond, with a killer smile that sometimes stopped men dead in their tracks. Clark was heavyset and jovial. When Christine wasn't doing her best to keep her girls corralled, she worked as a paralegal. Clark owned his own art supply business, and he traveled a lot.

Christine tousled Garrett's hair. "Hey, Wild One," she said. "Knocked over any gas stations lately?"

Garrett gave her a kiss. "Hey right back," he answered.

Clark helped himself to a beer then he sat down beside Garrett. Smiling, he clanked his beer bottle against Garrett's soda can.

An hour later with the pie cooling, the roast and green bean casserole done to perfection, and the Yorkshire pudding about to be cut, everyone was at last seated at the heavily laden dining table. Garrett took a moment to savor the scene. It was like something straight from a Norman Rockwell painting, and it warmed his heart.

Virginia was alternating between castigating Dale about the way he was carving the roast, and admonishing Garrett about the "bruised" wine. Elizabeth and Allison were pulling at each other's hair and calling one another insulting names. Christine busily harangued poor Clark about him never buying a motorcycle. And last but surely not least, Freckles sat patiently beside Garrett's chair, hoping for a handout. As one of her paws came to rest atop Garrett's thigh, Freckles made a begging sound that tugged at his heart.

Garrett smiled. No matter how random was every aroma, every action, every word, every laugh, and every tinkle of silverware and glass, each was exactly as it should be. Like snowflakes somehow born of thin air, the scene before him was being created naturally and without pretense; each part of it was unique in all of the world, and never to be duplicated in just the same way. But Garrett's joy was soon tempered, as he yet again wondered how many more such treasured gatherings he would share with his aging parents before they were finally gone. It was best that there was no discernible number, he realized, for the knowing of it would only tarnish such beloved moments as this.

And then he again thought of the mysterious woman he had encountered at Seaside, and he felt another pang of unexplained longing go through his heart. His mother had given him all the help she could, considering he had not shared the entire story. He had no way of knowing whether he would see that beautiful and ephemeral woman again.

But he silently resolved that if he did, things would be different.

Chapter 6

From a tenuous vantage point in one corner of the parlor, Constance watched with interest as Jay Morgan poured over Garrett's floor plans. Three days had passed since Garrett had seen her, and now workers had descended upon Seaside to begin their labors in earnest.

The men had begun working on the outside of the home first. Some of them were atop Seaside, eagerly tearing off the old roofing and throwing it to the ground. Others were removing the ancient clapboard siding and loading it into portable Dumpsters. While the sounds of their work resonated, Constance remained in the parlor and watched Jay as he now began making notes.

To Constance's disappointment, Garrett had not returned to Seaside since the night he had so surprisingly seen her. At first she wondered whether she'd scared him away. But then she decided that was probably not the case, since he seemed so intent upon completing this project.

Despite how little Constance knew about Garrett, she was certain of one thing. He loved this old house, and he was determined to restore it to its original beauty. At first Constance had been skeptical of Garrett's intentions. But now that the work had actually begun, she felt both joy and thankfulness that someone had at last purchased Seaside who might truly know how the house should appear.

She was surprised by how often Garrett had crossed her mind during the last three days. Since her fall from the widow's walk, he had been the only person to recognize her presence, but in her heart of hearts, she had also begun wondering if there might be other reasons. She had been without a man for a long time, yet it was more than that. His apparent determination to put Seaside right also intrigued her deeply. Did that make them kindred spirits? she wondered. Perhaps so . . . In any event she was eager to see him again, and when next she did, she would do her best to tell him her entire story.

Treading carefully, Constance wended her way out the front door and found a place to sit in the grass, where she could watch the workmen swarm over Seaside like so many busy ants. Although she had watched the world evolve for seventeen decades, she remained amazed at how much mankind had learned to do, and how quickly they could now do it.

It would be enjoyable to watch Seaside become whole again, she realized. And then what would happen? She could only assume that Garrett would live here permanently. And if he did, would he do so alone? Was he married? Did he have children? As such questions arose, she realized that they could only be answered with the passage of time.

Just then she heard the distant sound of a car coming up the road, and she turned to look. The moment Garrett's black vehicle came into view, she quickly stood up and began running toward the house. She could not confront him now, for there were others about. Running as fast as she could, she rounded the near corner of the house and entered quietly through the open back door, hoping against hope that Garrett had not seen her. Knowing that Garrett would seek out Jay, Constance again silently made her way down the hallway and reentered the parlor.

As Garrett stopped his Jeep before Seaside, he looked at the house and smiled. As luck would have it, he had not noticed the mystery woman. Even so, his mind went to her. Would he ever see her again? he wondered. Was she here even now, hiding somewhere about the property?

At long last his project was beginning, and seeing the busy workmen warmed his heart. Garrett enjoyed listening to music, but the various sounds of men working was the melody he loved best. Grinning from ear to ear, he happily trotted to the front porch and then entered the parlor, where he found Jay, steaming coffee cup in hand, examining Garrett's floor plans.

"Got any more of that?" Garrett asked as he walked into the room.

Without looking up, Jay took another swig of coffee. "Nope," he answered. "This stuff's for real workin' men only."

Garrett let go a little laugh as he cast his eyes about the room. A coffee station had been set up on a work-table along the far wall, so he went over and poured himself a cup, then went to stand alongside Jay. After he thought to himself for a few moments, Garrett's curiosity got the better of him and he decided to ask Jay something.

"By the way," he said nonchalantly, "have you seen anyone hanging around the house that doesn't belong? Like a beautiful blonde, maybe?"

Jay turned and looked at Garret like he had just been released from some institution. "What the hell are you talking about?" he asked.

"I thought I saw somebody like that here the other night," Garrett answered, "but now I'm guessing that it was probably only a shadow. I just thought I'd ask."

Jay snorted out a laugh. "With the bunch of guys I've got here working for me?" he asked. "Trust me, pal—if there'd been some gorgeous blonde lurking around, I'd have heard about it."

As Jay returned his focus to the plans, he took another swig of the excellent coffee.

"You know," he said, "for a genius professor, you're not a half-bad architect. Although you only paced off the rooms, these measurements seem spot-on."

"Wow," Garrett answered. "An honest-to-God complement."

"What the hell," Jay said. "So long as you're the money man, I have to be nice to you." At last he turned and looked at Garrett. "So how are you doing, ace?"

Garrett happily raised his coffee cup. "This is already a banner day, my friend," he answered. "Not only has our project officially begun, this morning I also accepted an offer on my condo! Which should relieve you, because now you know that you'll get paid."

"I was never worried about that," Jay answered. "Though I'd actually enjoy visiting you in debtors' prison."

After a couple more minutes of good-natured bantering, the two men got down to cases. Jay explained what was happening on the outside of the house, and he also gave Garrett a slightly revised timetable. Although he couldn't promise it, Jay thought that the entire project might now be completed a bit sooner than he first thought.

From her vantage point in the corner, Constance listened with great interest while Garrett advised Jay about such things as the correct style of crown moldings to use, what type of flooring should be laid, and so on. In each case, Constance noticed that Garrett was exactly describing how Seaside had looked at the height of her beauty. *What will it be like,* she wondered, *to again wander this house as it once was? Will doing so make me remember Adam even more vividly, thereby causing me only greater loneliness? Or will having this wonderful house fully restored finally give me some measure of peace?* Only time would tell, she decided. But first she would have to explain herself to Garrett, and that task filled her heart with trepidation.

Jay gave Garrett a sidelong glance. "What are you doing here, anyway?" he asked. "Shouldn't you be at your office, extracting every last cent from some unsuspecting consumer?"

"As a matter of fact, yes," Garrett answered. "I just wanted to see how things were going, and to let you know about the condo. But I'll be back later."

"Great," Jay said laughingly. "That's just what I need—a nanny."

"Don't think of me as a nanny," Garrett answered. "Just look at me as the guy who pays you."

"That'll help," Jay replied. "But if I had known you were going to be out here so often, I would've charged you a fee, just for watching."

Garrett laughed. "I've got to go," he said.

"Good," Jay answered. "And if I see a beautiful blonde hanging around, I'll get her number for you."

Garrett laughed. "Yeah," he answered. "Like you'd have a shot."

After giving Jay a hearty slap on the back, Garrett left the parlor, then walked down the front steps and got into his Jeep. In a matter of moments he was gone.

Constance was saddened to see Garrett leave. But as the day wore on and she watched the workmen continue to toil, she took solace in knowing that Garrett would return tonight. And if by then all the workmen were gone, she would reveal herself to him, no matter the outcome.

———————

Later that evening, Constance sat on Seaside's expansive veranda, watching the ocean birth wave after wave. All of the workmen had left about an hour ago, leaving her alone to await Garrett's return. It was a beautiful night and the wind was forgiving, causing the Atlantic to strike the shoreline gently. Such was oftentimes the case here in the early evening, when the wind lessened and the night creatures began warbling. This was normally her favorite time of day, but tonight was vastly different, because for the first time in more than 170 years, she would attempt an actual conversation with another human being.

Garrett had yet to return, and as the minutes ticked by, Constance became much more nervous. Even so, she was starting to get a feel for this man, this apparent architectural expert who had ordered the renovation of her beloved home. He seemed like someone who kept his promises, she realized.

Then her thoughts again turned to Adam, and once more she opened the locket hanging about her neck. In the dim light of evening she could barely make out his portrait, but it was no matter. She had looked at it so many times over the years that by now her memory of it rivaled the portrait itself. How she missed him! Even now he was the one true love of her life, and her passion for him remained so deep and strong.

As she closed the locket, her mind returned to the present. Garrett would be here soon, and with his arrival she must have a plan in place. Before now, she had always been able to remain here in this house seemingly forever, watching other people go about their lives. But because Garrett had so surprisingly recognized her existence, she felt that the time had come to share her many secrets, even if it was with just one man. With the knowledge that there was someone like him out there, she could no longer accept being merely a party to the world, but never a part of it.

As she sat thinking, the seed of an idea came to her, something that she could perhaps propose to Garrett if all else failed. But would he accept the premise? She knew not, and doing so would surely be her last, best hope.

Just then Constance saw the bright headlights of Garrett's Jeep round the far corner of the road and pierce the darkness. Suddenly more fearful than at any time since falling from the widow's walk, she left her chair and took refuge in the shadowy recesses of the house.

After exiting his jeep, Garrett stared up at Seaside, wondering whether he might ever again see the mysterious woman who haunted both his sleeping and waking moments. In truth, his feelings regarding her were torn. One part of him wanted her to be gone, so that he might find a measure of peace about all this. But the greater part wanted to see her again. Over the course of the last three days his strange longing for her had strengthened sharply. To his further frustration, he sensed that this surprising feeling would only intensify in the days to come.

Perhaps tonight I will find out why, he thought as he began walking toward the house.

On entering Seaside he quietly went from room to room, turning on all of Jay's electric lanterns. Although they lit the house well, each lent an unnatural hue that he found jarring. As best he could tell, "she" was not here.

Eager to see the progress that Jay's men had made, Garrett walked back down the front porch steps and around one front corner of the house. He held a lamp high and did his best to examine the work. Much of one side of the house had already been stripped clean of the boards, and he could see where some of the wood underneath had become moldy and rotten. These areas would be replaced with fresh lumber before the new clapboards were installed.

He then walked around the rest of the house, looking for other signs of work. All in all he was satisfied, and he could now understand Jay's optimistic reappraisal of the timetable. Given that the project was under way, and that he had also accepted an offer on his condo, this had been a very good day.

He walked back down to his Jeep, where he removed a few items before returning to the porch. After setting the electric lantern atop the porch railing, he settled into one of the folding chairs, lit a fresh cigar, and poured three fingers of Jack Daniel's into a highball glass. He would sit here for a time, he decided, before going home.

Sometime later—perhaps after half a cigar and three sips Jack Daniel's—his thoughts returned to the beautiful woman he had seen here three nights ago. He still couldn't get her out of his mind, given his total shock at seeing her brazenly sitting in his kitchen and crying her eyes out, not to mention her amazing beauty. Despite her distressed state, there had been an allure associated with her the likes of which he had never experienced. *Will she ever return?* he wondered. And if she did, might the two of them—

"Excuse me, Mr. Richmond?" a woman's voice suddenly asked from the darkness.

Garrett was so startled that he flinched sharply. He immediately stood up and peered into the gloom.

"Who's there!" he shouted.

As Constance slowly came into view, the cigar fell from Garrett's lips and the cocktail tumbler slipped from his hand. Her appearance was so identical to that of the woman in his dream that he literally could not speak. Sensing his overwhelming surprise, Constance gently took two steps nearer to stand fully in the light granted by the lantern. In some ways she was as frightened as he.

"So you are able to see me, after all," she whispered, her voice a sudden prisoner to her emotions. "For the last three days I have been wondering if it was really true, or but a dream."

For several moments Garrett's mouth worked up and down, but no words came. At last he found his voice.

"Yes . . . yes, of course I can see you," he answered. "Why wouldn't I?"

For the first time in a long while, Constance allowed herself just the hint of a smile.

"Well, Mr. Richmond," she said, "that is a rather long story, and if you will permit me, I would like to tell it to you. May I come up on the porch?"

"Uh . . . err . . . yes. Yes, of course, Miss, uh . . ."

Her legs trembling, Constance walked up the steps then came to stand before him at last.

"My name is Constance Elizabeth Canfield," she answered. "And there is much to which you need to be made privy."

Chapter 7

G arrett couldn't believe his ears. Constance Canfield and her husband, Adam, had given this home its lovely name. *So who could this woman be?* he wondered. *Some long-lost descendant perhaps, or maybe some squatter, looking for a handout?* Before he could answer, Constance produced another short smile.

"But before we converse," she said, "perhaps you should extinguish that cigar. It would be a shame to watch Seaside burn to the ground this night, would it not?"

"Uh . . . yes, of course," he answered. After a couple moments of searching he picked up the cocktail glass and then crushed the still-glowing cigar beneath one shoe.

"May I take a chair?" Constance asked politely.

"Yes," Garrett answered. "Please do."

As Constance took the chair alongside him, Garrett grasped the opportunity to look her over. Yet again, her beauty amazed him. This time her long blond hair was pulled back into a ponytail. She had large blue eyes, a rather short and straight nose, and full lips. She was a tall woman with a lovely figure. Her battered clothes, however, seemed to belie her beauty. She wore a simple red-and-white plaid shirt underneath a shopworn leather jacket, a pair of very old-looking jeans, and some blue and white Keds that had clearly seen better days.

Her clothes were not that unusual. It was their condition that was awful. They were rumpled and looked as if they hadn't been cleaned in a long time, adding further evidence to the chance that she might be a homeless person. Plus she carried no purse, which was odd for a woman of her age. Still unsure about how to begin a conversation, Garrett took a few moments to pour some more Jack Daniel's.

"Would you like some?" he asked.

Constance shook her head. "No thank you, sir," she answered.

After taking a generous swig, Garrett said, "So who are you, and why are you here at my home? This is the second night that I've seen you, and I don't understand. You seemed to be in a terrible way the first time. Do you need help of some kind?"

Constance closed her eyes for a few moments. *And just how do I answer such questions?* she wondered. *How on earth do I begin explaining myself to this man?*

After a while she nodded. "Yes," she answered. "That night I was in terrible straits. But I am in better form now, and there is much that you need to learn."

By now Garrett had calmed down, and he began regarding her with more skepticism than surprise. He could also see that her eyes were becoming shiny with the advent of tears.

"I'm listening," he answered politely.

"I know of no other way to say this," Constance answered, "so I'll just speak plainly."

While again trying to summon up her courage, she turned and looked out over the ocean.

"My name is Constance Elizabeth Canfield," she began. "I was born here in New Bedford, in the year of our Lord 1808. My husband was Adam Canfield, a whaler captain who died in a terrible storm while trying to round Cape Horn. On the same day that my beloved Adam died, I accidentally fell from the widow's walk atop this house and crashed onto the shoreline only feet from where we now sit. Adam perished, but for some unknown reason I did not, and was instead caught between the worlds of the living and the dead. I have existed here in this house since then, invisible to all the others who have come and gone, while also watching the history of the world unfold before me. In all that time, no one besides you has ever been able to see me or to hear me speak. Moreover, for some inexplicable reason only you can see the clothing I wear. That is why I have come to you this night, and why I have told you my story. Something about my existence has changed, and I need to know why you are so different from all the rest."

At last she took her gaze from the waves and looked at Garrett's face. By now her tears had come in earnest and were tracing their way down her cheeks.

Please, God, she thought. *Please make this man believe me . . .*

But to her deep disappointment, Garrett only shook his head.

"I don't know what you're after," he said, "but it must be something big for you to have made up a story like this! Did you honestly think I would swallow that? I know full well who Constance Canfield really was. All it took was a couple hours of research, something that you could have also done easily. So you tell me right now—who are you really, and what are you after? If I don't get an answer from you that makes sense, I'm going to call the police."

The sudden change in Garrett's tone stabbed at Constance's heart. But who could blame him? Her story was totally absurd, at best. As tears streamed down her face, she began trembling. She was unsure of how to continue, but continue she must, for she sensed that her very existence depended upon it.

"I beseech you, Mr. Richmond," she said pleadingly. "Every word I've just told you is the God's honest truth. I really am the same Constance Elizabeth Canfield who supposedly disappeared in 1840 and never returned."

Trying her best to compose herself, she wiped the tears from her cheeks and again cast her gaze out over the Atlantic.

"God's truth is," she added softly, "I never really left."

Her pleading tone softened Garrett's heart a bit, but her story remained completely unbelievable. Then he suddenly remembered his dream about her. He also abruptly realized that the longing he felt for this woman was increasing in intensity, and becoming nearly impossible to resist. It was as if his psyche was being ripped apart by two totally overpowering forces. One part of him wanted to dismiss this madwoman completely, but the other part suddenly wanted to believe her. No, he realized. It was far more than a case of simply needing to believe her. He wanted to pick her up off her feet, bend her body beneath his, and—

"Mr. Richmond?" Constance asked, interrupting his thoughts. "Are you quite all right?"

In an attempt to clear his mind, Garrett took a deep breath then scrubbed his face with his hands, a habit since his teen years.

"Yes, yes I am," he finally answered. Then to his own surprise, he added, "And although I don't believe you, I'd like to hear more."

To Constance's own surprise, she now hesitated. This was the first glimmering of any attempt on Garrett's part to believe her, and she didn't want to stifle that sentiment. But at the same time she now realized that if she told him everything at once, her tale would seem so unbelievable that he would dismiss her out of hand, and she couldn't risk that.

Then she considered playing the trump card that she had imagined, while sitting on the porch and await-ing his arrival. If he agreed, then later tomorrow she could tell him the rest of her tale and perhaps—just perhaps—he might start believing her. After taking a deep breath, she decided to forge ahead.

"I would be much pleased to tell you more," she answered. "But I also fathom why you're so hesitant to believe a story like mine. So if you will permit me, first I have an idea that might serve to put your misgivings to rest."

Garrett had to admit that he was intrigued. "And what would that be?" he asked.

When Constance explained, for the first time since seeing her, Garrett let go a short smile. What she had offered was ingenious, to say the least. He also knew that her idea was quite impossible.

"All right then," he said. "I'll come back tomorrow morning about the same time that I did today. You do what you offered, and then we'll see."

Although Constance was overjoyed, she did her best not to show it.

"Thank you, Mr. Richmond," she said. "I promise that I won't fail you."

"Call me Garrett," he told her.

"And you may call me Constance, should it please you to do so," she replied.

With their strange pact sealed, a quiet sort of peace reigned for a time. After a few more moments had passed, Constance decided to ask Garrett something else.

"There is one more thing I would request," she said. "And I will understand completely if you decline. But it would mean a great deal to me, because I have needed it for so very long."

"What is it?" Garrett asked.

Constance closed her eyes for a few moments before answering.

"Would you please take my hands into yours?" she asked.

Garrett's eyebrows rose questioningly.

"That's all," he asked, "to simply hold your hands?"

"Yes," Constance answered. "I have not felt the touch of another for so long. If you would but do this one thing for me I would be forever in your debt, no matter what happens on the morrow."

When Garrett stretched forth his hands, Constance replied in kind. And much to Garrett's surprise, from that point on, his life would never be the same.

Almost at once a wonderful sense of warmth and desire began to emanate outward from their joined hands. It was an indescribable feeling that they each sensed and soon permeated their entire beings. It was a blissful, joyful sensation that lifted the spirit and lightened the heart. At the same time, Garrett's unexplained longing for this woman suddenly became even more uncontrollable, and it took every last bit of willpower to finally release her. Stunned, he looked Constance in the eyes to find she had been as overcome as he.

Exhausted, Garrett fell back against his chair, trying to catch his breath. The same was true for Constance, as she too sought to regain her composure. After another few moments of silence, Garrett looked into her face.

"You felt it too?" he asked tentatively.

Still overcome, Constance only nodded.

"Did you know that would happen?" he asked.

Constance began to tremble again.

"No," she answered quietly. "I merely wanted to feel the touch of another human being after so long. What just transpired between us was entirely unexpected."

Garrett had to admit that he had never experienced anything remotely resembling what had just transpired between him and Constance. There had also been an undeniable sexual quality about it that, although fleeting, had been quite palpable. Despite all of his misgivings about this woman and her bizarre story, Garrett felt his defenses beginning to crumble.

"Can you explain it?" he asked.

Constance shook her head. "I cannot. I was as surprised as you. But after having lived this way for so long, I can tell you with certainty that there are forces operating in this world that mankind has yet to understand. I am the product of but one of them."

After looking out over the ocean again, Constance finally returned her gaze to his.

"With your permission I shall now take my leave," she said. "I have prevailed upon your time far too long, and given you a great deal to ponder. But I will keep my side of the bargain and be here tomorrow, as I prom-ised. Perhaps then you will start to believe me."

"Do you have a place to stay for the night?" Garrett asked, suddenly realizing that he did not want to see her go. "Would you like to sleep here? I would be happy to light a fire for you in one of the fireplaces."

Constance shook her head. "No, thank you," she answered. "I have a place, humble as it might be."

With that, she stood up and again looked Garrett in the eyes.

"Thank you for listening . . . Garrett," she said, tentatively using his first name. "If nothing else, at least after all this time I have finally shared a moment with another human being, and for that I am most grateful."

"Good night then," Garrett said, now even more aware that he would miss her badly. "I look forward to seeing you tomorrow."

Constance nodded. "Until the morrow . . ."

Constance then turned, walked down the steps, and disappeared into the night.

The moment she vanished, Garrett felt a sense of loneliness such as he had never before experienced. Moreover, he remained at a complete loss to under-stand how his earlier dream of her could have been so accurate. So too had he been totally absorbed in the experience of holding her hands—something else that defied explanation and description. He poured some more bourbon into the glass and swallowed it quickly, before again looking out over the restless Atlantic.

What just happened here? he found himself wondering.

Chapter 8

When he got to his condo, Garrett toyed with having some more bourbon then decided against it. He hadn't eaten dinner, but that no longer mattered. There was a woman on his mind just now, and he could not stop thinking about her. Even the blistering hot shower, followed by turning the handle onto full cold, failed to relieve his tension.

When at last he slipped between the cool sheets of his bed, his mind remained alive with questions. He had no doubt that this woman who called herself Constance Canfield was quite mad. Then again, there were many things about all of this that had yet to be answered. He also had no solution to his dream, or for what had happened between them when they held hands. Nor could he explain away his intense longing for this woman, so soon after having met her. And come the morning, what about this proposed scenario of hers? Could such a thing ever possibly work?

Just then an idea occurred to him. After thinking about it for a time, he switched on the nightstand lamp and reached for his cell phone. The number he dialed was a familiar one. When a sleepy-sounding voice answered, Garrett smiled to himself.

"Trent?" Garrett said. "It's me. Yeah, I know it's late. Listen, I need you to do me a favor. Meet me out at Seaside tomorrow morning will you, around eight o'clock? Yes, I know we have another presentation, but there'll be enough time for that. Why? Because I want you to go over the floor plans with me, and see if there's anything that I've missed. Okay, thanks. I'll see you there."

After shutting down the phone and turning off the light, Garrett's mind again began busily contemplating all the possibilities that tomorrow might bring. He had a very different reason for asking Trent to the house from the one he had explained to him.

As he continued to ponder these things and many more, sleep never came. Nor did any answers arrive with the dawn light as it began creeping through his bedroom windows. At around five-thirty, Garrett finally gave up and tossed the covers off his naked body. He shaved and showered, donned his favorite terry cloth bathrobe, and with a fresh cup of coffee in hand he went out onto his small condo balcony to greet the coming day. He liked his coffee strong and hot, and he could be a bear until he had his first cupful.

He would not miss this condominium. The offer he received yesterday had been slightly low, but because he would soon need more capital he had accepted without bargaining. The Realtor was disappointed that he hadn't made a counteroffer, but she understood. He wanted the money so he could concentrate fully on getting Seaside restored. On the plus side, he had purposely decorated the condo with inexpensive furniture, and because none of it would be appropriate for Seaside, he had listed the condo as "furnished." Letting all of this go was fine. He wanted it to be a new beginning, and it seemed that nothing could stop his dream now.

Even so, this would be a very busy time. The condo buyer was paying cash, and the seller's agreement had already been signed, so the closing would probably take place quickly. On top of his job and overseeing the restoration and teaching, he would also have to begin packing up what few personal items he would take with him. After his last meeting with Jay, he was no longer worried about whether Seaside would be buttoned up before winter. Although the place would be desperately

Spartan, he took comfort in knowing that he would soon rise each morning to the sounds of the sea.

Along with his thoughts of Seaside, the woman calling herself Constance Canfield again entered his mind. Clearly she had mental issues. For a moment he considered asking his mother to help her, but he saw no way to do that without seeming equally crazy. He didn't believe her wild tale, but at the same time he had absolutely no explanation for why he had dreamed of her before seeing her in the flesh, or the sensation he felt last night when holding her hands. His frustration mounting, he ran one hand through his still-damp hair.

Then there was also the bizarre scenario that she had concocted for this morning. Would she really go through with it? This was why he had called Trent and asked him to come out. He could imagine no way in which Trent and Constance might know each other. Therefore, if what she had in mind was some sort of joke cooked up between her and Jay, there would now be someone else there to call their bluff. Was this really just some huge prank? Maybe . . . but even that possibility did not answer his lingering questions.

His other concern regarding Constance was her continuing presence at Seaside. He felt sorry for her, but this could not go on. She told him last night that she had another place to stay, but where? The more he considered things, the more confused he became, especially about his growing attraction to her. It seemed to increase daily, but it had been especially pronounced last night, when he was in her actual presence. It was a heartfelt longing and a sharp sexual need that was causing him both joy and guilt.

His feelings for Constance defied definition, and he had never before reacted this way to a woman. He could not call it love. No, this was more like an obsession—a fascination with this beautiful creature that drifted in and out of his life whenever she chose. Constance was affecting him deeply, but this morning would settle everything. Assuming that Constance showed up and kept her side of the bargain, his suspicions about her madness would surely be confirmed, and he could then put all of this to rest.

But along with these worries had also come another and even more frightening concern. In all honesty, he was beginning to wonder whether he himself was going mad. Had he become some paranoid schizophrenic who saw people who weren't really there? Was his mother right, when she suggested that he had subconsciously created Constance as his "antebellum dream girl," and that her being in distress only added to her allure? He had no answers, and like his longing for

Constance, the fear for his sanity was growing by the moment.

Just then his stomach growled, reminding him that he had skipped dinner. He took a quick glance at his watch to find that it was six thirty. If he left soon, he could stop at his favorite diner and get some breakfast before heading out to Seaside.

Chapter 9

G arrett's mood lifted as he again watched Jay's men scrambling about the property. Like yesterday, some were working atop the roof while others were busily tearing off the siding. Jay's pickup was already here, but Trent had yet to arrive. *Good,* he thought. Garrett parked his Jeep and walked up the grassy knoll toward the porch.

Will she really show up like she said? he wondered. *Or has Constance been a figment of my imagination the entire time? Well, I'm about to find out . . .*

His tension rising with every step, Garrett entered the house then headed for the parlor, where Jay was dictating orders to a couple of his workers. Three more men were over at the coffee station, making selections from the doughnuts that Jay had brought. Constance was nowhere to be seen.

Feeling relieved, Garrett walked over to the coffee station. After saying hello to the workmen, he poured a cup of black coffee and took a sip. He then made his way over to where Jay was standing.

"Honey," he said, "I'm home."

"You hear that, guys?" Jay shouted out. "You all need to be on your best behavior, because Daddy Warbucks just arrived."

As the workmen laughed, Garrett joined in. He loved being around men who enjoyed a hard day's work and knew how to get things done. There had in fact been times when he believed he would have been equally happy as a construction laborer, and if for one minute he thought that he could afford to take a sabbatical from the firm and work here instead, he would do it.

Garrett looked back at Jay. "Thanks, dear," he said. "It's so heartwarming to know that you need me."

Jay laughed as he shook Garrett's hand. "Yeah," he answered, "about as much as a hole in my head."

Just then a familiar voice called out from the front door. "Hey!" Trent shouted. "Where is everybody?"

Garrett stuck his head out into the hall and beckoned Trent forward. "Down here," he said, "in the parlor."

Trent began trudging down the hallway. "The parlor," he grumbled to himself. "Who the hell has a parlor these days?"

When Trent arrived he spied the coffee and dough-nuts, and he made a beeline for them.

Jay shook his head. "Jesus," he said, "if I'd known there were gonna be this many freeloaders, I would've charged admission."

"I guess you'll just have to chalk it up to the cost of doing business," Garrett answered.

Jay turned and watched Trent eagerly munch a cin-namon doughnut. "So what brings you here today?" he asked.

Before answering, Trent swallowed hard. "I'm here on the boss's orders. I think he wants the benefit of my highly valuable input."

"Great," Jay said. "Another intellectual running around, making suggestions . . ."

Garrett beckoned Trent over to the aluminum table and showed him the floor plans. Like Jay had done with Garrett, he began telling Trent how the restora-tion was to be done. For the first time, Trent began to take an interest in Seaside, and he asked Jay a couple of salient questions.

Moments later, Garrett detected an unusual scent. It seemed familiar, but at first he could not place it. Then he realized that it was the same light, pretty fragrance that he had sensed last night while sitting with Constance on the veranda. His heart racing, he glanced about the parlor, but still saw no evidence of her.

And then, as if on silent cats' feet, Constance walked into the room. She came to stand directly behind Jay then turned and looked straight at Garrett. She was dressed in the same clothes as last night and there were dark circles under her eyes, lending the impression that she had not slept. Just as Garrett was about to speak to her, she quickly placed her index finger on her lips. Understanding, he relented.

His mind racing, Garrett watched with rapt fascination as Constance silently stepped in front of the table then looked directly at Jay and Trent. To Garrett's astonishment, neither they nor the other workmen took any notice of her. As Constance next looked at Garrett, he saw the beginnings of a mischievous smile cross her face.

Constance then stepped closer to Jay and she put her lips near his right ear. She blew lightly into Jay's ear and backed away. Jay quickly frowned, scratched his ear, and looked around. Then Constance stepped closer and repeated the gesture, this time more strongly. Jay's response was also more pronounced as he scratched his ear again, and then took a full step backward before glancing around once more.

"Dammit," he said, "there must be some houseflies in here. Freaking nuisances . . ."

Now Garrett was even more stunned. Even so, Constance had yet to prove her claims to his satisfaction. Sensing Garrett's continued skepticism, she moved to face Trent directly. She then gave Garrett another look, followed by a quick wink.

To Garrett's continued astonishment, Constance began making a series of bizarre faces at Trent, sometimes coming to within an inch of being nose to nose with him. She stuck out her tongue, pulled on her ears, and then finally made a threatening scowl, none of which Trent acknowledged in the slightest. Because Garrett could imagine no possible way that Constance and Trent might have met, he found this last gesture of hers to be the most compelling so far.

My God! Garrett thought. *For everyone else in the room, it's as if she doesn't exist . . . What in hell is going on? Could this woman actually be telling the truth? And if so, what would cause such a thing? And how is it that I see and hear her when no one else can?*

Wishing to also prove her command over the physical things of this world, Constance then walked around to the opposite side of the table and placed her lips down near one of Jay's pencils. She took a deep breath and blew it straight across the table, where it rolled off the edge and onto the floor. Grumbling again, Jay picked it up then mumbled something about the morning breeze.

Garrett then watched as she strode over to the far wall. Taking a deep breath, she let go a piecing scream that would have normally been heard throughout the entire house. But even now, Jay, Trent, and the other men in the room took absolutely no notice of it.

With that, Constance believed that for the moment, at least, she had done everything she could do to convince Garrett. Even so, if he needed more proof, there was one last thing that she could do. Although not now, because there were people about. That would come later tonight, when Garrett returned to Seaside, as she was now convinced he would. Then he would at last believe her, she prayed. After nodding at Garrett, Constance carefully wended her way among the men and left the room. She seemed able to move with complete silence and was apparently quite expert at avoiding human contact if needed.

Stunned, Garrett simply stood there, staring blankly at the open doorway.

"Garrett, are you still with us?" Jay asked.

As Garrett turned around, he realized that his knees were shaking and that he had broken out in a cold sweat.

"Are you okay, boss?" Trent asked. "You look a little pale."

While Garrett did his best to produce a smile, he wiped his forehead with a pocket handkerchief.

"Yeah, sure," he answered. "Too much coffee, probably."

"Well then, is it okay if I go to the office?" Trent asked. "The troops are probably wondering where we are."

"Yeah," Garrett answered. "You go on ahead. But I'm not feeling well, and I might take the day off. If you need anything, you can always reach me on my cell, okay? And I know we have a presentation today, but you can handle it, right?' "

"Sure, boss," Trent answered. Then the look on his face turned more serious. "And just for the record," he added, "being here today makes me realize that I was wrong about this place. When you get done with it, it's going to be beautiful, and I mean that. I know of no one else who could pull this off."

Those words meant a lot to Garrett, especially since nearly everyone had been of the opinion that he should never have bought Seaside. Now both Jay and Trent agreed with him, and because they were of the trades, their opinions mattered.

Trent smiled. "Take care of yourself," he said. "You do look kind of wiped out."

"Thanks," Garrett answered.

With that, Trent sauntered back down the hall and headed for work.

"I'm going to take a quick look around before I go," Garrett said to Jay. "Then I'll be out of your hair."

Jay smiled. "Okay," he answered. "See you later."

Garrett had no intention of actually inspecting the work. Nor was he feeling unwell, like he had told Trent. After what he had just witnessed he was desperate to find Constance, hopefully somewhere secluded where they might talk. Then he wanted to spend the rest of the day alone, trying to process all that he had just seen. He was taking a risk trying to find Constance now, because there were so many other people around. But something inside him said that he simply had to find her, if for no other reason than to see her again.

When a quick search of the house proved fruitless, he went outdoors. As if inspecting the ongoing work he walked all around the house but still did not find her, so he set off for the barn. After sliding one of the doors aside, he walked in.

All barns seemed to smell the same, he was reminded as he walked deeper inside. Regardless of how old or how new, they always reminded one of hay, dirt, dust, and leather. Despite how long this old barn had been empty, it too still smelled of such things.

After reconnoitering the first floor, he went to the stairs, where he paused, thinking. If Constance had wanted him to follow her, he decided, she would have beckoned him to do so. But she did not. No, he realized. She wanted to wait and talk to him later, when they could be alone.

When he lifted his face and looked up, he saw no movement, heard no sound. He did not know whether Constance was on the second floor, but it no longer seemed to matter. If she were there, seeking privacy from what had just transpired, he would let her have it. But he would return tonight and hopefully see her again.

Deciding to leave, he walked back to the house then down the grassy knoll to his Jeep.

Chapter 10

As Garrett drove away, Constance watched. She was standing in one of her favorite places in the old barn, before an open second-floor window that provided a wide view of the road leading in and out of Seaside.

This window was not far from her hiding place, and she had come to it hundreds of times over the decades, watching wistfully as home owners came and went. There had been many, and she could remember most of them by name. But the man who left Seaside just a few moments ago was the most important of them all. He could both see and hear her, and it was absolutely paramount that she learn why.

Then Constance let go a small smile, one of the few since her fall from the widow's walk so long ago.

Testing Jay and Trent had been a bit of fun, but in the end only Garrett mattered. While making faces and then shrieking at the top of her lungs, she knew she had no need to watch for Jay's and Trent's reactions, for there would be none. Only Garrett's responses were important, and she could tell by the look on his face that he had been highly affected. Even so, that did not mean he believed her. During the short time in which she had come to know him, she realized that he was a highly intelligent man, and surely not a gullible one. As her eyes welled up with tears, she lowered her head.

My Dear God, she thought. *I ask so much of him. If our roles were reversed, would I be half as receptive to all of this as he has been?*

She glanced around the second story of the barn again, thinking.

She was sure that Garrett would return tonight, because his curiosity about all this would now be far too great. If he remained skeptical, there was one more thing that she could do to convince him. She didn't particularly want to reveal it, but if she must, she would. And then Garrett would simply have to believe her, logic be damned.

Feeling tired, she walked back to her little hiding place in the far corner. It felt good to lie down on the tattered mattress, and although the barn itself was quiet, she could hear the distant sounds of the workmen. She found the sounds reassuring, and no matter what happened between her and Garrett, she could at least take solace in that.

As she lay there listening, her thoughts again turned to the strange effect he was having upon her feelings. She had no ready explanation for the wonderfully pleasant sensation she had experienced when touching his hands last night. And she was developing a sense of unrequited longing, which was at the same time wonderful, but frightening. Wonderful, because she had not felt this way about a man for so many decades. And frightening, both because she had no answer for what was causing it, and because of her continued love for her long-lost Adam. Along with every tiny increment of her growing interest in Garrett, there also came an equally painful rise in her guilt.

Some moments later she began feeling strangely, and soon she sensed her consciousness starting to drift away. It was a pleasant feeling, and it did not frighten her. Even so, despite how tired she was, she could not call it sleep. Instead it seemed a welcome departure from her consciousness, and she somehow realized that even if she wished to try and stop it, doing so would prove fruitless. She was being inexorably drawn to it like a moth to a flame. And so Constance gave herself over to it, and simply let it happen . . .

After some time had passed, she knew not how much, Constance felt someone gently shaking her by the shoulders.

"You must awaken, my love," Adam said to her. "It is such a lovely day. Were you planning to sleep it all away?"

Constance opened her eyes, stretched luxuriously, and then looked up at the face of her husband. Adam was staring down at her with those intense brown eyes of his, a wonderful smile stretched across his face. When she smiled back at him, he leaned down and gave her a deep kiss then stroked one of her cheeks. Although his hands were strong and calloused from his many years at sea, Constance always found them to be gentle and endearing.

"How fine ye are to me, wife," he said quietly.

Constance reached up and touched his face. He was clean-shaven now, but he would be putting to sea soon, and when he returned he would have a full beard.

"And how fine ye are to me, husband," she answered him.

Such were the loving phrases that they oftentimes said to each other. Adam had first uttered this to her only a few days into their marriage, and he had always remembered it. And Constance's reply, although nearly identical, was always equally heartfelt.

She rose up on her elbows and looked around. She and Adam were in a small cabin, located in the bow of Adam's personal sailboat. With a large picnic basket in hand, they had left Seaside that morning and sailed out onto the ocean. Even when he was between voyages, it seemed that Adam lusted for the sea. He had built this sailboat in their barn with his own two hands, and it had taken him several years to finish. Now it was a beautiful thing, and Constance enjoyed sailing almost as much as he did. But today she had grown weary after a couple of hours and retired to their small double berth to take a rest.

"Are ye hungry?" Adam asked her. "It has been hours since we have eaten."

"Indeed, husband, I am," she answered. "Let me open the basket and see what we have."

She rose from the berth, and with the picnic basket in her arms she then went up the few stairs and out onto the deck. By now the sun was slightly past the yardarm, telling her that it was a couple of hours after noonday. Adam had dropped the sails and tied off the wheel, allowing the boat to drift gently with the current. The sky was still a wonderful Wedgewood blue, with a few passing cumulus clouds and a gentle, north-easterly breeze. *A perfect day for sailing,* she thought.

As Constance opened the picnic basket, she was again reminded of how much she appreciated Eli, Emily, and James Jackson, the Negro family who helped her and Adam care for Seaside. Emily was a wonderful cook, and when she learned that Constance and Adam were going out for a sail, she had insisted on preparing the meal and packing the picnic basket herself. Emily had kept its contents all very hush-hush, causing Constance to smile as she began removing the food.

Emily had packed some of her wonderful baked ham, tomatoes and cucumbers in vinegar, a loaf of bread, a wedge of hard cheese, and two bottles of red wine. At the bottom of the basket were plates, utensils, napkins, and stemware. Adam appeared from belowdecks bearing a teak folding table that he had made with lumber left over from the boat. After setting it up alongside one of the boat's rows of side cushions, Constance laid out the dishes and food.

This is so lovely, she thought. *I wish our lives could always be so. But not long from now Adam will take sail again, and be gone for many months. I will miss him terribly, but the sea is as much a part of his blood as is his love for me, and I will always respect that.*

Adam smiled as he poured two glasses of wine. They lifted their glasses and gently touched them together in a toast.

"To my only love," Adam said. "Just as it always will be, no matter upon which of the seven seas I may roam."

Constance took her first sip of very good wine.

"Thank you, my darling," she said. "And always know that my heart feels the same."

They then ate in silence for a time, as the sun crept nearer the western horizon and the gentle waves of the Atlantic slapped the hull of their boat. It would take them some time to get home again, but Constance never worried when out here with Adam. He was one of the foremost captains in all of New Bedford, a distinction not earned without many years of hard experience.

While pausing for a moment in her meal, Constance looked out over the waves. They were ever restless, much like the feeling that had been growing in her for some time now. Despite their best efforts, she and Adam were still childless, and the thought of that always tugged hard on her heart. She could not know whether the fault was his or hers, nor did it matter, she supposed, but children would be of great comfort to her during Adam's long voyages. The thought that she might be barren seemed to forever hang about her neck like a millstone, constantly reminding her that there was a great part of her life that remained unfulfilled. After letting go a sigh, she returned to her meal.

The change in her had not gone unnoticed by Adam. Her mannerisms and the look on her face were always unique to whenever this perceived failure was yet again bedeviling her. He reached out and took both of her hands into his.

"This again, is it?" he asked gently.

Constance nodded.

"I'm sorry, husband," she answered. "But my lack of bearing a child still weighs heavily upon me. You could have had any woman you wanted, and only God knows why he blessed me so. But another woman would have surely given you children by now, and that's something that cannot be denied."

As Adam watched her eyes well up, he took her in his arms. Trying his best to smile, he used one thumb to wipe away a tear.

" 'Tis as much my fault," he said. "These great and terrible chases for the whales keep me away from thee far too often, and for far too long. So do not blame thyself alone, for I too must shoulder part of the burden."

Seeing that her sadness was still upon her, he took her face in his hands.

"It will happen, my love," he said. "I just know it. We're both still young and healthy. And we must also remember that when it does happen, it will be in God's time, rather than of our choosing."

After kissing her gently, he placed his palm upon her abdomen.

"For all we know, our child might be inside you already," he said.

Then he gave her one of his roguish, sea captain smiles that she had always found so irresistible.

"And if not," he said, "perhaps we should take the opportunity now, while we're alone."

Constance suddenly blushed. Never in her life had she made love with Adam anywhere other than in their bed at Seaside.

"You mean right now, here in the boat?" she asked incredulously.

Adam let go a short laugh. "Yes, my love," he answered. "Right now, here in the boat."

Before Constance could answer, Adam took her about the waist and gently lifted her to her feet. But as he began leading her toward the stairs, she had a thought and looked up at the sky.

"But, my darling," she said, "are you sure that there's enough time?"

This time Adam laughed fully. "Yes, my love, there's more than enough time. I've never failed to bring a ship home yet. In the meantime I'll let her drift."

Soon they stood before the cabin bed, where Adam began undressing her little by little. As her clothes came off and fell to the floor, Constance trembled slightly, just as she always did in anticipation of his touch. When at last they were both naked, Adam lifted her into his arms and laid her down upon the bed.

And at the precise moment he took her, she took him as well and she cried out with abandon, knowing that no one but her beloved would hear . . .

When Constance left her reverie, her shock was so great that she literally cried out loud and sat straight up on the old mattress. Her shouting out this way, she suddenly realized, was exactly as she had done only seconds ago, while still in Adam's arms. But now she was somehow back *here* again, in this time and world that she so disliked. Struggling to make sense of it, she wrapped her arms around her knees, her entire body trembling nearly beyond control.

This had been no dream, she realized. She had actually *been* there with Adam, back in her own time. But although she could remember that interlude while here in this time, while it had been happening she had had absolutely no inkling of what her future life would be like. Then she remembered something else, and her veins turned to ice water.

The reverie she had just experienced was something that had actually happened between her and Adam, one lovely fall day in the year 1837. Adam would leave on his last fateful voyage the following year, never to return. And despite their best efforts, Constance would stay barren, living alone in the great house with only the Jacksons to keep her company. Then one stormy afternoon two years later, she would fall from the widow's walk and somehow end up here in this day and age on the second floor of their old barn, her mind literally awash with fear. It was far too much to bear, and she began sobbing uncontrollably.

I understand nothing of this, she thought. *Certainly not why I have been imprisoned in time for all these years. Nor why this strange man named Garrett Richmond has suddenly entered my life and confounded me so. Nor do I understand my growing feelings for him, comingled with my guilt over my loving husband, which has now been even further reinforced by this incredibly strange voyage back into my past. This was no dream. Rather, I feel as if I had actually moved through time, and then returned. Will this occur again? Do I even want it to? What in God's name is happening to me?*

When at last her shaking stopped, Constance again walked to the open window and looked outside. All the laborers had quit for the day, and Seaside, although now more battered and torn up than ever, still somehow retained her stately grace. The sun was starting to go down, the sky over the ocean taking on that slowly changing violet hue that comes but once each day. With even more trepidation now filling her heart, Constance said a silent prayer.

Please, please return to me tonight, Garrett, she silently begged. *For there is so much that we must learn about one another . . .*

Chapter 11

"Heads up, Garrett!" Dale Richmond shouted. "She's on to something!"

Garrett watched with rapt attention as Freckles, her body and tail nearly rigid, crept slowly toward a clump of brush that lay about five yards ahead of him and his father. She was a wonderful bird dog, probably the best that Dale had ever owned, and she was certainly proving her worth today. It was late afternoon, the sun starting to give way to gloomy-looking clouds.

When Garrett took another step forward, Dale quickly chastised him.

"Stay where you are, son," he said. "We're already close enough. She'll do her job and then we'll do ours."

Stopping where he was, Garrett undid the safety on his twelve-gauge Browning over and under. This was the precise moment when all the hard work and practice came into play. For a split second he sensed the hairs on the back of his neck rise a bit, just as they always did before a game bird was flushed from hiding.

Just then Freckles took another careful step forward and a cock pheasant darted from his hiding place. Cackling proudly, he quickly took wing. Pheasants are fast flyers, and if the hunter is not quick enough the chance can be lost in a split second. Although Garrett had done this hundreds of times before, each time was a new experience.

He raised the Browning quickly, pulled the gun sight across the climbing bird's flight path, then pulled the trigger. The Browning roared once, its bird shot killing the pheasant instantly. When the dead bird fell, Garrett recognized both the thrill of victory and the fleeting sense of guilt that any responsible hunter always felt.

Freckles gleefully bounded over, picked up the pheasant in her mouth, then brought it to Garrett and dutifully dropped it at his feet. Garrett reached down and tousled her ears.

"Nice shot!" Dale said as he walked over to where Garrett was standing. "I always knew you had quick reflexes. Your gun went off before mine even reached my shoulder."

Garrett laughed. "Yeah, well," he said, "I'm not sixty-three years old. When I'm as decrepit as you, I probably won't be able to do half the things you can."

Dale laughed, then reached down and picked up the dead pheasant. After admiring it, he reached behind himself and dropped it into the rucksack sewn into the back of his hunting vest. That made two birds this afternoon, which was the Massachusetts daily limit. He then looked up at the sky.

"Good thing we got this last one when we did," Dale said. "It looks like rain. Plus, if we're going to eat these birds tonight, we need to get them home to your mother."

Garrett broke open his gun, removed the shells, and put them into one pocket of his hunting vest. As they neared Dale's truck, Garrett smiled a little. He loved hunting game birds with his father. It was the only kind of hunting they did. Dale had taught him to shoot as a teenager, and had begun taking him out pheasant hunting soon after. Garrett had taken to it quickly, and he now sometimes borrowed Freckles and went out on his own. He enjoyed the hunt, but there were occasions when he appreciated the walking and the solitude even more.

While continuing his walk alongside his father, Garrett's thoughts again turned to Constance. After his unsuccessful search for her, he simply couldn't bear being bottled up in his office. And so after fibbing to Trent, he had called his dad and asked if the two of them could go hunting this afternoon. Dale had been ecstatic and told Garrett to come straight over to the house. But hunting was the lesser of Garrett's motives. Just as he had needed to talk to his mother privately a few days ago, he now also wanted to talk to his father one on one, and out here had seemed the perfect venue.

Garrett valued both his parents for good advice, but in different ways. His mother was the more analytical of the two, who always put her trust in facts and science. Dale, on the other hand, was more spiritual and much more willing to admit that not everything needed a scientific explanation simply to be true. It was that metaphysical sort of question that Garrett now wished to ask his father.

When they got to the truck, Dale put down the tailgate and lifted Freckles into the back. Then the father and son sat down on the tailgate, watching the dark clouds gather. They were parked atop a small knoll that overlooked a rolling valley, the leaves of its trees crimson and gold with the advent of winter.

Dale grabbed a cooler that lay in the truck bed and pulled out two longneck beers, handing one to Garrett. Father and son sat quietly, enjoying the moment.

After a time, Garrett set down his half-consumed beer.

"Dad," he asked, "could I ask you a question?"

"Sure," Dale answered. "What is it? Do you have a problem of some kind?"

Garrett thought about that for a moment.

"No, not really," he answered. "My question's more of a general nature."

Dale took another slug of his beer.

"Then fire away," he answered.

"You believe in the hereafter, right?" Garrett asked.

Dale found that a rather unusual question coming from Garrett, because like his mother, he had never been particularly religious.

"Yes," Dale answered, "I do. I've always found that a sense of faith helps get me through all the tough stuff."

"What about reincarnation, ghosts, things like that?" Garrett asked. "Do you believe those sorts of things are possible too?"

On hearing that question, Dale began perusing his memories.

"I've seen a lot of things I couldn't account for, Garrett," he answered, "especially during the fog of war that was Vietnam. I've seen people that I've pronounced dead, only to watch them come alive again. And I've performed simple surgeries during which I thought the patient would surely survive, but didn't. I suppose that being a surgeon has given me a unique perspective on life, death, and perhaps even the hereafter. As far as your question about reincarnation and ghosts is concerned, all I can say is that there are many things we have yet to understand. And as such, we must at least admit the possibility that they exist."

Garrett thought about his father's answer for a while, then picked up his bottle and took another drink.

"Like God?" Garrett asked.

"I don't know an awful lot about God," Dale said. "But I believe in him."

Dale again gazed out at the magnificent view.

"If he can create the world in seven days," he added, "then I sure as hell believe that he can create ghosts and reincarnation, if he wants to. But when all is said and done, there's only one thing I know for sure about the relationship between God and surgeons."

Garrett looked at his father quizzically.

"And just what is that?" he asked.

"The answer's simple," Dale said. "God doesn't think he's a surgeon."

Garrett couldn't help but laugh out loud.

"You might be right on that one," he answered, "but I never saw you that way."

Dale smiled again then clinked his beer bottle against Garrett's.

"Thanks, son," he answered. "I'll take that as a compliment."

Garrett hadn't gotten a definitive answer from his father, but then again, he hadn't really expected one. There were no real truths about reincarnation, or ghosts, or coming back from the dead. In the end he realized that he hadn't been looking for an answer, so much as a reassurance that such things might actually exist, thereby allowing him to believe Constance's mad story. It was always good talking to his father. Dale had a beneficent way about him that made Garrett feel welcome, and protected. Being out here with his father had been exactly the tonic he needed.

"A penny for your thoughts," Dale said.

Garrett smiled as he turned to look at his dad. "Sorry about that," he answered. "I was just off somewhere, thinking."

"Yeah," Dale answered, "I can understand that. But my sense is that there's something more going on here. It isn't like you to ask these sorts of questions. Are you sure there isn't something you need to talk about?"

Garrett returned his gaze to the darkening skyline.

"For now, I'm just going to have to figure this out on my own," he answered. "But if I ever need to come to you about it, I know you'll be there."

"Of course I will, son," Dale answered. "And so will your mom."

Garrett looked at his watch.

"Would you mind if we got going, Dad?" he asked. "I'd like to be back at Seaside before it gets too late."

"Yep," Dale said.

"Sounds good," Garrett answered. "And thanks for today. I needed this time with you."

"Well, you're already a hell of a good shot," Dale answered. "Now, if you'd only let me teach you how to play poker . . ."

Garrett laughed.

"One sin at a time, Dad," he said. "One sin at a time."

Dale nodded.

"And regarding your questions about God," he said, "well, there's only one more thought that I might add."

"What's that?"

Dale fished around in his hunting jacket for his truck keys, then looked into Garrett's eyes.

"If you want to hear God laugh," he said, "just try telling him your plans."

Chapter 12

After arranging some newspaper and kindling in the dining room fireplace, Garrett struck a match and set them ablaze. They caught fire quickly, and he soon loaded on some heavier pieces of wood. As the fire's warmth crept throughout the room, he sat down against one wall, thinking.

Because he ate the pheasant dinner with his parents, he had arrived here at Seaside later than he had wanted. By now the night had fallen in earnest. But that hadn't mattered, because he hadn't really come here to view the ongoing restoration. He was really here in hopes of finding Constance.

He had done another search of the house, but Constance was nowhere to be seen. Perhaps that didn't matter either, for she seemed able to come and go like some sort of wraith. If she wanted to find him, she would do so in her own good time. Would she come to him tonight? he wondered. He hoped so, for he urgently needed to talk to her. The events of this morning had rattled him deeply, and he was desperate to know more.

Garrett took a fresh bottle of bourbon from his knapsack, and poured some into a Styrofoam cup. It tasted good, and as he sat watching the fire he realized he could wait here all night, if need be. But what if he never saw her again, and he couldn't ask her the many questions that had been plaguing him? Could he live without knowing the answers? And perhaps worse, could he live with the answers if he learned them?

From here he could faintly hear the sounds of the ocean, crashing against the shoreline. Combined with the crackling sounds of the fire, they made for pleasant companions. He knew that once the restoration was complete he would love living here, and that nothing could stop him now. Nothing, he supposed, except perhaps Constance.

And what of her wild story? Part of him wanted to believe her, but he still couldn't shake the feeling that he was the butt of some huge practical joke. Hence his need to be with his father, and to ask those questions. There also remained the nagging mysteries of his increasing longing for Constance, and the sensation they both had felt when they touched hands.

He simply could not believe her, because there were too many reasons against it. First, of course, was that her story was so preposterous. And second, the idea of believing her scared him a little, because if what she said was true, then he seemed destined to become part of her mad existence. Or was he simply going crazy? he wondered. Was Constance nothing more than some woman he had dreamed up, a hallucination that—

"Garrett?" he heard Constance say from across the room.

Garrett immediately came to his feet. Constance was dressed the same as this morning, but tonight her hair lay down about her shoulders. She still carried the same dark circles under her eyes, reaffirming that she had had little sleep. She stood in the doorway tentatively, staring at him with questioning eyes.

"Constance . . ." he said. "You're here . . ."

She entered the room and went to him.

"Yes," she said. "I knew that you would come."

Garrett beckoned her to sit down with him. As he offered her some of the bourbon, she refused. When next she looked into his eyes, he saw desperation.

"Do you at last accept my word?" she asked simply. "Please say that you believe me . . . you simply must do so . . ."

Before he could answer, Garrett suddenly felt that unique sense of longing that always overcame him whenever she was near. It was becoming a familiar sensation by now, but no less potent. And he could tell by the look on Constance's face that the same feeling was overcoming her too.

Garrett sighed and scrubbed his face with his hands.

"I don't know what to believe anymore," he said. "I can't help but think that this morning was just some sort of cruel joke, cooked up by you and Jay. But what I can't explain is why Trent was apparently taken in too. Had you ever seen him before today?"

"Only when he has been here with you," she answered. "I do not know him."

While staring at the fire, Garrett thought for a moment.

"And just why is it so important that I believe you?" he asked.

"Because since the night you first saw me in the kitchen, everything has been uprooted," Constance answered. "You are now a part of all this, whether you wish it or not. And until we unravel it, neither of us will find any peace. Deep down, I believe you know that."

Garrett shook his head.

"I'm sorry, Constance," he said, "but this is just too crazy. Can you really blame me? Would you believe some stranger who came out of nowhere and tried to convince you of such a bizarre story?"

Constance felt her heart breaking. She had feared this reaction, even though she had done her level best to convince him. There was only one more card up her sleeve, but she was reticent to play it because it would give so much away. Then again, what if he banished her from this place? Where would she go? How would she live? Seaside was all she had known for the last 170 years, and the thought of having to leave here was causing her insurmountable worry. And so Constance made her choice. Even though it was something that could never be undone, it was her last, best chance of convincing Garrett.

"Will you allow me the pleasure of showing you something?" she asked.

"That depends," Garrett answered. "Is it another parlor trick?"

Constance shook her head.

"No, Garrett," she said. "This is no trick. But to fully comprehend both Seaside and me, you must see it."

Constance stood and picked up the electric lantern.

"Please follow me," she said.

"Where are we going?" he asked.

"To the barn."

"But this barn is empty," he protested. "There's nothing there to see."

This time when Constance looked into his eyes, her gaze seemed to penetrate his very soul.

"Yes, there is," she answered. "I can discern that you're a highly intelligent man, Garrett. But even for you, everything in this world is not always as it appears."

As Constance left the room, Garrett followed her through the house and outside. The night was cool, the stars were bright, and dew lay heavy upon the grass.

Garrett had already inspected the barn, and he knew that it was empty, so he could not understand why Constance was taking them there. But he had decided to give this woman one last chance to convince him.

Constance slid one of the doors aside. Switching on the lights, she led him to the far right-hand corner. The barn floor was made of wooden planks, each one dark and dank from the passage of so many years.

"What are you looking for?" Garrett asked. "Can't you see that there's nothing here?"

Constance paused in her search and looked at him again.

"Oh, but there is," she answered. "For example, did you know that there exists a cellar beneath this floor?"

"There isn't one."

"Yes, there is," she answered. "One needs to only find the trapdoor. It has been such a long time . . ."

After some more searching, she finally saw what she was looking for. In the far corner of the floor there lay a metal handle. The area beneath the handle had been carved out to match so that the handle itself lay flush and unnoticeable.

"Where did that come from?" he asked incredulously.

"It was always here," Constance answered. "You see, Seaside was once a part of what you now call the Underground Railroad. My husband, Adam, was an abolitionist, and we helped many slaves pass safely through here on their way to Canada. The cellar was already here when we bought Seaside, but he and Eli expanded it greatly."

"Eli . . . ?" Garrett asked.

"Eli Jackson," Constance answered. "The head of the black family that once inhabited the guesthouse."

Garrett was stunned. The cellar was so well hidden by both the barn floor and the surrounding foundation that even his expert eye had never suspected its existence. His curiosity rising hugely, he grabbed the large handle, and together they struggled to open the old trapdoor. Its rusted hinges creaked mightily, but they finally got it up and over.

Garrett took the lantern from Constance then lowered it near the opening, trying to peer into the gloom below. The door had been substantial, revealing a large square hole in the barn floor. A set of ancient steps led down into the darkness.

"And you want us to go down there?" he asked.

"Yes."

"When was the last time you did this?" Garrett asked skeptically.

"Nearly one hundred and seventy years ago," Constance answered. "I never visited after that, for fear of revealing it to any of Seaside's previous owners. As best I know, no one else has ventured there since."

"What's down there that's so important?" he asked.

Constance shook her head.

"If I told you, you would never believe me. You simply must trust me, Garrett. What I have to show you has not been seen by anyone for a very long time."

"All right," Garrett said. "We'll do it. But you should go first, because you know the way. I'll follow you down."

When Constance turned to look at him, he saw genuine gratitude in her eyes.

"Thank you," said. "This means more to me that you could ever know."

Holding the electric lantern before her, Constance started down the steps. When she reached the bottom she called to Garrett, telling him to come down. Garrett couldn't see much as he carefully navigated the creaky old steps, wondering the whole time whether they might give way and send him tumbling into oblivion. When at last he reached the bottom, he stopped and looked around. What he saw staggered him.

He had expected to see only one room, but instead there were several interconnecting chambers, each of them reinforced with wooden timbers. As Constance walked about with the lamp, she showed him several rows of ancient iron bunk beds, their linens torn and dirty from the passage of time, tables strewn with eating utensils, and timeworn lanterns mounted upon many of the timbers. It was impressive, to say the least.

"How did you and Adam get the slaves into the cellar without being seen?" Garrett asked.

"Tunnels," Constance answered.

"Tunnels . . . ?"

"Yes," she said. "Whenever Adam was between voyages, he and Eli worked tirelessly on the tunnels. When Adam was away, Eli and his son, James, continued the work. There are two main tunnels; one leads from here into the woods for further escape to the next station, and the other leads from here back to the house where it joins with the cellar."

"Are the tunnels still passable?" Garrett asked.

Constance shook her head.

"I do not know," she answered. "I was always afraid of trying to use them, for fear of a cave-in."

"Was this what you wanted me to see?" he asked her. "I can easily believe that this was a station for the Underground Railroad, but that doesn't mean that your story is true, or that you had any hand in it. I'm afraid I'm going to need more than this, Constance."

"No, Garrett, this is not all," she said. "Nor is it even this room that I especially wanted you to see. That place lies farther on. So please follow me again. And mind your step, because there is no way of knowing whether it remains safe."

Beckoning Garrett to follow her, Constance walked across the dirt floor and entered a tunnel carved into the right-hand wall of the first room. Holding the lantern high she treaded carefully, with Garrett following behind her. After a few moments they approached another room, this one several times larger than the first. The moment they entered, Constance broke down and began crying.

"It's all still here . . ." she said, her voice a near whisper. "I can hardly believe my eyes . . ."

But Garrett was stymied, for he saw nothing save for another room, its ceiling, walls, and floor also made of earth and heavily reinforced with old timbers. He couldn't possibly imagine why Constance had become relieved to the point of tears.

"Do you mean the room itself?" he asked her. "Is that why you're so happy—because you've discovered it hasn't collapsed?"

She turned and looked at him with tearful, but joyous, eyes. It was the first time he had ever seen her genuinely happy. Constance put down the lantern and wiped her tears away.

"This is but a part of it," she said. "As I told you before, there is far more here than meets the eye."

"What are you talking about?"

"Will you indulge me for a moment?" she asked.

"All right," he answered. "What do you have in mind?"

A hint of a smile crossed Constance's lips.

"I'm going to hold the lantern high," she said, "and when I do, I want you to pick up a handful of dirt and throw it against the far wall."

Garrett looked at her quizzically.

"And just what is that going to accomplish?" he asked.

"You will see," she said. "I'm asking you to do this because it will be more believable for you this way."

After everything Constance had shown him, Garrett could hardly refuse. Even so, he felt foolish because he knew that it would accomplish nothing. But in for a penny, in for a pound, he decided.

After Constance lifted the lantern higher, Garrett obediently grabbed up a handful of dirt then vigorously tossed it toward the far wall. The totally unexpected effect was so mesmerizing that he would remember it all his life.

Instead of hitting the wall, the dirt seemed to strike something first, some sort of invisible barrier that stood between him and it, yet allowed him to look through it and see the wall some distance behind. When the dirt struck the transparent barrier it fell straight to the floor, but not before creating ripples that wavered gently toward its outer edges, much like when one drops a pebble into a still pond. Speechless, he simply stood there, gazing at it while the rippling effect slowed and then stopped altogether.

"My God . . ." he said, his voice cracking with incredulity. "What just happened there?"

Certain that he had been seeing things, he threw another handful of dirt, and to his sheer amazement, the same thing happened. The dirt struck the invisible barrier and fell straight to the floor while yet more ripples emanated outward in concentric circles, only to be absorbed by the sidewalls of the room.

Garrett turned toward Constance.

"What the hell *is* that?" he demanded.

Constance put down the lantern then she walked across the room to where the invisible barrier stood.

"Watch," she said simply.

Reaching up, she opened her hands and then closed them again, as if she were grasping handfuls of pure nothingness. And yet as she did so he could see more ripples forming in the barrier. With a strong pull, Constance yanked the barrier down. When it fell to the floor the invisible barrier suddenly became an old tarpaulin, its age and existence betrayed by its mildewed surface, and its hundreds of wrinkles.

Yet again Garrett simply stood there, speechless. But it wasn't the sudden and impossible appearance of the old tarpaulin that was the most spellbinding. It was what it had been hiding behind it, on the floor of the cavernous room.

The chamber was filled with furniture. But not just any furniture, for everything he saw dated from the antebellum period. There were beds, desks, tables and chairs, wall hangings, a china cabinet, sofas, and many other items too numerous to name. And to his even greater surprise, every piece seemed to be in nearly brand-new condition. But what he could not understand were the "why" and the "how" of all this.

He turned and looked at Constance.

"What in the world . . . ?" he asked. "Where did all this come from, and why is it here? And what about that invisible barrier that you just pulled down? Even though I saw you do it with my own eyes, I still can't believe it!"

Before answering, Constance gathered up the old tarpaulin and put it in one corner of the room. Then she walked over to where Garrett was standing and she looked him in the eyes.

"Everything you see before you was taken from Seaside," she answered.

"But how did it all remain in such pristine condition?" Garrett asked. "I've never seen a collection like it. It all appears as if it was put here yesterday."

Constance ran her fingertips over one of the tables, remembering.

"I don't know why it all remained in such excellent condition," she answered. "I can only say that it must have something to do with the invisible cloak that I created for it."

"*You* created that?" Garrett asked incredulously. "How is it that you can do such things?"

Constance sighed.

"There is still so much you do not know," she answered.

Garrett was dumbfounded. The discovery of these furnishings was certainly surprising enough, but how Constance had hidden them from the world was astonishing.

"Was it magic that you just did?" he asked.

"I do not believe so," she answered. "I am not even sure that I know what magic is. Aside from being invisible to others, what you just saw is the only unnatural ability granted to me after my fall from the widow's walk. I actually discovered its existence by accident one day."

"So what is going to happen to all these things?" Garrett asked. "To the right person they're worth a fortune."

"That is for you to decide," Constance answered.

"Me?" Garrett asked.

"Of course," Constance said. "You purchased Seaside lock, stock, and barrel. Therefore anything in the house or on the surrounding property belongs to you."

"But if all these things came out of Seaside, then they must've belonged to you and Adam, right?"

"Yes," she answered, "they did. They were gifts, given to us by my parents immediately after we purchased the house. But they're rightfully yours now. And besides, Garrett, I want you to have them. You are the only person who has chosen to restore Seaside to its former beauty, and in order to finish this project you will need every one of these things. I can think of no other person on earth to whom I would rather give them."

Garrett was speechless. In truth he had been worrying about not only where to find enough genuine antique furniture to fill Seaside, but also about how much it would cost. This was a bonanza, a gift to him beyond price. And of even greater importance was that when the restoration was done and all the furnishings were returned to the house, Seaside would again be exactly as she was in 1840. Moreover, Constance would presumably be here to show him where each piece had originally stood.

"But didn't the bank want all of this furniture when it foreclosed?" he asked. "I'd think that they were very angry when it came time to auction off the property, and every scrap of its interior furnishings came up missing."

Constance smiled a little.

"You are correct," she answered. "When it came time to auction off Seaside, all the furniture was already stored here for safekeeping."

"But you certainly couldn't have moved everything by yourself," Garrett protested. "And if you were completely unable to communicate with people, then there was no way to ask for help. So how on earth did everything get down here?"

"The slaves," Constance answered, "plus much help from the Jackson family. The Jacksons convinced them to do it, in hopes that Adam and I might one day return here. But without Adam and me to continue helping, Seaside was no longer a true station, and the slaves left. The Jacksons eventually gave up hope and departed, as well. I was so sorry to see them go."

Garrett turned and looked at all the furnishings again. He had never seen their like. It would have taken him untold years and countless dollars to accumulate such a collection as this. But he also knew that the furniture and the invisible barrier that had lain before it were not the real issues here. Yes, Constance wished for him to have the furniture for Seaside. But her continual, desperate question would come again very soon, and he would need to give her an honest and heartfelt answer. Only moments later, Constance looked at him and cleared her throat, politely separating him from his thoughts.

"It is now time to answer me once and for all, Garrett," she said. "And this time you must tell me the truth, no matter what it is. After all you have seen this day, can you at last accept my story?"

Garrett took a deep breath and let it out slowly. He could not believe what he was about to say. But seemingly before he knew it, he had uttered the words.

"Yes, Constance," he said softly. "I do believe you now. I never thought that I would be saying these words, but I am, and I mean them. Before today, dismissing your story was the only logical answer. But after seeing all the amazing things you have shown me, believing in you isn't just the right conclusion. It's the *only* one."

Constance immediately broke out into tears of happiness.

"Oh, thank God!" she said excitedly. "After all this time, at last someone can see me and hear me, and believes in my story!"

Then her happiness suddenly lessened a bit, and she looked at him again with questioning eyes.

"I cannot begin to thank you for your trust," she said. "But you must also know that we are only at the beginning of this journey, rather than at its end. We must discover why it is that you are so different from everyone else. Because if we don't, I fear the worst will befall both of us."

Before Garrett could ask her what she meant, he suddenly realized that he was trembling. The truth of Constance's situation had settled in at last, and he honestly did believe her story. He also knew that she was right—they were just beginning this journey together, and that they must somehow find the answers to the many questions confronting them.

"I do believe you, Constance, I really do," he said to her, his voice choking with emotion. "But I have so many questions I hardly know where to begin, or how to find the answers."

When Constance stepped closer and put one palm upon his cheek, each of them immediately felt the same sense of deep need and overpowering desire that had engulfed them only a few nights ago, while sitting on the veranda. Suddenly realizing what was happening, it was all Constance could do to pull her hand away. As the wonderful sensation faded, they each realized that this issue, and many more like it, would have to be resolved one way or another.

Just then Constance felt a quick bolt of fear go through her. The two of them were about to enter into some great puzzle that may have no solution. And if they could not unravel it, something in her heart told her their lives might become forfeit.

As Garrett recovered from the passion that had flowed through him, he took a deep breath and smiled a little.

"I do believe in you, but I have a question," he said.

Constance gave him a light smile.

"Then please ask it of me," she said.

Garrett sighed and shook his head a little bit.

"What now?"

Chapter 13

After leaving the barn, Garrett and Constance settled down before the dining room fireplace and talked late into the night, until Constance fell asleep atop Garrett's sleeping bag. Garrett remained so stunned over Constance's amazing revelations that he found sleep impossible, and he stayed awake until dawn, whereupon he drove into town to pick up some breakfast and coffee. Because today was Saturday and Jay's crew would not be working, he'd have plenty of privacy to talk to Constance again.

Back at Seaside now and seated on the veranda, he took a welcome sip of coffee. His tiredness was starting to seep through, and he needed the caffeine. Then he looked out over the restless waves again, contemplating everything that Constance had told him.

That Seaside had once been a station for the Underground Railroad had been interesting, but not enough to convince him of Constance's story. That had come later, with the amazing invisible barrier that she had used to hide all the furniture in the cellar, safe from the bank's clutches. When he saw it he had been absolutely stunned, and he had no choice but to believe her.

The many things she later told him about her life during the past seventeen decades had been no less fantastical, yet he now believed all of that too. Constance's story was one of despair, hope, triumph, and tragedy. But the greatest question—the riddle that truly united their existences—was how and why Garrett was the only known person in the world able to see and hear her.

He also sensed that she was holding something back. Something important, he feared, that could have a profound effect upon their lives. If asked, he would be unable to explain why he felt that way. All he knew was that he had become as certain of this unknown danger as anything in his life. By now, he also realized that there would be no point in trying to push Constance regarding this issue. She was the kind of woman who revealed things little by little, and he would respect that. In the end, what choice did he have?

Although he suspected she had more to tell him, he remained amazed by what she had already confided.

She had "lived" here anonymously for more than seventeen decades while watching Seaside's previous owners come and go; some of them good people, and some not. And not once in all that time had she ever set foot off the property. She had been forced to steal clothing whenever she could. And although none of Seaside's previous owners could see or hear her, she was still forced to remain stealthy at all times. She had also explained to him that she had been a very successful midwife, a skill taught to her by her late mother.

The more Garrett thought about it, the more he realized just how lonely, scary, and nerve-racking Constance's existence must have been during all that time. Being a party to the world but never a part of it, she was always worried about being discovered, despite no one being able to see or hear her. And it was those same attributes that would become not only her saving graces, but also her most maddening obstacles against achieving a normal life.

Last night she had also shown him the pitiful little area in the barn with the ragged mattress and what few personal possessions she called her own. When he asked why no one had ever discovered it, she told him that like in the barn cellar, she kept this place hidden with an invisible barrier. He immediately insisted that from now on she would live in the main house. Although she would have to carefully avoid Jay's workers, he knew that she was up to the task. Garrett had also decided to set her up in one of the second-floor bedrooms, and to get her some new clothes.

Because Constance's fall from the widow's walk seemed to be the catalyst for everything, he found that part of her tale particularly compelling. She had awakened on the rocky shore completely unharmed and fully unaware of her strange plight. That very same day she had discovered a newspaper that had been left in the guesthouse, announcing the loss of Adam's ship with all hands. The newspaper date told her that several months had passed, yet for Constance it seemed to be the very next day after her fall. She could only assume that she had spent all that time lying unconscious on the rocky shoreline and invisible to everyone, although she had no idea how or why she had survived the ordeal.

The paper also stated that because Mrs. Canfield was nowhere to be found and her husband was lost at sea, their mortgage had fallen into arrears and foreclosure proceedings would be instigated against Seaside. And so Constance remained at Seaside for the next 170-odd years. Because she never grew older or became ill, she eventually came to realize that she was neither fully alive nor dead. Something about this enchanting place and her fall from the widow's walk had trapped her between worlds, and she had no idea how to escape her fate.

Then a man named Garrett Richmond purchased the property and began a proper restoration. And with that he had seen her in the kitchen, the first person to do so in all that time. It had been that single, shocking experience which had thrust everything into motion, and it was now up to the two of them to try and find the way back for her. For in his heart Garrett truly believed what Constance had said to him last night. Unless they could get to the bottom of everything that had happened here, some unknown danger might indeed threaten both their lives. Just then another thought struck him, and he shook his head with disbelief.

My God, he thought. *I'm sharing my house with a ghost . . .*

Mere seconds after his mind created that thought his heart rejected it. Constance was no ghost, nor would he ever again allow himself to think of her as one. Although he knew that she was not truly whole in the same way as other people, she still seemed a fully flesh-and-blood woman. She was a real person to him, and not only would he refuse to think of her in any other way, but he would also do his best to convince her of the same.

How much Constance has seen! he suddenly realized. The more he considered that thought, the more staggering it became. The Civil War, the dawn of the American industrial age, World War I and World War II, the Great Depression, the Cold War, and the rise of this current technological era; all of which she had experienced solely through this unique prism called Seaside. She had also watched the families who had owned this great house; their trials and tribulations, their joys and defeats, their lives—and in some cases—perhaps even their deaths. He knew that Constance must possess a truly unique perspective on this day and age, and he wanted to hear more about that. But most of all he wanted to help this beautiful woman who was trapped between worlds, and for whom his heart was starting to care so much.

Sighing softly, he looked back out over the waves, thinking.

He knew he had to help her, of that much he had become certain. But how? he wondered. He had no real idea about what had happened here so many years ago, plus he knew nothing about mysticism, or any other forces of nature that might have caused Constance's situation. He would not tell her so, but it disheartened him whenever he tried to think of a way to unravel this terrible conundrum. He felt like a young lamb lost in the woods, with danger lurking at every turn of what would soon become a rudderless quest for answers. He had no idea what that first step would be, but he must do his best to find it.

And what of his ever-increasing feelings for her? he soon wondered. The more he came to know her, the more he cared for her. Was he falling in love with this beautiful and intelligent woman from the past? And what about his dream of her, so lifelike in its perfection, which had occurred shortly before he had first seen her in the flesh? How was something like that possible? Then there was also the wonderful feeling each of them always shared, whenever they touched. What would become of them, as together they tried to unravel everything that had happened here? And despite her continuing love for her lost husband, how would Constance eventually come to feel about him? Would she—

"Good morning," he heard Constance say.

Garrett turned to see her standing in the doorway. Although she wore the same dingy clothes as last night, today she appeared freshly scrubbed and well rested.

"Good morning to you too," he answered.

He gestured to the empty lawn chair.

"Come sit next to me and we'll have some breakfast. I went into town and got it while you were still sleeping.

And by the looks of you this morning, the hot water and upstairs bathtub must be working fine, right?"

Constance nodded.

"It was wonderful," she answered. "Over the course of so many years, I have oftentimes had to make do with much less. Even so, it sometimes remains difficult to accustom myself to these modern conveniences."

Constance came and sat down next to him. When Garrett handed her a Styrofoam cup of coffee, she took it in her hands tentatively, as if unsure whether to drink it. Then she took a small sip and nodded her head.

"It's good," Constance said. "But there are still countless things that went unsaid last night. And it will probably take many more nights of talking before you even begin to understand all that has happened to me, and the way that I have become."

Garrett nodded solemnly.

"Go ahead," he answered.

"Well," Constance replied, "there is food, for example. Ever since my fall from the widow's walk I have never needed food, or anything to drink, either. I just don't require them to survive. It's strange, I admit, but there it is. Over the many years I have oftentimes tasted food, but mostly only to remind myself of it, or to discover the flavor of something new. And so I do eat from time to time, but usually only to satisfy my curiosity. And since my fall from the widow's walk, I haven't been ill for a single day."

"What did you do in the wintertime?"

"What do you mean?"

"When it got cold out in the barn," he answered. "You certainly couldn't have stayed there all winter long. So what did you do?"

"I had no choice but to come into the house," she answered, "and to do my very best to avoid the people, and to not make any noise. I became good at it. I also spent a lot of time in the cellar, where they didn't often go."

Yet more amazing revelations, Garrett thought. *She's right. There does seem to be a great deal more for me to learn.*

He reached into the McDonald's bag and produced an egg sandwich, which he handed to her.

"Have you ever had one of these?" he asked.

Constance shook her head.

"No," she answered, "but I've seen them on television. I've always been curious about them."

She removed the paper from the sandwich and took a tentative bite before swallowing some more coffee. Garrett watched with amused interest.

"It's a shame you don't eat more," he said to her. "There are so many wonderful things in the world to try."

Constance smiled at him then wiped her mouth with a paper napkin.

"Perhaps," she said.

After taking another sip of coffee, Constance gave Garrett a small smile.

"I spent all of last night talking about myself," she said. "But I know so little about you. Please tell me."

Garrett smiled and shifted in his chair. After again casting his gaze out across the waves, he did his best to tell her about himself, his family, his education, his practice, and his passion for architecture.

"And there you have it," he said to her, "my life in a nutshell."

Moments later he shook his head and laughed a little bit.

"And then all of a sudden, along comes this beautiful woman who is sitting in my kitchen and crying her eyes out," he added. "All the rest of it you already know."

Constance sat there quietly for a time, thinking. When at last she finally spoke, what she had to say would prove intriguing.

"You know," Constance said, "perhaps your buying this old house is part of whatever mystical plan is being carried out here."

"What do you mean?" he asked.

"You just told me that ever since you were a young boy, you have been oddly attracted to this house,"

Constance said. "And that it always exerted some sort of 'magical' pull on you, as if trying to draw you near. And then there is your fascination with my time's culture and architecture. You may not have thought about it this way before, but every time you rode by Seaside on your bicycle, or you drove past in your car, I was here, and I looked exactly the same then as I do now. It's almost as if it was arranged that I should be here, waiting all this time for you to come of age, to buy this house, and to then be the only person in the world with the ability to realize my presence. Do you not see? Whether we wish to admit it or not, all these things are just pieces of the larger puzzle. Even so, everything returns to the question of 'why.' Why us, Garrett? And why here and now, after so much time has passed?"

Garrett was both intrigued and impressed by the way Constance had just phrased things. He had in fact never considered that even as a young boy coming out here to admire Seaside that she too was here, a fully grown woman who looked exactly the way she did now. Had she ever seen him as he rode by on his bicycle, or later in life as he enviously drove past the house in his car? Or didn't it matter, given that if she did see him, he would have appeared to be just a simple young man to her, with probably no importance in her life whatsoever?

After thinking about things again, Garrett realized that there was more to tell her and he decided to recount his dream. He then went on to tell Constance that the dream was an exact duplicate of his experience when he had heard her crying in the kitchen, and gone there to first see her.

Although Constance said nothing at first, the expression on her face said that she was stunned. A few moments later she finally found her voice.

"But that's . . . impossible . . ." she said softly, her tone a near whisper. "Unless you want to characterize it as a premonition of some kind, I suppose . . . But you must realize that I know nothing of metaphysical things, Garrett, despite that my existence seems to be so entangled in such matters. Even so, this business of your dream may be a clue toward helping us unravel all this."

Garrett nodded.

"Yes," he answered. "I've considered that too. But like you, I haven't the faintest notion of how to try to start."

"It is interesting . . ." Constance said quietly.

"What is?" Garrett asked.

"Your dream of me was a premonition about what would happen in the future," Constance answered. "And two days ago I had a similar experience, but mine was a remembrance of something that had actually happened in my past. It seems that I went back in time to share an afternoon with Adam on his sailboat. But it wasn't a dream. It was real, I just know it; as real as my time here and now, talking with you."

Constance went on to describe her flashback to Garrett. She too left nothing out. Because each of their tales had included intimate specifics, it was as if they both already knew that they must be completely honest with each other, if they were to ever solve this labyrinthine riddle.

"What do you think it all means?" Garrett asked.

Constance shook her head.

"I have no idea," she answered. "But I do believe that if either of us experiences such an occurrence again, we must be certain to tell the other."

"Yes," Garrett answered simply. "And you know," he said, "I would love to hear about Adam. I'm already aware that he was a whaling captain who was lost at sea. But I don't really know any more than that."

With the mention of her late husband, Constance felt her eyes begin to well up with tears. After brushing them away, she removed the locket from around her neck, opened it, and handed it to Garrett. Garrett regarded Adam's portrait with interest before returning it to her.

"He was a handsome man," Garrett said.

"And the love of my life," Constance answered.

"I'm sorry for your loss, Constance," Garrett said. "I can only assume that when you love someone that much, the passage of time doesn't really change things."

"Although I have never heard it phrased quite that way, you are correct," Constance answered. "To understand Adam, you first need to understand a bit of what those times were truly like. Whale oil was king, and whalebone was used to make many things. Adam was a sailor, heart and soul. And he was also an abolitionist—something that he told me before we were married—and I also took up the cause. In truth, I believe he came to hate his seagoing profession. Sometimes the stories he told me about killing and harvesting the whales were enough to make me literally ill. But it was a living, and I suppose his love for the sea helped to ameliorate some of his revulsion. In any event, when I learned of his death I was devastated, and I have been ever since. I fear that in this life I was meant to truly love only one man. And that man has already come and gone."

Garrett's heart went out to her. Soon after, he realized something else. Now that he had heard Constance's story about Adam, he realized just how much Constance must have loved him. Then he saw her gaze become a bit more pensive.

"A penny for your thoughts," Garrett said.

"To tell you the honest truth," she answered, "I much preferred 1840 to today."

"But women have come so far since then," he said. "Things are very different now, than when you were a woman in 1840."

"Yes," Constance answered. "In some ways women have come far, and that is a good thing. But in other ways, they have lost much too."

"What you mean?"

Before answering, Constance took a deep breath, remembering.

"Back then, Garrett," she said, "there was an understood gentility about things. I know that this will sound contradictory, but despite our relative lack of rights, men took care of their women. I of course cannot speak for every woman from that time, but in my experience, most women were treated with true respect. Men opened doors for them, bowed to them, and kissed the backs of their hands, and spoke in far more loving and respectful ways than they now do. Forgive me for seeming old-fashioned, but it's as if all of the rights and privileges that women have fought for and won throughout the years have been paid for with a contradictory increase in crassness and crudity. Sometimes, I must admit, I find myself unsure of whether the trade was a fair one."

Garrett had to admit that he found her comments interesting. Despite all her accumulated knowledge, he realized that she remained a product of her time, and he would respect that.

"I'm sorry, but I must leave here soon," he said to her. "I've got to get back to my condo and get some sleep. Will you be all right on your own tonight?"

Without answering, Constance left her chair and walked to the rail of the veranda. She stood like that for several minutes, her back to him and her long blond hair flowing lightly in the onshore breeze. The sun had come up, and it shone on her face, highlighting her lovely features. As the sea wind passed her by, it absconded with the scent of her perfume, bringing it to him. At that moment he was sure that he had never seen a more beautiful woman as she simply stood there, serenely looking out over the ocean. Finally she turned and looked at him.

"I've been surviving here on my own for one hundred and seventy-some years, Garrett," she said. "Even so, I would be lying if I said that I won't miss you, because I will. But I do hope that I will see you again soon, for there remains so much unsaid between us."

She walked back over to him then she bent down and gave him a light kiss on one cheek. Even with slightest brush of her lips against his skin, he felt his physical desire for her increase massively, and if left unheeded, might soon go beyond his control. As if she had sensed it also, she then backed off a little bit and stood looking at him.

"Until later, then," she said.

Without further ado Constance walked back into the house, leaving him alone on the veranda. After sitting there for a time and staring out at the ocean, Garrett gathered up his things, got into his Jeep, and drove away.

Chapter 14

Once he got to his condo, Garrett checked his voice mail. One from Jay, with an update about a slight change in materials he wanted for the new roof. The second was from Trent, just to rattle his cage. After deleting them, he went out onto the balcony.

Whenever he sat here these days, he couldn't help but think how disappointing this view was when compared to that at Seaside. But it didn't matter, because in about two more weeks he would be staying at the house full-time. What would that be like, he wondered, with Constance also there?

He hoped that he could help Constance, but he harbored no illusions about how impossible that might be. He'd never been particularly religious, nor did he have any interest in what might be called "the metaphysical arts." Being an architect meant that he was part artist and part scientist, and it seemed to him that whatever happened to Constance so long ago had nothing to do with either of those disciplines. Even so, he now believed that her plight was linked to forces of the universe that might be known to only a chosen few, if anyone. And that, he realized, would only make helping her all the tougher.

Even so, like his father he was at least willing to admit the possibility of esoteric dynamisms in the world. He needed a mystic, or a medium, someone who dabbled in such strange happenings, or who could at least point him in the right direction. This would be a walk into uncharted territory, and he found the prospect daunting.

Last night Constance told him that since her fall from the widow's walk she had never left the property. Maybe it was time for him to change that. The more he thought about it, the more surprised he became that she hadn't already raised the issue, for one might have thought her desperate to see how the world had changed. It then occurred to him that her staying at Seaside might have been due to fear. No matter, he decided. He would ask her anyway, and if she chose not to go then so be it.

One corner of Garrett's mouth wryly turned up again as he considered the realities of such a bizarre situation.

If Constance did say anything to him in public, he would have to resist the inclination to turn and look at her. Or, God forbid, he might slip up and actually answer her back! He shook his head with skepticism. Clearly, taking Constance out into the world would be risky.

He yawned sleepily. Because he had gotten no rest last night, the need to sleep became overpowering. He shuffled into his bedroom, where he pulled the shades and turned off his phone. After removing his clothes, he settled into bed.

But just as sleep overtook him, Garrett's vision seemed to explode into countless shards of blinding white light. The moment the shards disappeared, he realized that he was no longer in his condo. He had inexplicably traveled to another place, and he was making love to a woman.

When next he opened his eyes and looked down, to both his horror and delight the woman in his arms was Constance.

She lay beneath him as he held her, galloping with him, begging him for more. Stunned beyond belief, he looked into her beautiful blue eyes and found himself entranced. The same exquisite sense of sexual longing that he had felt when they first touched hands several days ago was upon him yet again, and strengthening past any hope of control. All he could think about was taking her, just as she relentlessly begged to be taken.

To his great shock, he saw that they were in the master bedroom at Seaside. The room was furnished with antebellum furniture and illuminated with whale oil lanterns, telling him that he had somehow gone back into the past. No detail had been overlooked, and a fire burned brightly in the master bedroom fireplace, its flames casting ghostly shadows across the walls and ceiling. He and Constance were in a huge four-poster bed, and as she ran her fingers through his hair and begged him for more, he at last looked back down onto her face and took her. When he did, it was far and away the most intense experience of his life. When he was at last spent, he rolled over onto the magnificent bed unconscious.

Hours later, Garrett woke up to find that he was back in his condo. After waiting another ten minutes for his mind to clear, he threw on his trousers and shirt, and left the bedroom. Grabbing up his bottle of Jack Daniel's and a clean cocktail glass, he shuffled out onto the patio and sat down. The sun was beginning to set, and stars were gradually taking its place. To his further astonishment, he had slept the entire day away.

After pouring three fingers of whiskey with shaking hands, he drank it all at once, and then immediately poured some more. His nerves were beyond the point of being frayed. He wasn't sure whether he had experienced a hallucination, and the very idea of such a thing frightened him right down to his core. His mind awash with questions, feelings, and fears, he tried to calm his breathing and make some sense of it all.

What he had just experienced with Constance had been so genuine that had anyone asked him, he would have sworn it was real. He had been there and made love to Constance, he just knew it. But at the same time, how could that be? The more he tried to understand, the more confused he became. Perhaps of even greater consequence was that he seemed to have somehow actually gone back in time, only to return to the here and now.

Should he tell Constance about it? he wondered. And if he did, what would be her reaction? Did he really want her knowing that he was falling in love with her, and that this dream—if indeed it really was a dream— was something that he had relished? Would she accept his explanation? Or, God forbid, would she instead feel violated by it?

He quickly gulped down some more whiskey, but even now the alcohol was having no effect on his nerves. He desperately wanted to feel numb, but as if it were being denied by some higher power, that sensation still eluded him. His body trembling noticeably now, he suddenly felt more lost and alone than at any other time in his life.

He then put down his glass, placed his head in his hands, and wept.

Chapter 15

While Garrett desperately tried to calm himself, several miles away Constance was enjoying the veranda at Seaside. The onshore breeze was strong tonight, causing the waves of the Atlantic to bear whitecaps as they rushed the coast.

She would be lying if she said she did not miss him, for he had already become a huge presence in her life. She also knew that he would do his best to help her escape this terrible existence. But like Garrett, she had absolutely no idea about how to do so, and that realization was depressing.

She liked Garrett very much, and she had to admit that her feelings for him were growing. But Adam remained the love of her life, and even now Constance could not bring herself to love another. Then again, during her purgatory here at Seaside there had been no real chance for any such affairs of the heart. What will it be like, to live here with Garrett? she wondered. Just how attracted to him would she eventually become? Was that something that she unconsciously wanted?

Only time can provide the answers to such things, she thought. *And even then, I may not wish to know them.*

Suddenly her head began to swim. As the feeling intensified, she soon realized that she was experiencing the same sort of disorientation that had overcome her, just before being taken back in time to Adam.

Suspecting that another such flashback was imminent, Constance stood from her chair and hurried on shaky legs into the dining room. When she reached there she fell to her knees, her mind once again totally consumed by the same strange and overpowering phenomenon as before. Moments later she curled up onto Garrett's sleeping bag, unconscious.

"For Christ's sake, can we get on with it, Canfield?" the man in the black waistcoat shouted angrily at Adam. "Or were you planning on hiding behind your woman and your house servants all day? I always said that you are a coward, and you're starting to prove me right!"

Stunned by what she was seeing, Constance was doing her best to fight back tears. She was dressed in a light blue hoop skirt, silk slippers and a high hat, its satin ribbons tied into a large bow beneath her chin. She was standing on the long, narrow patch of ground that lay between Seaside's veranda and the rocky Atlantic shoreline. It was an early fall day, the tree leaves just starting to turn. Also dressed rather formally, Adam stood beside her. Eli, James, and Emily Jackson were also here, their dark faces bearing stark expressions of concern.

Some distance away stood two other men, both of whom Constance knew. One was Jack Rackham, an infamous New Bedford tavern and brothel owner. Rackham was a large and very vain man, with piercing dark eyes and a balding head over which he always combed loose strands of dark hair. But today the sea wind had dislodged those carefully arranged tresses, causing them to fly about and make him look faintly ridiculous. From time to time Rackham regarded Constance with a hugely libidinous glare, as if at any moment he might dare scoop her up and carry her off.

Rackham was not a fellow with whom to trifle. Rumor had it that he had by now killed five men; three of them by formal duel, and two more whom he had beaten to death following verbal altercations in his infamous tavern. Be it fisticuffs or firearms, he was clearly adept with each.

The other man was named Yancy Kilgoyle and was well known for doing most of Rackham's dirty work; he had reputedly killed even more men than his vicious employer. He was a short, greasy-looking creature who also wore a waistcoat suit, plus a top hat. His eyes were close set, and his longish, dark hair protruded haphazardly out from under his hatband.

But Rackham's lecherous glances were not what bothered Constance the most. Soon her hands began shaking so badly that she could no longer hold her parasol, so she placed it gently on the ground. Trying to fight back tears, she did her best to calm herself. However it was to no avail, because there was nothing she could do to stop what was about to happen.

Very soon now, either Jack Rackham or her beloved husband, Adam, would be dead.

Adam had been home from his most recent sea voyage for only two months. During that trip he had taken a liking to a young, Irish crewman of only fifteen years named Sean Fahey. Fahey had clearly been scared and inexperienced, and when Adam asked him about himself, Fahey confided that he had been shanghaied out of Rackham's saloon. This was not the first time that Adam had heard of such goings-on in Rackham's place, and now that he had firsthand knowledge, he was infuriated. During his long times at sea he had seen many examples of forced servitude, and he hated them all. For Adam was not only an abolitionist. He despised slavery in any form, and to his mind being shanghaied certainly qualified.

Upon arriving home, one of the first things Adam did was go to Rackham's tavern and confront him about the Fahey boy. Rackham had smiled nastily and told Adam that not only was he free to make money any way he chose, but that if Adam knew what was good for him, he would hightail it straight back out the door for the coward that he was.

The argument escalated until Rackham slapped Adam across the face, whereupon Adam immediately demanded the satisfaction of a duel. Rackham quickly accepted, and the time and place were set right there and then. The weapons of choice would be pistols. Yancy Kilgoyle would serve as Rackham's second, while Eli Jackson would serve as second to Adam.

Overcome with fear, Constance turned and looked at the table that had been set up on the grass. Each man had brought with him four loaded pistols, all of which lay atop the table. By mutual agreement, this would be a duel to the death. If each man missed the other, they would take up fresh pistols and try again. If one or both of them was wounded but the injuries were not serious, they would try again. Until one of them laid dead, or one or both of them had sustained a wound that was considered mortal, the process would continue to its bizarre conclusion. Eli and Yancy would also be responsible for reloading the respective weapons, if need be.

My God, Constance thought. *This is insane! There are even rules for this madness! Why must men be so honor bound?*

Rackham looked at Adam and Eli then he beckoned them nearer. As they approached, Rackham smiled, revealing several holes where teeth had been.

"I have something to tell the both of you," Rackham said. "After I've killed you, Canfield, my man Kilgoyle is going to murder this here manservant of yours. And when you're both lying dead at my feet, I'm going to give that pretty little wife of his to Yancy. Then I'm going to drag Constance into the house, where we will get to know each other much, much better."

At Rackham's obscene mention of the women, it was all Adam could do to keep from choking him barehanded. But that would do no good, for it would leave Yancy Kilgoyle as a witness, and then he would have to be killed too. *No,* Adam thought. God willing, he would simply have to kill Rackham first. Because if he failed, what happened next was unthinkable.

Instead of answering Rackham, Adam pulled Eli aside. Eli was a big man and a good shot, but most importantly, Adam trusted him. Placing his face close to Eli's, he began issuing some final orders.

"Now you listen carefully to me," Adam whispered. "If I'm killed, I want you to run like hell back to the gun table. Scoop up all the pistols you can carry then hurry back to Constance and Emily, and the three of you head straight for the barn as fast as you can. Open the cellar door and get all the male slaves up and out as quickly as possible, and arm as many as you can. That's the only thing that will stop Rackham and Kilgoyle from raping both of our wives. Doing so will forever reveal Seaside as a slave station, but that can't be helped. Do you understand me, Eli?"

Before answering, Eli turned and again glared with hatred at the two other men.

"Yes, sir, but if you fall dead, first I'm gonna pick up a couple of those guns and shoot both them bastards dead."

Adam shook his head vehemently.

"No, Goddammit, you listen to me!" Adam said. "If you try that, Rackham will kill you! If I'm dead and Rackham remains alive, your only hope will be in numbers. And those numbers can come only from the barn! Promise me you'll do as you're told!"

"All right, then," Eli answered angrily. "But once I do everything you say, I'll see to it that both them bastards lay dead, one way or the other."

"That's up to you," Adam answered. "Now let's get on with this."

"If you're done conspiring with your pet manservant, what's say I get to killin' you, eh?" Rackham shouted. "I ain't got all day, Canfield!"

Then he gave Constance another lecherous look.

"And besides," he added, "I got other business to attend to after you're dead."

Adam and Eli turned and walked back to their wives. By now both women were crying openly and they desperately begged their men to stop this madness, despite the shame it might bring upon them.

Adam shook his head.

"No, my love," he answered. "I may have been impetuous in this, but my path is set now. If I fall, follow Eli's orders to the letter."

Then he reached out and caressed her cheek.

"And never forget, my darling," he said softly, "how fine ye were to me."

As Adam and Eli began walking to the gun table, something Adam just said stabbed at Constance's heart.

"*Were . . .*" Constance thought. *He said: "* . . . *how fine ye were to me.*"

Upon reaching the table, Adam selected one of his pistols then he carefully checked the load. The place where this would happen was already laid out. A sword had been stuck into the ground nearby, and two more swords, each one ten paces away in opposite directions, had also been shoved into the ground, marking where the combatants would turn and fire. Because all that remained was for the duel to begin, without further ado Adam and Rackham walked to the center sword, whereupon they turned their backs to one another.

Adam was a crack shot, but this was his first duel. And although he had been in many scrapes during his time at sea, he had never been forced to kill a man. He knew that this must be done, but deep in his heart he wondered whether his nerves would hold, and if his aim would run true.

"At long last," Rackham whispered over one shoulder, "I'm going to get a taste of that pretty wife of yours."

Adam cocked his pistol then pointed it straight up into the air, as did Rackham.

"I'll see you in hell," he said quietly.

Rackham smiled again.

"You first . . ."

Eli Jackson and Yancy Kilgoyle came to stand side by side before the gun table. Kilgoyle turned and looked at Jackson.

"Would you like to do the honors?" he asked snidely.

Eli shot a steely glare at Kilgoyle.

"No," he answered. "This is your sort of thing, not mine. But no matter what happens, I'm gonna kill you sure. Maybe not today, you bastard, or even tomorrow. But in the end, I'm gonna wear your guts as a necktie."

Kilgoyle only laughed.

"Then let's get on with it," he answered, " 'cause my itch for your woman is gettin' stronger by the second."

Kilgoyle turned and looked at the two combatants.

"On my command," he said, "you will march one pace at a time toward your respective swords, where you will then turn and fire at will. Moreover, it has been decided that this will be a fight to the death. Does each of you agree to these terms?"

"I do," Adam answered.

"Gladly," Rackham said.

"Very well, then," Eli replied.

The next few seconds were the longest of Adam's life. Everything seemed to occur in slow motion; the singing of the birds was lengthened, the clouds passed overhead more languidly, and the offshore breeze magically softened to a mere caress. Had the circumstances been different, he would have welcomed all of it. But such was not the case, because one of them was about to die.

Then Kilgoyle said the words.

"On my count, you may commence walking!"

As Kilgoyle counted out the paces, each man marched diligently toward his impaled sword. At the count of ten, Rackham and Adam swiveled quickly, took aim and fired.

Her heart in her throat, Constance watched as the pistol muzzles flashed and gunpowder smoke swirled about the two combatants. She watched in horror as Rackham's ball hit Adam squarely in the left side, spinning him around and down onto the ground. Constance was about to run to Adam when Kilgoyle's voice rang out again.

"No!" he shouted. "It has been agreed that no quarter, nor aid, shall be given! Now get back to your place, woman!"

Seeing Adam bleeding and suffering was tearing Constance's heart out, but she had no choice. With tears running uncontrollably down her cheeks, on trembling legs she walked back to again stand alongside Emily.

Adam agonizingly came to his feet. He put one hand inside his shirt, and when he withdrew it, it was covered with blood. Even so, he managed to stagger back over to the gun table and put down his weapon.

Rackham was already there, gloatingly checking the load in his next pistol. He waited until Adam looked at him, then he made a show of glaring lecherously at Constance.

"One more ball," he said Adam. "I only need to put one more ball into you, and then I get to put myself into her."

After selecting another of his pistols, Adam glared hotly at Rackham through his pain.

"You're forgetting one thing," he said.

"And just what, pray tell, might that be?"

"Your ball found the wrong shoulder," Adam said. "And my gun arm still wants you."

Yet again the two men went to stand back to back at the single sword impaled into the grass. By now Adam could barely stand, and he wavered from side to side.

Steady on, he said to himself. *Whatever happens, this will be your last shot and it has to count, or else . . .*

Once again Kilgoyle began calling out the paces. Adam staggered along to the count as best he could, desperately hoping that he would not fall. At last the two men reached the count of ten, whereupon they turned and fired.

Yet again, Constance watched in horror as the two gun muzzles flashed and acrid gunpowder smoke filled the air. But this time Rackham missed and Adam prevailed, the ball from his gun striking Rackham squarely over his right eye. Rackham was literally lifted backward off his feet and thrown some distance to the ground, dead where he lay.

At once Adam did his best to hurry back to the gun table, where he dropped his spent weapon and picked up another fresh pistol. He quickly cocked the pistol and placed the muzzle squarely against Kilgoyle's forehead. Eli immediately approached Adam and took hold of him, helping him to remain standing.

"Eli . . ." Adam said breathlessly.

"Yes, sir . . ." Eli answered. "I'm here for you . . ."

Adam looked Kilgoyle squarely in the eyes. He briefly pointed his pistol at the body of Jack Rackham then he quickly reinstated it squarely against Kilgoyle's cranium.

"Now, then," Adam said to Kilgoyle. "You and my man here are going to pick up that worthless corpse and tie him across his empty saddle. And then you are going to leave. If you so much as darken my door again, I will shoot you on sight. Do you understand me, you dumb bastard?"

Shaking nearly beyond control, Kilgoyle nodded stupidly.

"Then get to it . . ." Adam said.

When Adam started to falter, Emily and Constance took him into their arms and gently laid him down upon the grass.

Adam looked up at Constance and gave her a weak smile.

"Emily can tend to me for now, my love," he said. "Go and get a pistol from Eli, and then point it directly at Kilgoyle while they load Rackham's body onto his horse. If Kilgoyle so much as breathes wrong, shoot him."

As much as Constance wanted to stay with him, she knew that she must do as he ordered.

"I will, husband," she said.

But just as Constance accepted one of the pistols from Eli, she suddenly felt her head start to spin. The feeling became stronger and stronger, until she began losing consciousness. Soon everything around her began to melt into nothingness, and . . .

Crying aloud, Constance awakened with start. At once she curled into a ball, the way a little child might do after having a terrible nightmare. Covered with sweat and breathing heavily, she frantically looked about herself to find that she was back in Seaside's dining room, lying atop Garrett's rumpled sleeping bag.

The fire she had set in the hearth earlier this evening was little more than embers now, telling her that she had been gone for some time. As if it might somehow grant her a modicum of safety, she skidded across the floor to the far corner and pulled her knees up tight against her chest, sobbing.

She would remain that way until dawn ascended over the Atlantic.

Chapter 16

"I don't mean to pry, honey," Dale Richmond said to his wife, Virginia. "And I'm not asking you to betray any confidences. But I do have a question for you about Garrett."

The Richmonds were enjoying their first cups of coffee before making breakfast. They loved these mornings together, and for as long as Dale could remember, he had asked the same Sunday morning question of himself: *Am I feeling religious today, or merely spiritual?*

If the answer was "religious," he went to church. And if the answer was "spiritual," he stayed home and made a big breakfast with his wife. He would then retire to the couch, where he reclined with Freckles at his feet and read the Sunday paper from beginning to end. Lately, the spiritual answer had been winning out over the religious one.

After taking another sip of coffee, Virginia put down her cup and looked into Dale's eyes. She wasn't sure what he was getting at, but she suspected that it might have something to do with Garrett's private conversation with her. Although she was hesitant about discussing it, she hadn't entered into any sort of professional relationship with Garrett. That said, there was no issue, save for that of any mother questioning whether to reveal her child's innermost thoughts.

The unsettled nature of her gaze was not lost on Dale.

"What?" he asked.

"What do you mean, 'what'?" Virginia asked. "If you have a question for me about Garrett, just ask it."

Dale shrugged his shoulders.

"I'm sort of worried about him," he said. "The other day when we were out hunting he asked me several rather cosmic questions, none of which I answered well, I'm afraid. For better or worse, I got the impression that he was doing some real soul-searching. Then again, he's got a lot on his plate just now, and it could've been nothing more than that."

Dale reached out and put one hand atop Virginia's.

"I'm just wondering if you've seen a change in him," he said. "I know I have."

At first, Virginia hesitated. But she and Dale had never kept secrets from each other, and this was no time to start. Besides, she was rather concerned about Garrett too. Over the next ten minutes she explained her conversation with him. While sipping his coffee from time to time, Dale listened attentively. When Virginia finished, he let go a long sigh.

"Good Lord," he said. "That was certainly some dream. So you're the shrink . . . can you tell me what it means?"

"I think his subconscious was trying to create his perfect dream girl," she said. "And as I told Garrett, the fact that she seemed to be straight out of the antebellum period and that she desperately needed his help only added to her allure."

Thinking, Dale went to the refrigerator and produced a carton of jumbo eggs.

"Is scrambled okay?" he asked.

"Sure."

"This is what we get for having such willful children, Ginnie," he said as he cracked four eggs into a mixing bowl. "But Garrett is especially stubborn, and we both know where that came from."

Virginia snorted out a short laugh.

"Your side of the family of course," she said.

"Yeah, right," Dale answered. "What is it you used to say to your clients when they were telling whoppers? 'It's your dream, so make it as big as you want.'"

Virginia laughed.

"You remember that one, eh?" she answered. "I'm duly impressed."

Dale went back to the refrigerator and retrieved some smoked bacon, which he unwrapped on the cutting board. The moment the familiar scent hit the air, Freckles bounded up from her dog bed and began whining plaintively.

"Not yet, girl," Dale said. "But once it's cooked, if there's any left over, it's all yours."

As if she were actually answering him, she let go a happy bark.

"How the hell does she always seem to understand you?" Virginia asked. "It's like the two of you can communicate, or something."

Dale smiled as he pulled another frying pan from the cupboard, placed it on the range, and then set the burner on medium.

"It's all about the bond between man and dog," he said. Then he laughed a little. "Being a woman, you wouldn't understand."

Virginia rolled her eyes.

"Yeah, that must be it," she answered. "We women just never learned to speak 'dog.'"

Virginia watched lovingly as Dale began frying the bacon. Their marriage had been a long and wonderful one, and they were looking forward to the remaining years. She felt better now after telling Dale of her conversation with Garrett. And because of that, she decided that turnabout was fair play.

"Okay, buster," Virginia announced. "I've shown you mine. Now show me yours."

Dale turned around and looked at her quizzically.

"In case you haven't noticed," he said, "I'm in the middle of cooking breakfast, and this is not the time to play 'doctor,' even though I am one. But if you're still interested later on . . ."

Virginia laughed.

"No, dummy," she answered. "I mean your conversation with Garrett."

"Ah," Dale said. "Now I get it. Oh well, a boy can still dream."

Dale swiveled back around and started turning the bacon.

"His questions were largely metaphysical," he answered. "He wanted to know if I believed in the hereafter, reincarnation, and that sort of thing. Like I said before, I got the impression that he was doing some soul-searching, and that he wanted my guidance. I'm afraid I wasn't much help, though. Does any of that reflect in his conversation with you?"

"No, not really," Virginia answered. "Then again, a few days transpired between my conversation and yours, so maybe my answers influenced his questions to you. But there's a bigger issue here, Dale."

"Which is?"

"Well, there's nothing wrong with wanting to renovate an old house and then live in it. As a matter of fact, my guess is that when it's done, it will be absolutely charming. That's not the point. What concerns me are his motives. It's almost as if he is so obsessed with the past that he really wants to live there. And if that obsession becomes strong enough, then it's unhealthy. He's already stretched pretty thin, and now his preoccupation with restoring the house isn't helping. Plus, when I spoke to him I got the impression that he had more to tell me, but he didn't for some reason. That's not like him, and the more I think about it, the more it all worries me. It's almost like that old house actually has some weird power over him."

Dale placed four slices of whole wheat bread into the toaster then he poured another cup of coffee before returning to his chair. As he sat there thinking, Virginia could see the concern registering on his face.

"What is it?" she asked gently.

Dale sighed and looked into her eyes.

"Ginnie," he asked, "do we have a son who's in trouble?"

Thinking, she worriedly rubbed her forehead.

"I only wish I knew."

Chapter 17

Garrett was still sitting on his balcony when the sun came up. The alcohol had eventually calmed him, but not so much that he couldn't function. He then cleaned up, changed his clothes, and left for Seaside in search of answers.

While driving, he still agonized over whether to tell Constance about his "flashback." They had previously vowed to tell each other everything, but this seemed a special circumstance. If the nature of his experience had been less intimate, there would be no doubt. But as things stood, he didn't know what to do. He was now experiencing the same sort of phenomena as was Constance, and that realization disturbed him to his core.

He was desperately concerned that if he told her, she would feel violated. But in the end he realized that she must know, because anything that might help in their quest for answers could not be ignored. Clearly if they were to solve this mystical riddle, no scrap of information could be deemed too sensitive to hide from one another. The flashback he had experienced last night concerned him for other reasons, as well. Would there be more of them, for example? He desperately hoped not, because they were highly cathartic events that he feared might do true psychological damage, if left unchecked. He also longed to tell the story to his mother but knew that he couldn't, for fear of sounding like a complete lunatic.

There is some reason why these things are happening to us, he thought as he turned onto the road toward Seaside. *There simply must be. But it's all such a mystery! And every day I become more convinced that until we solve it, we will never escape its grip.*

When he neared Seaside he did not see Constance. He parked the Jeep out front, and because it was a nice day he left its top open. After grabbing up a brown paper bag from the back, he took a moment to admire the house.

Garrett was pleased with what he saw. Even one with no knowledge of architecture could see that the house was coming along. Jay's men had begun installing the new siding, and several others had started repairing the widow's walk. Soon now, repairs would also be made to other areas such as the veranda, the side porches, and so on. From the very beginning he had believed that Seaside would be an absolutely beautiful house, and with each passing day he became surer of it.

As an architect, he had always preferred overseeing restorations and remodeling, as opposed to building new structures. It was true that designing a new work gave him a great deal of latitude. But restoring an old building, especially one with a significant history, ensured that future generations could enjoy it as well.

Because it was Sunday and there were no workers about, the house seemed unusually quiet. After putting the brown paper bag down on one of the kitchen counters, he called out Constance's name but got no reply. She must be in the barn, he decided.

That was when he heard her call his name. Walking back down the hall, he checked each room and found her sitting on the dining room floor, her back against one corner and her knees pulled tightly against her chest.

He quickly walked in and sat down beside her. She looked exhausted, her face red and blotchy from hard crying. He soon guessed that she was again bereft of sleep. Knowing that he would be risking the same onslaught of sexual longing he always felt when touching her, he nonetheless stroked her cheek. As he did, the feeling overcame him briefly and then vanished when his fingertips reluctantly left her skin.

"Are you all right?" he asked softly. "Did something happen?"

Constance looked at him with beseeching eyes.

"My God, Garrett," she said, her voice a near whisper. "I suffered another flashback last night, and it was awful. Like the first one, this was something that actually happened. And also like the first one, I was quite unaware of my future life in the here and now."

Exhausted, she laid her head on his shoulder.

"You should tell me about it," he said.

Constance nodded slightly.

"Yes . . ." she answered. "But first, I have a question for you."

Garrett smiled.

"Of course," he answered.

"Did you by chance bring coffee?" she asked. "I must admit that since you've come into my life, I've developed an affinity for it. And doughnuts . . . the truth is I've been stealing one each morning while Jay's workmen are here. I like the way they taste too."

Garrett smiled again.

"Why yes, madam," he said. "I just happen to have a thermos of coffee and two cheese Danish waiting in the kitchen."

"Bless you," she answered.

Two cups of black coffee and a Danish later, Constance began telling Garrett about her flashback. As she described it, she was very careful to include all the details. Retelling it was difficult for her, and she paused several times. But when it was over, a great weight seemed to have been lifted from her shoulders.

The two of them were sitting cross-legged on the dining room floor, drinking the remains of the coffee. When Constance finished her story, Garrett sighed and leaned back against the wall.

"I knew that there was dueling in the antebellum period, and that in some areas it even lasted straight through the Civil War," he said. "After that it fell out of favor, and most states passed laws against it. But I of course had no idea that Adam had participated in one, or that he nearly lost his life. I assume that because he died later at sea, he was able to overcome Jack Rackham's bullet wound, right?"

Constance nodded.

"It took several months, but Emily and I nursed him back to health. The ball broke one rib then went cleanly out his back. The most important thing in those days was to keep the wound clean, because we didn't have any antibiotics, and surgeons were few. But Adam pulled through, God bless him. He saved us all that day. Although he hated the notoriety, he became known in New Bedford as 'the man who killed Jack Rackham.' "

Garrett leaned his head back, thinking about something Constance had told him. She disliked this day and age, she had said, and wished that she could return to her own time and be with Adam. But it wasn't just missing Adam that made her feel this way, Garrett knew. As she had told him, she believed the time in which she previously lived had been far more genteel and halcyon, despite being so different. *Perhaps what they say is true, after all,* he thought. Maybe there really is no place like home.

Garrett knew that he must tell her about his own flashback, yet she seemed so vulnerable right now that he remained hesitant. On the other hand, because she had just shared her experience with him, this might be the best time. After letting go a long sigh, Garrett looked into her eyes.

"I have something to tell you too," he said softly. "I've been questioning whether to, but I decided that you must know."

"What is it?" she asked.

"Before I tell you," he said, "you must understand that I had absolutely no control over what happened. It was as if I was possessed, and being controlled by forces far stronger than I."

Constance looked at him quizzically.

"Go on," she said.

"I had my first flashback last night," he answered. "And like your experiences, it was no dream. I was really there, and yet I was not. And even now I'm hesitant to tell you, because I'm so worried about how you might react."

Constance shook her head.

"You must never feel that way," she answered. "Do you not see? To ever find our way out of this, we must be completely honest with each other. So please, Garrett, please tell me all of it, no matter how difficult it might prove. I promise I will do my best to understand."

Still fearing that he might lose her trust forever, Garrett began telling the story. As he did, Constance blushed and cast her eyes to the floor. But even during the most awkward parts she never distanced herself from him. When at last he was done, she looked back into his eyes.

"My God, Garrett," she whispered.

"I know," he answered. "And there's something I have to know from you, Constance."

"Yes . . . ?"

"While this was going on, were you 'there' with me? Were you aware of what was happening?"

As Constance began crying again, she nodded.

"Yes," she answered, her voice shaking. "I was there with you. It happened right after I reexperienced Adam's duel with Yancy. I went unconscious again, and the next thing I knew, I was in your arms."

Garrett ran his hands through his hair, thinking. There was another question he wanted to ask but wasn't sure he dared. At last he decided.

"There's something else that I must know," he said gently. "Forgive me for asking this, but did you want it too? Please tell me that I didn't take you against your will . . ."

As if she were ashamed, Constance looked down at the floor.

"Yes, Garrett," she answered, her voice now a mere whisper. "I daresay that I wanted it as badly as you, and was equally compelled. I had decided not to mention it, unless you did. Was it wrong of us?"

Vastly relieved that Constance didn't feel violated, he sighed.

"I don't know," he answered. "But I'm sure of two things."

"And what are they?" she asked.

"I don't think we could have stopped, even if we had wanted to," he said. "We were in the grip of some force far larger than ourselves, I'm convinced of it."

"And the other thing?" she asked.

"I'm not sorry it happened."

Constance looked at the floor again, thinking. It was becoming clear to Garrett that she had something important to say, and she was trying to find the courage. When he reached out and put one hand on her shoulder, the familiar sexual undercurrent ran through him again.

"What is it?" he asked. "I know that this must have upset you greatly, but as I told you, there was literally nothing we could do about it."

Constance shook her head again.

"No," she answered, "it is not what you think. What really concerns me goes much deeper. And because of that, there is something that I must now know from you. But you will probably be as unwilling to answer my question, as I am afraid to hear your reply."

"What is it?" he asked.

Constance took a deep breath.

"Are you falling in love with me, Garrett?" she asked.

Although he might have expected this question from her, it still rattled him deeply. Not so much because Constance had asked it, but because he must now reveal his true feelings about her. For more reasons than he could count, he still struggled mightily with telling her the truth. But they had come this far, and being deceitful would not only harm their relationship, but it might also impede their search for answers.

And here it is at last, he thought. *The one question that I have feared asking of myself, despite knowing its answer for some time now. So be it, then.*

Garrett took Constance's hands into his own and looked into her eyes.

"God help me, yes," he admitted. "I have loved you from the first moment I saw you in my dream. And I have more passion for you than for any other woman I have ever known. Forgive me if my love for you is unwanted, but I simply can't help myself. It dwells deep inside me, and to ignore it would not only be a lie to you, but also a betrayal to me."

Constance quickly stood and went to stand before one of the dining room windows. Rather than ask her to return, Garrett remained silent. After a time, she turned and looked at him.

"This mustn't happen, Garrett," Constance said. "We simply cannot allow it. I still love Adam, despite what occurred between us."

"And what about us?" he asked. "You can't tell me that you feel nothing for me, Constance. I don't know how deep your feelings run, but I believe that you care, and perhaps far more than you'd like to admit. Call me crazy, but I can sense it. You're so deep inside me, it's almost like I breathe with you."

Her silent tears came again, this time more out of frustration than fear. Wrapping her arms protectively about herself, she stared at him almost as if she were seeing him for the first time.

"Yes, Garrett," she said. "You are right—my feelings for you are growing, and they scare me. Although Adam is still the love of my life, it is becoming harder and harder for me to keep my love for him from turning into even more passion for you. And may God forgive me, although what transpired between us has made me feel guilty, I'm not sorry that it happened, either."

Whatever was going on between him and Constance, it was progressing quickly and affecting each of them, he realized. And because of his great desire for her, he could not convince himself that their growing attraction for one another was wrong.

Constance then closed her eyes briefly, her shoulders slumping down gently, as if in defeat.

"Do you have any idea how difficult it is to remain faithful to someone who has been gone for so long?" she asked. "No, of course you don't. How could you? I always believed that Adam would remain the one true love of my life. And then, for the first time in more than one hundred and seventy years, a man comes along who can both see and hear me. And with his coming, everything changes."

There was a pained look on her face now as she shook her head back and forth.

"I am mightily confused, Garrett," she said quietly. "It is as if something foreign is taking control of my heart. And until we solve the riddle of whatever is going on here, I fear that my feelings for you will only grow."

Having heard enough, Garrett purposefully walked to her and held her close. Aside from his experience during the flashback, this was the first time he had truly taken her into his arms. And although she still remained hopelessly trapped between worlds, she felt to him like any other warm, flesh-and-blood woman might. Placing two fingers beneath her chin, he lifted her face to his.

"I understand," he said. "I really do. But trying to condemn yourself over this is not proof that your feelings are wrong, or any guarantee that they won't deepen."

Constance gently freed herself from his embrace then she looked blankly about the room.

"It is this house, Garrett," she said quietly.

"What are you talking about?" he asked.

She raised her arms and gestured toward the room.

"It is this *house*," she repeated. "*Seaside* has done this to us. Can you not see it? There is more going on here than meets the eye. I just know it. Something about this place has changed us. A spell, an enchantment, or even a curse perhaps, call it what you will. But to my mind there is something about this house that put you and me together this way, and it is forcing us ever closer. It is almost as if Seaside has a plan for us that will not be denied, no matter what we do."

This time it was she who initiated the embrace, and he was glad for it.

"God, Garrett, what are we going to do?" she asked.

Constance needed reassurance, he realized. Plus, he wanted to lighten her mood. He knew a way to try and accomplish these things, but would she go along with it?

"Well," he said, "I have an idea, but it's going to require that you leave Seaside and actually venture out into the world. Do you think you can handle that?"

Constance shook her head questioningly, then she turned and gazed out the dining room window again. It was a pretty morning and the window was partly open, allowing them to hear the gulls crying outside.

"I don't know," she answered softly. "It has been so long . . ."

"Well, there's one way to find out," Garrett said.

He smiled and gave her a comforting wink.

"What say we go for a ride?"

Chapter 18

G arrett laughed as Constance let go another joyful shriek. He had never seen her so happy, and it warmed his heart. They were in Garrett's Jeep, heading down the road that led toward New Bedford.

At first he had had a difficult time persuading Constance to leave the house, but after some friendly coaxing she finally agreed. He could understand her apprehension. For more than 170 years she had never departed the property. There hadn't seemed a safe way to do it, plus going out alone had always scared her.

Moreover, they weren't totally sure at first whether Constance could really leave the property, even if she wanted to. Because she had never tried, she had no way of knowing what might happen. For all they knew, she could be somehow bound to Seaside by the same strange set of circumstances that kept her imprisoned between life and death. The idea of tempting the fates this way scared her, and Garrett sympathized. But they had to know, and so Garrett helped Constance into his Jeep, and they tentatively drove off the property, wondering whether at any moment Constance might disappear, or worse. By now they were well on their way, and everything seemed all right. Their test run was proving successful, and Garrett was pleased.

At first the Jeep ride scared her silly. She had never gone this fast, and it seemed to her as if they might crash at any moment. But she soon became accustomed to it, although from time to time she would still let go a happy shriek. She found stop signs and stoplights to be particularly troublesome to fathom, but by the time they reached the city limits she was more relaxed and enjoying herself.

For his part, Garrett was considering the "rules" to follow when going out in public with Constance. He could listen to her, but if there were people about, he shouldn't speak to her. Other unexpected issues would surely crop up as well, like her not wearing the shoulder harness in the Jeep. When she first got into the vehicle, Garrett had begun strapping her in when she gently stopped him, explaining that it would appear as if the shoulder harness was somehow being suspended in midair.

This is going to be one hell of a learning experience, he thought.

When at last they entered New Bedford, Constance gawked at everything with awe. Despite all that she had seen on television and read in the newspapers, witnessing modern life was far more impressive. She watched the people, stared at the buildings, and marveled at how all the street traffic managed to so cleverly avoid crashing at the various intersections. Whenever Garrett looked over at her, she had a huge smile of amazement on her face, and he was glad to see it after their heartfelt conversation of less than one hour ago. Many important things had been said then, and they were both glad to be preoccupied with something else.

Garrett headed straight for Dartmouth Mall, where he soon found a remote parking place for the Jeep. Laughing again, Constance ran her fingers back through her hair in an attempt to look more presentable. After checking to see whether anyone was in earshot, Garrett looked over at her and smiled.

"So tell me," he said quietly, "what do you think about this newfangled form of transportation called the automobile?"

"How marvelous!" she said. "And so fast too! I am actually beginning to think that living in the here and now might not be such a bad thing!"

Garrett laughed a little.

"Well," he said, "I'm glad to hear you say that, because there's so much more for you to see and learn."

Constance regarded Dartmouth Mall with interest.

"So this is what a mall looks like," she mused. "I have seen them on television, but I did not realize they were so big. Why did you bring us here?"

Garrett looked around again to make sure there was no one nearby. He was starting to get the hang of this, he hoped.

"I need to fulfill my promise to you," he answered.

"What promise?" she asked.

"I said that I would buy you some new clothes, remember?" he answered. "And I also promised to buy you a new bed and dresser, so that you could begin sleeping in the house full-time."

"Thank you, Garrett," she said, "but you needn't do this. I am getting along all right, just as things are now."

Garrett shook his head.

"That's not good enough," he said. "No offense, but I'm tired of seeing you in those same clothes all the time! Plus the weather is turning colder, and you can't sleep in that damned barn forever."

Then he laughed a little again.

"Besides," he added, "because you gave me all of that exquisite furniture in the barn cellar, this seems the least I can do. Now get out of the Jeep and let's get going. I can't honestly say that mall shopping has ever been one of my favorite experiences, but with you along, who knows?"

When they entered the mall, Constance became even more thunderstruck. Today was Sunday and the place was mobbed. Hordes of young people were texting relentlessly on their cell phones, and Garrett thought for the hundredth time that if this was what they called socializing, they could have just as well stayed home. Given the many glittering stores lined up one after another, Constance was at first overwhelmed.

No sooner had they gotten inside than Constance stopped walking. When she turned and looked at Garrett she wore a concerned expression on her face.

"We must be careful about this," she whispered.

"What do you mean?" he whispered back.

"The way that we walk together," Constance answered. "If we are not cautious, we will raise suspicion."

"How so?"

"It is only logical," Constance answered. "You must always remember that no one can see me but you. So if I walk ahead of you, the chances are good that someone will walk into us. That is probably also true if I walk alongside you."

"So what do you suggest?" he asked.

"I will walk behind you," she answered. "And I will stay close. I am not familiar with this place, so when you see a store that you think is appropriate, go inside and I will follow you. And if I say something to you, for heaven's sake do not turn around and reply."

Garrett suddenly realized that this would be more complicated than he had first thought. Constance left his side and went to stand behind him.

"Ready?" she asked.

"Yes," he answered.

Constance laughed a little.

"You failed your first test," she said.

"Huh?"

"You answered me," she said. "You are not supposed to do that, remember?"

Garrett began leading her deeper into the mall. He tried his best to avoid other people, but the going was tricky. After a couple of minutes he felt the need to ask Constance whether she was still behind him but knew that he shouldn't. He would just have to trust her. A bit later he entered a fashionable women's clothing store, where he came to a stop and waited for her to speak to him.

"Do not worry," she said. "I am still with you. There are fewer people here, so I think it is probably all right now for us to walk together."

She came up alongside him and gave him a smile.

"Hello, handsome," she said.

Although this time Garrett didn't answer her, he couldn't help but laugh out loud. When he did, a couple of women shoppers turned and looked at him oddly.

"Do you see?" Constance asked. "Like I said, we must be careful. Now then, I suppose the best thing for me to do is to walk around this place and point at the things I need. If it is something you don't like or do not wish to purchase for me, shake your head. Otherwise, I suppose that you will have to pick up my choices and carry them in your arms."

Garrett nodded slightly.

"Very well, then," Constance said. "Let us go."

As Constance strolled through the store, she was amazed by the vast variety of clothing available to her. In her previous life there had only been a few stores in New Bedford and the selections were very limited, but here there were literally mountains of clothing from which to choose. The sizes were different from what she remembered, so when she found something, she whispered to Garrett to find a medium, and Garrett gathered it up into his arms.

"Am I taking too much?" Constance asked tentatively.

After looking around, Garrett shook his head.

"Then I am finished," she said, "and I will never know how to thank you."

Constance followed Garrett to the register, where she watched with rapt fascination as he used some sort of a plastic playing card to pay for everything. She could hardly believe that no cash had traded hands.

With that, they left the store and began walking through the mall again. Garrett next entered a ladies' shoe store, where he sought out and found the cowboy boots. Stopping before them, he nodded slightly. Although genteel women never wore such things during Constance's previous life, she liked them.

"So you think I should have a pair of those?" she asked.

Again, Garrett nodded slightly. While examining the selection, Constance stopped before a pair of shiny black leather boots with fancy tooling and she pointed at them.

Garrett looked down at her worn-out sneakers and did his best to ascertain her shoe size. On finding the appropriate boot box, he picked it up and the two of them walked farther into the store. After Constance also picked out a pair of Nike sneakers and a sensible pair of women's shoes, Garrett paid for the items and they left the store. Because there was so much to carry, Garrett got a shopping cart before he and Constance continued their explorations. But Garrett soon found himself blushing slightly, and the sudden change in his expression was not lost on Constance.

"Is something amiss?" she asked.

Garrett shook his head. Not being able to talk to her was maddening, but in this particular instance he didn't mind. He knew that there were some other things that she probably needed, but had been ladylike enough to not discuss. He rightly suspected that she needed some new "unmentionables," and he soon decided that the best way to get the point across would be to simply visit an appropriate store.

A few minutes later, they found themselves standing before a Victoria's Secret store. As Constance stood looking at the giant advertisements of scantily dressed women, her jaw literally dropped. During her previous life, such things were scandalous beyond all reason and would have probably landed their creators in jail. As it was, she simply stood there, fascinated by the garish displays. She soon gave Garrett an incredulous look.

"You are not suggesting that we enter there, are you?" she asked tentatively.

Garrett nodded.

"But it is so outrageous!" she protested.

Smiling, this time Garrett couldn't help but to answer her verbally.

"It's not outrageous, Constance," he answered softly. "It's commerce."

Without giving her another chance to protest, Garrett strode inside the store and Constance had no choice but to follow him. All the items for sale immediately entranced her, and Garrett shadowed her as she wandered from table to table, pointing to the things that she needed. Garrett couldn't help blushing all over again, and when the time came to check out, he felt a bit foolish standing in line with his arms full of ladies' unmentionables. When at last he reached the register, the young female associate gave him a crafty smile.

"Planning on a big night, are we?" she asked mischievously.

It was all Garrett could do to resist turning and looking at Constance, but he managed.

"Well . . ." he answered. "Not really, I guess."

The salesgirl smiled again.

"That's a pity," she said. "Because whoever is getting all this is a very lucky girl."

While trying his best to remain unflustered, Garrett paid quickly, and they were soon out of the store and back into the hubbub.

"We should leave now, Garrett," Constance said. "I have already squandered too much money, but I thank you from the bottom of my heart."

Eager to be free of the mall so that he could talk to her once again, Garrett pushed the shopping cart out through the front doors and they returned to the Jeep, where he placed all of the packages into the back. Still no one had parked nearby, it seemed. After the two of them got into the Jeep, Garrett again looked around warily. At last he could speak openly to her.

"I really like the things you picked out," he said. "For a girl from the past, you've got great taste in this day and age."

As Constance laughed again, he found himself doubting that during the entire time of her imprisonment at Seaside she had ever been this happy.

"Thank you," she said. "And thank you again for all the nice clothes. I am eager to go home and try them all on!"

Garrett smiled and shook his head.

"Nope," he answered. "Before we go home, we have to get you a new bed, remember?"

It was clear by the look on Constance's face that she was starting to feel guilty about all this. He had done so much for her already that she wasn't at all sure about letting him buy her a bed as well.

"Are you certain?" she asked. "It would be nice to sleep in the house, but—"

"No more 'buts,'" Garrett said as he fired up the Jeep. "You're going to be sleeping inside the house from now on, and that's the end of it."

With that, Garrett promptly drove to a furniture store with which he had previously done business. After parking the Jeep, he and Constance went inside. They strolled for a while among the various beds, and at last Garrett chose a large four-post affair and a matching armoire. They then wandered over to where the mattress and box springs were displayed, and while they stood there looking at them, a saleslady walked up.

"Can I be of help?" she asked. She was a tall redhead whose name badge read CLAIRE.

"We—uh—I mean *I'm* looking for a new bed," Garrett said. "I've already picked out the frame, so now I need a mattress to go with it."

"Do you know what size?" Claire asked.

"A king," he answered.

As he looked to his right for approval from Constance, he was aghast to find that she was nowhere to be seen. Despite that Claire was standing right next to him he began blatantly gawking all about the store, trying to find her.

"Is there something wrong?" Claire asked.

"No . . . no," Garrett answered. "I was just looking around at the other mattresses."

Then he saw something that truly took him aback. A little way down the aisle of mattresses, Constance was lying atop one, and he desperately hoped that Claire would not notice the depressions that she was making in the plush pillow top. Closing his eyes, he took a deep breath. Then Claire gave Garrett another curious look.

"Are you quite sure that you're all right, sir?" she asked. "I'd be happy to go and get you a glass of water, or—"

Garrett shook his head.

"No, no . . . thank you all the same," he said. "But I am in a bit of a hurry, so could we write these up now?"

Realizing that she had just made an easy sale, Claire smiled broadly.

"Certainly," she said. "Please come this way."

Forty-five minutes later, Garrett and Constance were once more ensconced in his Jeep. Laughing broadly, Garrett turned the ignition key, and the trusty vehicle roared to life.

"So tell me," he said. "Did you have fun testing out the mattress?"

Constance immediately blushed.

"That was so unlike me!" she answered. "I suppose that I am so overly glad to be here with you I could not help myself!"

Garrett smiled broadly at her. This was more like the real Constance, he supposed. He also knew that even if she had been a woman of this time, she would still be the most beautiful and vivacious one he had ever known. And he had meant every word of what he had said to her back at Seaside. He loved her with all of his heart, and no matter what obstacles might lay ahead of them, his love for her would never fade.

While Constance settled into her seat, Garrett pointed the Jeep homeward, toward Seaside.

Chapter 19

G arrett poured a glass of red wine then leaned back luxuriously against his new sofa. He'd purchased it—and a cocktail table—from Claire, and paid handsomely to have them delivered immediately. Although he had first considered bringing some of the antique stuff into the house, he wasn't ready to explain that to Jay and the workmen. Constance was upstairs, trying on her new clothes, and had eagerly promised to model some of them for him.

After taking another sip, Garrett put his wineglass down on the cocktail table. He had built a fire in the dining room fireplace, its heat spreading nicely throughout the room. Although this was only a small taste of the comfort he hoped to eventually savor here at Seaside, it was a welcome respite just the same.

After a time he lit a cigar, letting its pungent smoke drift across his palette.

He had deeply enjoyed his time with Constance today, and she had shown him a childlike quality that he suspected hadn't surfaced for many years. For a few precious hours they were able to escape their awful predicament. But now that Garrett was back at Seaside, his worries about their future and his growing feelings for Constance began to crowd in on him again. He must begin trying to unravel this mystery, if for no other reason than that the pull he felt toward Constance was undeniable, and impossible to fight.

Perhaps he should have never bought this old house, but what was done was done. Either way, he and Constance were now involved in a riddle they might never solve. He loved Constance, and he wanted her here with him forever. But at the same time he remained unsure of her feelings for him. Her undying love for her late husband, Adam, never seemed to wane, and Garrett knew that until it did, his desperate love for her might remain unrequited.

After taking another sip of wine, he carefully tapped the ash from his cigar into an old ashtray he had found in the house. For a precise architect who worshiped organization, his life had certainly become quite the mess.

Clearly, this predicament had something to do with the concept of time. In the beginning he had considered Constance to be a total prisoner of time, but in some ways he had been wrong. She was only partly time's captive because she moved along with it. Yet she also seemed to defy time in that she never aged. It was as if time were somehow both her friend and her enemy. The concept of time also played a huge part in their flashbacks. Each one had been firmly rooted in the past, the most perplexing aspect perhaps being that the experiences had felt so real, rather than dreamlike.

Sighing deeply, Garrett put down his cigar and scrubbed his face with both hands. This was all so maddening. Even worse, he had no clue about how to proceed. And that notion discouraged him, largely due to the sheer incomprehensibility of the problem. To his mind, whatever forces drove all this seemed far beyond human understanding or a mere mortal's power to change them.

And what would be the outcome, he wondered, if he and Constance never found the answer? What would it be like living here with her decade after decade while he grew older, and she remained the same young and beautiful widow that she was now? Given how much he loved her, would that be such an awful life? Or would the nature of it eventually tear their relationship to shreds, and cause him to leave Seaside forever? If so, then what would it be like without Constance in his life, now that she meant so much to him?

So many questions, he thought, *and not a single answer in sight.*

Just then Constance walked into the room. She was wearing a white shirt with a pink pullover sweater, a pair of navy clam diggers, and her new sneakers. She looked freshly scrubbed, her hair was down, and as she neared he could smell the Chanel No. 5 she had chosen earlier today. As she sat down beside him, he told her how lovely she looked.

"Thank you," she said quietly. "You have been so good to me that I do not know how I will ever repay you."

Although Garrett could never be sure whether Constance might eat or drink something, he poured her a glass of red wine anyway. She tasted it approvingly then set it back down on the table.

Garrett smiled at her.

"Not thirsty?" he asked.

Just then he saw a look of worry overtake her face. It was slight, but noticeable. As if she had just read his mind, she walked across the dining room and stood, staring into the hearth. Concerned, he put down his wineglass and went to her. She was gripping the fireplace mantel with both hands, her head slightly bowed as she stared into the mesmerizing flames.

"What is it?" he asked her. "I haven't known you for very long, but I can tell when you're upset."

When she turned around to face him there were tears in her eyes, some of which had begun streaming down her cheeks. When he tried to wipe them away, she surprised him by backing off a little.

"What's wrong?" he asked again. "Please tell me. I can't bear seeing you this way."

"Did you really mean what you said?" she asked softly.

As Garrett stepped nearer, he could smell her lovely perfume.

"About me loving you?" he asked.

"Is it really true?"

"Yes, Constance. God help me, every word of it."

When she began crying again, this time her body trembled slightly. He could sense that she was holding something back; something that she perhaps had wanted to say to him for some time now but hadn't been able to find the courage. When she looked into his eyes again, there was a questioning expression on her face.

"Do you think it possible to love two people at the same time?" she asked quietly.

Before answering, Garrett reached out and brushed an errant lock from her forehead.

"I don't know," Garrett answered. "I'm not sure that anyone does."

On an impulse he put his arms around her, and this time she entered his embrace gladly. As her body pressed against his, he again felt the overpowering sexual attraction for her take command of him. Seconds later, he unexpectedly felt his consciousness begin to slip away. He quickly looked into Constance's eyes and could easily tell that she was experiencing the same thing. He tried to say something to her, but the best he could do was to soften their fall as they both slumped to the floor.

Garrett soon awakened to a living nightmare.

He was terrified and had absolutely no idea where he was. All he knew was that he was in a very dark room. The room was moving to and fro sickeningly, and its entire floor was covered with freezing cold, ankle deep water that sloshed back and forth. There was absolutely no light, nor any way to know when the room might shift violently yet again.

He heard Constance scream, her outburst telling him that she was somewhere inside this terrible place too. Then the room shifted drastically once more, literally throwing him across the floor. It took every ounce of his strength to stand up, but at last he succeeded.

"Constance!" he screamed. "Constance, where are you?"

A few moments later, Constance screamed again. This time her outburst gave him a better sense of her location. Struggling as best he could against the terrible swaying, he crawled on all fours toward her voice. He soon called out again, and to his relief this time she answered him.

Just then the room shifted violently again, this time to an even greater degree than before. As it did, an unseen door in the ceiling flew open and swung all the way over onto its opposite side, leaving an opening. Through the space Garrett could now see an occasional lightning flash, and watch rain literally pour down into the room. In a few moments, he realized, this chamber might well be flooded entirely.

Pausing in his search for Constance, he used the occasional lightning flashes to try and find her. And then, during one especially bright burst he saw her for a split second on her knees, about five paces from his position.

With the room still lurching horribly and rain pouring in unabated through the opened door, he again struggled across the floor on his hands and knees.

When at last he reached her, he put both of his arms around her, and the two of them stood up. With the coming of the next lightning flash, for a split second Constance was able to look into his eyes.

"I know where we are!" she screamed. "Follow me! If we stay here, we die!"

Constance turned and began leading Garrett in a direction different from where he had come. After a few more steps there came another flash of lightning, allowing him to glimpse a set of stairs up ahead. When they reached the stairs Constance clambered up them and Garrett followed her. At last free of the terrible room, Garrett looked around himself and witnessed an absolutely unbelievable sight.

They were standing topsides on a huge sailing ship in the dark of night. There was a terrible storm raging, the likes of which Garrett had never seen. He knew very little about ships, but even he could tell that this vessel was in dire straits.

The ship seemed to be powered only by sail, for he saw no smokestacks. Two of the masts had already come crashing down and lay atop the deck, hopelessly entangled in their own sails and rigging. Crewmen were scrambling across the decks and up the remaining masts, trying to secure everything as best they could, but even to Garrett's untrained eye, their efforts seemed too little and too late. When he turned to look behind him, he saw that the ship's wheel had been tied off.

Suddenly, another lightning flash cracked across the sky, followed by even more fierce thunder and lashing rain. While he and Constance did their best to hold on to some rigging near the starboard gunwale, the ship lurched violently again, nearly capsizing in the angry sea.

Just then he saw something glint during another of the lightning flashes, and Garrett narrowed his eyes, doing his best to see what it was. When at last he understood, he could scarcely believe it. It was a brass plaque, affixed to the forward wall of the wheelhouse. The plaque read:

THE AMERICAN WHALING SHIP INTREPID
BUILT AND COMMISSIONED IN THE YEAR OF OUR LORD,
1830 A.D.
MAY GOD WATCH OVER HER

Despite the storm howling all around him, the name "*Intrepid*" spurred something in Garrett's memories. Moments later he remembered, and although he knew that he was right, he still couldn't believe it.

Can all of this actually be happening? Garrett's frantic mind shouted at him. *Are Constance and I actually standing on the deck of the* Intrepid *on the night she met her terrible fate? And if that's true, then—*

Garrett immediately turned to look at Constance. She was still standing right beside him, holding on to some of the rigging for dear life. As the ship lurched drastically again, it was all the two of them could do to keep from being washed overboard. But through it all, Constance seemed to be quite mesmerized by something. She stared straight ahead toward the bow of the ship, her gaze unmoving despite the continuing terror. When Garrett tried to shout at her, she refused to answer, even though his lips had been mere inches from her ear. It was as if she had become hysterically frozen in the moment, all her thoughts and energy focused on a single thing.

Trying to understand, Garrett turned and looked through the blinding rain in the same direction. When the next flash of lightning arrived and its radiance dashed across the deck, at last Garrett saw the reason for Constance's supreme stalwartness.

Adam Canfield, captain of the *Intrepid,* was standing in the bow of the ship and peering intently into the darkness. It had to be Adam, for something in Garrett's heart told him so.

Garrett could not see Adam well, because Adam's back was to him. Adam stood almost proudly in the bow, his arms outstretched to either side, his hands grasping opposing rigging lines to help keep his balance. The bravery being displayed was overwhelming, and like Constance, for a time all Garrett could do was to stand and watch. It was at that exact moment Constance let go of the rigging and tried to scrabble her way forward across the pitching deck.

As Garrett realized what she was doing, his heart was torn between allowing her to try and reach her beloved husband, or grabbing her up to keep her as safe as possible while the *Intrepid* pitched violently in the hellish storm. He could not know for certain whether what he and Constance were experiencing was real. If he let her go and she went overboard, would she truly drown?

He had always heard that it was impossible to die in one's dreams, which lent credence to letting her try and reach her husband. But this felt like no dream, Garrett realized. The cold was mind numbing, the harsh storm wind and rain stung his face like a thousand needles, and the groaning hull and masts called out to him torturously, as if begging to be released from the storm's terrible fury. He knew in his heart that this beleaguered ship would soon end up on the bottom of the ocean.

Suddenly a wave clambered up the port side and literally exploded over the gunwale. It washed across the deck with such force that it literally picked up a crewman in its maw, then swept the screaming man directly across the deck and tossed him over the opposite gunwale like so much debris. People were dying here, and Garrett knew that he could never forgive himself if something happened to Constance.

For better or worse, Garrett reached down and grabbed her by the waist then held her to him, imprisoning her tightly. While trying to keep her immobile with one arm, he used his other arm to again grab some rigging in an attempt to keep them both from being swept overboard.

Enraged, Constance screamed at him and banged on his arm with her fists in an effort to free herself. When she found that she could not break Garrett's grasp, she began screaming Adam's name at the top of her lungs.

It was then that Garrett first realized none of the crewmen could see or hear them. For the time being at least, he had again joined Constance in her anonymous netherworld. But then to his great surprise, he saw Adam suddenly turn and stare directly toward them. However, instead of looking *at* them, Adam seemed to stare straight *through* them. After several more moments of this, Adam gave up and returned to searching the dark sea lying up ahead.

When Constance saw Adam turn back around, she began screaming and hitting Garrett again with even greater ferocity. It was all he could now do to keep control of her, and hold on to the rigging at the same time. And then, from out of nowhere he saw a giant wave bearing down on them. It was like nothing he had ever seen before. Towering nearly thirty feet high, the deadly, froth-tipped giant raced directly toward the *Intrepid*'s port bow. When it hit, Garrett and Constance watched in horror as it took Adam overboard.

Just then Garrett felt his consciousness slipping away again. With Constance still wrapped tightly in his arms, they too splashed into the cold, dark ocean.

Chapter 20

When Garrett awakened, he found himself lying on the dining room floor. Constance lay on her side next to him, still unconscious. Instinctively, he placed two fingers against the side of her neck, checking for a pulse. To his relief he found that she was alive, her heartbeat steady but slow.

The fire in the hearth had gone out, and the dining room had grown cold. The night sky was still visible through the windows, and when he checked his watch it said a little past 2:00 A.M. He was almost surprised he and Constance weren't soaking wet, again causing him to wonder whether it had all been real, or just a dream.

When he stood up he had to shake off some lingering dizziness, but he soon recovered. Bending down, he picked Constance up in his arms and carried her to the sofa. For a time he debated whether to try and rouse her. It would be another five hours or so before Jay and his crew arrived, which gave him ample time to try, should Constance not awaken on her own.

After bringing in some more kindling and firewood, he set another fire and nursed it until it was burning strongly. He checked on Constance again, then walked into the parlor and made a fresh pot of coffee on Jay's setup. There were some leftover doughnuts in the box, and although he knew they would be stale, he didn't care. Next, he went out to the veranda and brought one of the folding chairs inside the house so that he could watch over Constance, then returned to the dining room with a cup of black coffee and a rather dry cinnamon doughnut.

Despite the poor quality of the food, he was so hungry and thirsty that they actually tasted good. Once the doughnut was gone he went back into the parlor for more coffee and then returned to watch Constance again. She had changed position on the sofa but had yet to awaken.

As he sat staring at her lovely face, his mind became crowded with questions that had no answers. Clearly he had experienced another flashback. Coupled with the one from the night before, this now made two events in as many days. But why had they happened? And when Constance awakened, would she remember it as he did, or had she perhaps suffered an entirely different experience all her own? Totally stymied, Garrett sighed deeply then scrubbed his face with both hands.

Just then he remembered the plaque that had been affixed to the wall of the *Intrepid's* wheelhouse. Part of it had read: *"May God Watch Over Her."* Garrett shook his head. *God certainly wasn't much help that night,* he thought.

Now more than ever he knew that he must find the answers, despite his trepidation. These psychic events were coming faster, which concerned him deeply. Did this mean that their lives would eventually become nothing but a nonstop series of these bizarre occurrences? he wondered. Although Garrett had never been afraid of much, the awful nature of such an existence terrified him.

Constance groaned a little, separating Garrett from his thoughts. He looked down at her lovingly and gently stroked her face. How much he cared for this woman! She had come into his life as if on a summer breeze, yet still seemed equally capable of vanishing just as quickly. Even so, he no longer worried that she might abandon him. But he also knew that if she did ever leave Seaside and strike out on her own, not only would he worry about her all the rest of his days, but his heart would be irreparably broken, as well.

He shuddered to think of the pain she would feel when she awakened. Knowing that Adam had died was awful enough, but actually going back in time and seeing it happen was horrible beyond imagining. For several moments he tried to understand why such a thing would be forced upon her. Had the powers behind all this actually wanted Constance to witness her husband's death?

At last she groaned a little more and opened her eyes. As she gazed at her surroundings, a confused expression overtook her face. He immediately reached down and took her into his arms. She did not fight him, and he could feel her tears moisten his cheek as she clung to him. After a time, she raised her head and again looked into his eyes.

"Are you all right?" he asked gently.

"I watched him die . . ." she said softly.

"I know," Garrett answered. "I was there too. Do you remember?"

"Yes," she said, "I remember. You kept me from going to him. I was so angry that I struck you. I am sorry, Garrett, but it was just so awful . . ."

Trying his best to comfort her, he reached down and stroked her face.

"I can't begin to know how you're suffering," he said, "but if I had let you go to Adam, you both might have died. That was something I just couldn't risk. Even now, we still don't know whether what we experienced was real, or just a dream."

Constance sat up on the couch a little more. As she did her head swam, but after a few moments the dizziness abated. She looked longingly at Garrett's coffee cup.

"Is there more?" she asked.

He smiled at her.

"Yes," he answered. "But don't tell me you're actually thirsty?"

Constance shook her head.

"I just want to taste it. And are there additional doughnuts? One of those would be welcome too."

Garrett laughed a little.

"Yeah," he answered, "but they're stale as hell."

"No matter," Constance answered.

"Okay," Garrett said. "I'll be right back."

While Garrett was in the parlor, Constance took a moment to look around the dining room. The new couch and cocktail table were certainly a blessing, and the fire that Garrett had set was comforting. But as she thought back to the episode aboard the *Intrepid,* she again felt chilled by what she had witnessed. Like the two times before, seeing Adam again had been a great shock. But this latest episode had been vastly different, in that she actually saw him die.

Garrett returned with the coffee and a doughnut. After finishing them both, she set the cup on the table.

"Thank you," she said.

Garrett leaned back against the sofa and looked at her. Despite the pain she was feeling, he knew that she was trying to be brave. He didn't want to push her, but he also felt that they should discuss their experience now, while it remained fresh in their minds.

"I have a lot of questions about this," he said. "And I don't suppose you have any more answers than I do, but I'd like to ask you a few things, just the same. Given everything that you've just been through, do you feel up to it?"

Constance nodded. "I will try," she answered.

"This was my second flashback," Garrett said, "and the first episode we've shared that we both remember. Do you have any idea why that might be?"

Constance shook her head.

"We slumped to the floor unconscious," Garrett added, "and I tried to break our fall. We woke up in the hold of that ship, which brings me to another question. You said that you knew where we were. How was that possible?"

"I have visited the *Intrepid* several times," Constance said. "Never while Adam was out to sea hunting whales, but he enjoyed taking me aboard sometimes, when she was tied up at the pier. How he loved to show me all the things that made such a grand ship work! Even so, I am not sure how I knew that we were in one of the holds. I guess that's just another of our unanswered questions.

"I feel so guilty for not saving him," Constance added. "I am not angry at you for holding me back. Even so, I still believe that if I could have gone to Adam, he might have lived."

Garrett shook his head.

"I understand how you feel, but you're wrong," he said gently. "It was the *Intrepid*'s destiny to go down that night. You couldn't have saved Adam, any more than you could have helped all those other poor devils aboard that condemned vessel. Surely you must know that."

"I suppose so," she answered. "But if there really are forces at work here that are causing flashbacks in time, then why are we experiencing these specific ones? What possible good could it do either of us to witness Adam's death?"

"I may have an answer, Constance," he replied. "But I'm not sure that you want to hear it."

While trying to decide how to begin, Garrett took a deep breath and stared at the floor for a few moments. When he looked back into her eyes, they were questioning.

"Until being on the *Intrepid*, I had never seen anyone die," he answered. "And now that I have, I've learned something. Hearing that someone has died is far different from actually seeing it happen. Until this most recent flashback, you had only been told that Adam was dead. And because of that, I suspect you always wondered if there had been a mistake, and that by some miracle he might still be alive. But now you know, Constance, because you've seen it happen. And if there was ever any doubt in your heart about Adam's fate, at least you now have some sense of closure."

When she began crying quietly again, Garrett simply let it happen. He couldn't begin to know how much she was hurting. Perhaps even worse, there was absolutely nothing he could do about it. Seeing her husband perish that way must have been like hearing about his death for the very first time. He also realized that she was quite probably the only woman in history who had first heard about her husband's demise, and was then forced to go back in time and actually witness it.

But why? he kept wondering. Why were all of these things happening to them? Why was he the only person on earth who could see and hear her? Had he been specifically chosen for some reason? And if so, why him?

"You are right," she finally said. "At long last, I do have my answers about Adam. I was sometimes tempted into thinking that he might have survived that day, even though by this time he would of course be long dead. And now that I know he's actually gone . . ."

Garrett nodded. He wanted to sympathize with her, and see her through this crisis as best he could. But at the same time he couldn't help thinking that with Adam truly gone, she might at last feel free to love him.

Then he sighed and shook his head a little as he realized how selfish he was being. This wasn't about him; it was about her and her feelings, and he would do everything in his power to help her through it. If she came to love him, so be it. And if not . . .

"I cannot know why this is happening to us, Garrett," she said. "Nor do I know how all of this is going to end. But we must find our answers soon, because after this most recent flashback, I have come to realize something. Do not ask me how I know, I just do."

"And what is that?"

Before answering, Constance wrung her hands worriedly.

"We are running out of time," she finally answered.

Chapter 21

That evening Garrett stared out his college office window, watching the students pass by. There were so many of them, each one preoccupied with his or her own little world. He could still easily remember his own times here, first as an undergraduate student, and then later as both a master's and Ph.D. candidate. He had loved those days, and compared to now they seemed blissfully carefree. Part of the reason for that, he knew, was that he loved learning and it had always come easily to him.

While letting go a sigh, he returned to his desk and sat down. The clock on his desk said five minutes to six, and he would have a visitor soon.

His flashback with Constance on the deck of the *Intrepid* had seriously rattled them both. Again, the experience was far more real than any dream he had ever known. It was as if the two of them had actually been aboard that ship, and when they were thrown overboard, he was certain that they would die. The entire thing had been a terrible and awe-inspiring experience. But then they had each awakened safely back in the dining room at Seaside, both of them dry as a bone and with exactly the same memory of what had just occurred. He desperately needed to find out what was happening to them, and that was why he was here in his office tonight. Just then came the anticipated knock on his office door.

"Come in," Garrett called out.

John Jacobs opened the door and stepped tentatively into the office.

"You asked to see me?" he asked.

"Yes, John," Garrett answered. "Please come in and sit down."

As John took one of the guest chairs opposite the desk, Garrett could see that the young man was nervous. Garrett could easily understand that, because it wasn't every day a student was unexpectedly summoned to one of his professors' offices. John sat tenuously on the edge of his chair, as if it might suddenly bite him.

"Have I done something wrong?" John asked nervously. "If this is about my last paper, I know I made a few mistakes, but—"

Garrett quickly waved one hand, cutting John off.

"No, no," he said. "There's nothing wrong. I've asked you here because I was wondering if you would like to take on a little project for some extra credit. If you're too busy right now, I can certainly understand. But if you could help me out with this, I would greatly appreciate it."

Obviously relieved, John finally relaxed a bit. He was a tall and lanky young man in his midtwenties, with closely cropped, dark hair. He always gave Garrett the impression that when the good Lord made John, all God had left at his disposal was sinew, bones, and sharp angles. John was a Ph.D. candidate, one of the few Garrett had known with that rare combination of both an artistic and an analytical side. So much so, in fact, that once the young man completed his studies, Garrett was considering asking him to join his firm. Most important of all, Garrett trusted him.

"What can I do for you?" John asked.

Garrett leaned back in his chair.

"I need some research done," he said. "And I think you're just the guy for it. But first, I need to tell you that this must be accomplished with discretion. Anything you find out, you bring to me, and me alone. Got it?"

"What sort of information do you need?"

"I'm going to try my hand at writing a novel," he answered. "It's going to be about a person who gets trapped in time between the worlds of heaven and hell. You don't really need to know anything more about it than that, John. But what I do need from you is a list of people who may be experts in such things—psychics, mediums, soothsayers, or anybody else that can shed some light on the topic for me. Then bring the list back here to me, and I'll take it from there. In return, I'll exempt you from your next paper."

"How much time do I have?" John asked.

"I know this is short notice," Garrett said, "but I'd like to have the distilled list one week from now." He took a few moments to open his schedule and flip through it. "Shall we say, one week from today?"

"Sure," John answered. "I can do that."

"I'm afraid I can't tell you how to get started," Garrett added, "but I'm assuming that Web browsing will be your best bet, at least at first. And John, please make sure that you do a good job of weeding out all the weirdos, okay? I don't have time to deal with crystal ball gazers and tarot card readers. I want only people who are legitimate sources—hopefully academics, if possible, whose credentials can be verified."

"I understand, professor," John answered. "And I thank you for putting your trust in me. I'll do my best. Truth is, it kind of sounds like fun."

Garrett smiled.

"Great," he said. "In that case, I'll see you back here, one week from today. And, John, if you run into any snags or have any questions, just give me a call here on my office phone and leave a message."

John stood from his chair.

"Anything else?"

Garrett shook his head.

"Nope," he said. "Just bring me a good list, okay?"

"Will do."

With that, John left the office and closed the door behind him.

Satisfied, Garrett returned to the office window. Nothing out there had changed during the course of his discussion with John, just as he knew it would not. In his experience, every university had a sort of sameness to it, a kind of commonality that he had found boring, yet endearing at the same time.

After thinking about it, he had decided that putting one of his brightest students on this problem was his best option. The work would go faster, and once he had a distilled list, he could start making phone calls to try and find someone who actually might be of help to him and Constance. He hadn't enjoyed misleading John about supposedly writing a novel, but there had been no alternative. The only question was—what would John find in all his searching?

Only time will tell, Garrett thought. *But if Constance and I are to ever discover a way out of this, that list had better hold somebody who can help us, and help us quickly.*

Chapter 22

One week later, Garrett again sat in his college office, glumly staring down at the list of ten names that had been supplied to him by John Jacobs. Garrett had already called six of them, each one proving useless. Thinking, he leaned back in his chair and closed his eyes.

It wasn't his student's fault, he knew. If anybody could have provided a list of people who might be of potential use, it was John. The six people Garrett had already called were very different from one another in their approach to all things metaphysical. One of the men, whose gravelly voice suggested that he was well into his eighties, seemed to immediately forget whatever Garrett told him. Another of them, a woman this time, had seemed promising until she started asking

Garrett about his marital status. And yet another man suggested that Garrett take up astrology and examine the stars for his answers, because such knowledge could only come from God himself.

Sighing, Garrett looked at the next name on the list, a woman from some remote village in Oregon. He punched in the number and talked to her for a time, only to discover that she too could not help him. When the last three people on the list proved no better, he finally tore up the sheet of paper and unceremoniously dropped the pieces into his wastebasket.

Garrett was becoming extremely discouraged. He and Constance seemed to be up against something that they simply could not understand, much less find any way to escape. More and more now it was not only Constance for whom he worried, but also for himself. There had been no flashbacks for a week, but something in Garrett's heart told him that there would be more of them, provided a solution to their bewildering problem wasn't found.

Feeling the need to move, Garrett stood from his chair and began quietly pacing back and forth before the office windows, thinking. After a time he stopped, folded his arms across his chest, and again looked down at the many students continuously scurrying here and there. Just then he saw a professor he recognized, presumably on his way back to his office. Garrett knew this man well, and he suddenly realized that he might actually have some answers, or at the very least point him in the right direction.

Why didn't I think of him sooner? he thought. *He's nearing retirement, but he's still sharp as a tack and just might be able to help.*

Smiling lightly, Garrett realized that this was the first true ray of hope he had encountered since this bizarre episode started. He returned to his desk and waited for another ten minutes or so before calling him. When the other man picked up the phone, Garrett greeted him happily, and then asked for an appointment. When the fellow agreed, Garrett hung up the phone and smiled.

Chapter 23

As Garrett and Constance crossed the grounds of Boston College, he smiled widely at her apparent amazement at seeing the campus. By now the two of them had become proficient enough at avoiding other people that they could walk side by side, which also made discreet communication far easier.

While they walked, Garrett kept reminding himself that Constance was no longer totally a woman of antebellum times. Conversely, neither was she a woman totally of modern times, and nothing could have sufficiently prepared her for venturing out into the real world. She was the product of more than seventeen decades, he realized, and he would always do his best to respect that.

It was a cool and crisp Tuesday afternoon, the trees still shedding their leaves as they prepared for winter's onslaught. They were on their way to meet Dr. Jim Baker, a professor and a friend of Garrett's.

As Garrett and Constance walked toward the building that housed Jim's office, Garrett couldn't help but notice how intently Constance was watching the other young women. Although she had seen many women at the mall the other day, these females were different in that they were actually attending college. Because such a thing was unheard of back in Constance's time, he could well imagine her amazement, which also caused him to wonder if she was jealous. At last he decided that she probably was not, because despite all that she had endured, she was perhaps the most grounded woman he had ever known.

As they approached the building, Garrett said, "Is there any particular way that you want to handle this? I've been in Jim's office before, and I know that there are two guest chairs opposite his desk, so I assume that I will sit in one and you will sit in the other. And I also suppose that you will be free to talk to me, because he won't be able to see or hear you. So if there's anything you want to say to me, or if there's any question that you want me to ask, please tell me, because I have a feeling that I'm going to need you in there."

Constance nodded.

"I only hope that he can help us," she said. "And like you said before, if he is unable to help, then perhaps he can point us toward someone who can."

When they entered the building, the halls were filled with students, some of who greeted Garrett. As they went, Constance slipped in behind Garret like she had done at the mall, so as to help avoid running into anyone. At last they found themselves at Jim Baker's door, where a small brass plaque read: DR. JAMES BAKER, PH.D., PROFESSOR OF AMERICAN HISTORY. Garrett knocked and soon heard Jim welcome him inside.

As they walked into the office, Garrett held his breath for a moment, wondering if by some chance Jim might sense Constance's presence. When Jim did not, Garrett breathed a little sigh of relief. Walking across the floor, the two men shook hands heartily. After exchanging a few pleasantries, Garrett took the guest seat on Jim's right, and Constance took the other.

Jim's office was larger than Garrett's, with a more spacious window that looked out onto the quad. Garrett had always been envious of his friend's dark-paneled bookcases, hardwood floor, and huge antique mahogany desk.

Dr. Jim Baker was a large and jovial man. He was beloved by his students for his pleasant nature and for not taking himself too seriously. His gray hair was thinning, which he had complemented with a neatly trimmed beard. His glasses, which hung from a string about his neck, were only for reading.

Smiling again, Jim leaned forward and put his palms flat upon his desk.

"Now then," he said, "what is it that a lowly history professor can do for the famous wunderkind of the architecture department?"

"Truth be known," Garrett answered, "I'm going to try my hand at writing a novel."

Jim raised his eyebrows.

"Impressive," he said. "Architect *and* novelist. And after that you'll compose your first symphony, I suppose? Just kidding, Garrett. But in all honesty, shouldn't you be talking to somebody in the English department?"

"Nope," Garrett answered. "You're exactly who I need to see."

"How so?"

"I've gotten it into my head that I want to write a novel about someone who should have died but was instead trapped between life and death for some unknown reason. I was hoping that given your expertise in American mysticism, you might have some knowledge of such things, or could maybe point me toward someone else who might be able to help. What I really need is background information. I know that I've got a lot on my plate right now, and starting a novel is the last thing I need to be doing. But I've got this idea in my head, and I need to get it out and onto paper."

Jim nodded judiciously.

"Although I've never tried my hand at writing a novel," he said, "I know the feeling well. It was like that when I wrote my Ph.D. dissertation. I'd get an idea, and I just had to write it down before I lost it."

"Exactly," Garrett answered.

"Most people don't know it," Jim said, "but American history is replete with mysticism, spells, magic, and all manner of weird things. From the witch trials at Salem, to the vampires that once supposedly inhabited New Orleans, and the many esoteric practices of Native Americans, there is literally too much information to absorb. The class I teach about such things barely scratches the surface. But other than vampirism, I can't say that I'm overly familiar with what you're suggesting."

"Question him more about Salem," Constance said to Garrett.

At first, Garrett had to fight the inclination to turn and look at her because she had been so quiet until now, and he had almost forgotten that she was there. After shifting a little bit in his chair, he looked back at Jim.

"You mentioned Salem," Garrett said. "Can you think of anything in that history that you believe could help me?"

"No, but I know someone who might."

Jim opened his laptop and brought up his contacts list. After searching through the list for a few moments, he came upon the name he wanted and wrote the particulars down on a pad. He tore the page off the pad and handed it to Garrett. Garrett read the information then looked back at Jim questioningly.

"Dr. Brooke Wentworth?" he asked. "Sounds positively regal."

"I know," Jim answered with a smile. "Truth be told, Brooke and I were once pretty close, if you know what I mean. Anyway, for my money, she's the foremost authority I know in the kind of things that you're talking about."

Garrett looked back down at the piece of paper Jim had given him. It listed the woman's name and phone number. *It's not much,* he thought, *but at least it's a place to start.*

"Brooke, huh?" Garrett asked, half to himself.

"Yep," Jim answered. "As best I know, she's the world authority."

"Okay, then," Garrett said. "And just where do I find her?"

Jim smiled and leaned forward a little more.

"Why, in Salem, my friend," he answered. "Where else?"

Chapter 24

The following morning was dark and rainy, causing Garrett to drive carefully as he and Constance headed north to keep their appointment with Dr. Wentworth. Under normal conditions the drive from New Bedford would run about two hours, but because of the heavy rain he expected it to take longer. Despite Dr. Wentworth's Ph.D., Garrett remained skeptical about whether she could help them. But she was their only remaining lead, and to ignore her would be foolish.

As Garrett drove, he and Constance talked of many things. He never tired of hearing about her life. While the windshield wipers slapped back and forth and the Jeep's knobby tires sang upon the road, at last they came to the heart of Salem. The weather had cleared,

and the sun had begun drying the rain-soaked buildings and streets.

Garrett had always thought Salem an interesting place.
Much of Salem's current identity was still reflected in its
role as the location of the Salem witch trials of 1692. The
police cars were adorned with witch logos, a local public
school was known as Witchcraft Heights Elementary,
and several Salem high school athletic teams were named
"The Witches." Gallows Hill, a site of numerous hangings, was currently used as a sports field. Today's tour-
ists knew Salem as a weird mix of historical sites, New
Age Wiccan boutiques, kitschy Halloween celebrations,
and a vibrant downtown that boasted more than sixty
restaurants, cafés and coffee shops.

About twenty minutes later the GPS system said that
they had arrived at their destination. Garrett stopped
the Jeep and looked out his window incredulously. The
home standing before them was nothing like they had
expected. They were parked before a walled mansion,
with a huge wrought-iron gate that bore the single
word FAIRLAWN. Fairlawn lay about fifty yards ahead,
serenely basking in the Massachusetts sunlight. Still
wet with rain, manicured lawns seemed to stretch into
infinity on either side of the drive.

Built entirely of stone, the mansion stood three
stories tall, reminding Garrett of those huge, English

country estates one sees in the movies. He always wondered how anyone afforded to maintain them, much less navigate their mazelike interiors. Ornate windows with leaded panes graced all three floors, their glasswork glinting prettily in the sunlight. Ivy had long ago conquered much of the facade, adding a welcome splash of color to what would have otherwise been a monotonous shade of gray.

"Hardly what I was expecting . . ." Garrett said wryly.

"I daresay not," Constance answered. "I understand nothing about the device that let us here, but are you quite sure that it is correct?"

Garrett turned and again looked toward the mansion.

"There's only one way to find out," he answered.

Garrett inched the Jeep toward the speaker setup standing near the gate. He pressed the button and waited.

"May I be of service?" a rather imperious sounding voice asked.

"Dr. Garrett Richmond to see Dr. Wentworth," Garrett answered. "I have a three o'clock appointment."

"One moment, sir," the speaker voice answered.

After about twenty seconds of silence, the speaker crackled again.

"Thank you, Dr. Richmond. You may proceed."

The twin gates soon parted, allowing them access. The circular drive before the mansion was wide, and Garrett pulled the Jeep off to one side before shutting down the engine. He and Constance walked the short distance to the massive front doors, where Garrett rang the doorbell.

After a few more moments passed, one of the great wooden doors opened to reveal a butler standing there, dressed in full formal livery. He looked to be in his late fifties, with balding gray hair and an expansive midsection.

"Dr. Richmond?" he asked politely.

"Yes. And you are . . . ?"

"William," the butler answered. Despite how long his tenure in America might have already been, it had done little to blunt his English accent. "This way, please."

Garrett and Constance followed William into the grand foyer. For several nervous moments they each wondered whether William could see Constance, but if he did, he gave no appearance of it. While breathing quick sighs of relief, Garrett and Constance took a moment to look around.

The two-story foyer was huge and built from solid mahogany. Its inlaid hardwood floors sparkled with cleanliness. The vast room was beautifully furnished with exquisite sofas, tables and chairs, none of which looked like they had been used a day in their lives. A great marble fireplace stood in the wall on the opposite side of the room and was adorned with flying cupids that, although continuously trying to reach each other, were doomed to perpetual failure.

Over the fireplace hung a huge portrait of an elderly man. Behind him was a scene showing several factories, each one unapologetically belching dark smoke into the air. The great portrait appeared old, and although the man seemed familiar to Garrett, he could not place the name. Given Garrett's great love of architecture, he could have gladly spent an entire month respectfully admiring this majestic house.

William then led them down a spacious hallway and into yet another great room, one nearly as large as the foyer, and decorated just as beautifully. The right-hand wall held a line of twelve French doors that looked out over but one portion of Fairlawn's spacious grounds. Because the day was unusually warm, each door stood partly open to accept the afternoon breeze, which bothered the curtains pleasantly and carried with it the familiar smell of wet leaves. Here too there was a massive marble fireplace adorned with angels. Like the foyer, this room was decorated with upholstered furniture, Oriental rugs, and numerous oil paintings.

At the far end of the room, Dr. Brooke Wentworth sat behind a massive Louis Quatorze desk. Rather than acknowledge their presence, she remained riveted to something she was reading. When William beckoned Garrett to sit in one of several upholstered chairs opposite the desk he did so, silently followed by Constance. For several moments Garrett and Constance simply sat there, with William standing guard next to them like some obedient gun dog awaiting his master's next command.

"Thank you, William," Dr. Wentworth said at last, her attention still riveted upon her work. "You may leave us now. Please tell Millicent that I would like a full tea service sent in. And have her include some of those lovely blueberry scones, should we have any left."

"Yes, madam," he answered. "Will there be anything else?"

"Just a few quiet moments with my visitor," she answered.

"Very good, madam."

With near military precision the large man turned briskly on his heel, left the room, and closed the sliding doors behind him.

Even now, Dr. Wentworth did not look at Garrett. Realizing that silence was in order, he wisely remained quiet.

While waiting, Garrett took a few moments to regard her. She was a trim and astute-looking woman who appeared to be somewhere in her midfifties. Her face was attractive, and she was impeccably dressed. Her graying auburn hair was cut rather short. She wore a ruby necklace overtop a well-tailored pink suit, accompanied by matching ruby earrings. Tortoiseshell reading glasses lay perched near the end of her nose, allowing her to gaze over them when needed. Taken as a whole, she seemed every inch a highly intelligent, extremely wealthy, and very capable woman.

Garrett smirked a little. *Jim Baker never gave me a heads-up about any of this. Just like him to send me into the lion's den without any warning, the bastard . . .*

After a few more moments, Dr. Wentworth finally removed her reading glasses and looked into Garrett's eyes.

"You told me on the phone that you would be coming alone, Dr. Richmond," she said.

Her words stunned him.

"But I am alone, Dr. Wentworth," he finally answered.

"No, you're not," she said. "And before we go any further, I need a promise from you that there will be no more lies."

Garrett was at complete loss, as was Constance. Until now, they had been quite certain that he was the only person in the world who could see and hear Constance. Completely stymied, he realized he had no choice but to come clean.

"You're right," he answered apologetically, "and I'm sorry for misleading you. There is a woman with me, but I thought I was the only one who could recognize her presence."

"I can't 'see' her, per se," Dr. Wentworth answered. "But I know that she is sitting beside you, just as surely as I know that the sun rose this morning. I can detect her aura, and from that I already know she is female. I cannot, however, converse with her. I can only assume that it is her presence in your life that has brought the two of you here. If you wish to have my help, you must tell me everything."

Garrett gave Constance a questioning look.

"It is all right, Garrett," Constance answered. "I don't know why, but I trust her."

Garrett looked back at Dr. Wentworth.

"Constance says yes," he said.

"Very well," Dr. Wentworth answered. "But first things first." She then stared in Constance's direction. "Let me have a look at you."

To Garrett's and Constance's surprise, when Dr. Wentworth left her desk she did so via an electric wheelchair. Although she was obviously handicapped, her disadvantage did nothing to compromise her regal bearing. As she maneuvered the chair closer to Constance, she looked at Garrett.

"It was a car crash," she said quietly.

"Excuse me?" Garrett asked.

"Four years ago, a drunk driver did this to me. No reason for it, really. William was driving, and he got the worst of it. Nearly killed him. That was the question you were asking yourself, was it not?"

"Yes," Garrett answered. "I'm sorry."

"Don't be," Dr. Wentworth answered. "Life is seldom fair, professor."

Seated directly across from Constance, she held out her hands.

"Please, my dear," she said, "take my hands and place them upon your face so that I can get a sense of you."

After Constance did as she was asked, Dr. Wentworth ran her palms and fingertips over Constance's face and hair, trying to glean a mental picture of her. When she was finished, she returned her hands to her sides.

"So beautiful," she said. Then she looked at Garrett. "How old is she?" she asked.

"Thirty-two," Garrett answered.

"Cut down in the prime of her life," Dr. Wentworth said. "Please tell me how it happened."

Just then someone knocked on the doors. After Brooke bid her entry, one of the maids wheeled a silver tray into the room. It was laden with a full tea service and two platefuls of scones. She quietly served Garrett and Brooke then departed as smoothly as she had arrived.

"Would Constance like some?" Brooke asked.

Constance nodded at Garrett, and he served her some tea and a scone. After sipping the very good tea he explained everything to Brooke, including his love of Seaside and its restoration. When he finished, he sat back in his chair.

"You tell me that Constance fell from her widow's walk and onto the shore," Brooke said. "And that she awakened in the same state in which we now find her. That is to say, her condition has remained unchanged for seventeen decades."

"That's right," Garrett answered.

"And that her husband, Adam, the sea captain, died when his whaling vessel capsized off Cape Horn?"

"Also true," Garrett answered. "As fate would have it, they perished on the very same day."

Just then Garrett saw Brooke blanch. She soon began shaking her head, and whispering something under her breath that sounded something like, "No, it can't be . . . the odds against you two ever finding each other are simply too great . . ."

Concerned, Garrett tried to look into Brooke's eyes, but it did him no good. She was staring off into space, seeing nothing, still muttering to herself. After a time Brooke seemed to calm down.

"The *mora mortis* . . ." she said quietly, as if Garrett and Constance weren't there.

"What did you just say?" Garrett asked.

"I take it that you do not speak Latin, Dr. Richmond," she said.

"No."

"The *mora mortis*," Brooke repeated. "I knew of its supposed existence, but the odds are so impossibly high . . . just the same, though, that could be it. My God, could it really be happening?"

"What is she talking about?" Constance asked Garrett.

"I have no idea," Garrett answered. He again turned his attention toward Brooke. "What are you saying, Dr. Wentworth?" he asked her.

"Please call me Brooke," she said. "And now, the two of you must come with me."

"Where are we going?" Garrett asked.

"Someplace where no other outsider has ever ventured," Brooke said.

With Garrett and Constance in tow, Brooke maneuvered her chair across the massive room and toward a pair of elevator doors. She then pushed one of the elevator buttons, the twin doors hissed apart, and the three of them entered. On reaching the basement floor, Brooke used a wall switch to illuminate the subterranean room.

As they looked around, Garrett and Constance could hardly believe their eyes. The room was nearly as large as the one they just departed. Clearly they had entered another study, but this one was quite unlike any they had ever experienced.

The entire room was finished in dark hardwoods, and whoever had ordered the job had spared no expense. The walls were lined with bookcases, none of which rose to a height of more than four feet, presumably so that the many hundreds of volumes would be accessible to Brooke. The fourth wall held a lovely marble fireplace, with a hearty fire burning in the hearth that dispatched welcome heat and some rather ghostly shadows across the room.

Against the opposite wall there stood a huge mahogany desk that was literally strewn with papers, and reading and writing tools. Before the desk stood a lovely leather couch. A massive Oriental rug lay in the center of the floor, and the numerous light fixtures all appeared to be original Tiffany. Every inch of available wall space seemed taken up with historical artifacts and works of art that had apparently been gleaned from various places all over the world. Taken as a whole, Garrett couldn't begin to imagine the value of this secret room.

Brooke beckoned Garrett and Constance to sit on the sofa then she maneuvered her chair to the book-cases, where she began perusing the many hundreds of volumes. When at last she found the two books she wanted, she eagerly freed them from their breth-ren then blew the dust from them before going to the desk. She opened one of the books and quickly began thumbing through its pages in an apparent search for some specific information. When at last she looked up at Constance and Garrett, she was positively beaming.

"What is this place?" Garrett asked.

"It's my sanctuary," Brooke answered. "Aside from me, my father, and a handful of servants, you two are the only other people to ever visit here."

"Your father?" Garrett asked.

Brooke nodded rather sadly.

"Yes," she answered. "He died some twenty years ago, and as his only child, I inherited this house. This study was originally his, and everything in it was col-lected either by him or me from various places around the world. As best I know there's nothing else quite like it—at least not in private hands, anyway."

"It's amazing," Garrett said. "I've never seen its rival."

"Nor are you likely to," Brooke said.

"Yes, I'm sure that's all true," Garrett replied, "but what I don't understand is—"

Brooke quickly held up one hand, stopping him.

"May I call you Garrett?" she asked. "I do believe that I can help the two of you, at least to a certain extent. But as laymen, you have no idea of the complexity of that which has taken you into its grip. We are most likely dealing with forces beyond human ken. Even so, I still believe that I can aid you, provided you wish to pay the steep price involved."

Constance looked at Garrett with worried eyes.

"Of what price does she speak?" she asked Garrett.

"Constance wants to know what you meant by that last part," Garrett said to Brooke. "What is the price that we must pay?"

"All things in good time," Brooke answered. "To give you a proper explanation, I must start at the beginning. And starting at the beginning also means telling you my story."

Chapter 25

Leaning back in her chair, Dr. Brooke Wentworth gazed directly into Garrett's eyes.

"To understand what's happening," she said, "you first need to know about my father, James. He was also a Ph.D., and his discipline was archaeology. My mother died while giving birth to me, and as a consequence, my father began dragging me all over the world with him on his many expeditions. If there was such a thing as a real-life Indiana Jones, then that was my dad. He risked his life more times than I can count in dense jungles, on archaeological digs, and anywhere else he thought he might find a valuable artifact. He also taught at Harvard, where I eventually received my degree in anthropology. Later came my car crash, which relegated me to this chair. That's when I quit teaching."

"Forgive me, but what does any of this have to do with our situation?" Garrett asked.

Brooke gave him a smile.

"Patience, young man," she said. "We're getting there. As I was saying, although my father and I shared many of the same interests, I soon became more intrigued with the metaphysical realms. As we traveled the world I studied under various swamis, gurus, rabbis, monks, and priests—virtually anyone who could give me insight into the very powerful forces that truly shape and control our world. Now I spend my days here in Salem, overseeing my ancestral home and managing several charitable foundations."

" 'Ancestral'?" Garrett asked.

Brooke nodded.

"I'm sure that you're more than curious about how my father, a college professor, might have become so wealthy," she said. "The truth is he inherited it all, and then I from him when he died. Did you notice the portrait in the foyer?"

"It's impossible not to," Garrett answered.

"That man is my great-great-great uncle," she said, "and at one time he was one of the richest industrialists in America. As you can imagine, being even obliquely related to such massive wealth has its advantages."

"Of course," Garrett said.

"A massive trust left to my father allowed for all of this, and was what really paid for his many adventures," Brooke added. "Even so I was not spoiled, despite being an only child. My father had a saying: 'Give your children enough to do something, but not enough to do nothing.'"

"Well said."

Brooke beckoned about the room.

"Many of the books and artifacts you see here are one of a kind," she said, "collected by my father and me during our travels. We compensated their owners fairly for each of them. Even so, many are by now quite priceless—especially the two volumes that I just pulled from the shelves and brought to my desk."

Brooke lifted one of the books so that Constance and Garrett could see its old leather cover, and then the writing that lay inside. The pages looked ancient and were nearly falling apart. They had not been printed on a press, but were instead handwritten in a language that Garrett could not read.

"Is that Latin?" he asked.

Brooke nodded.

"This book is called the *Carta Umbrarum*, she answered. "Translated into English, it means: *The Book of Shadows*. My father found it during one of his archaeological digs in Southern Italy. It dates from the fifteen hundreds. When he first saw it, he thought that it was probably an old handwritten copy of the Bible, which at one time was the usual way priests and monks reproduced it for distribution throughout the world. But because he read and wrote Latin fluently, he immediately realized that it was something else altogether."

"And that is?" Garrett asked.

"Believe it or not," Brooke answered, "it's like a book of spells. Sorry, let me rephrase that. It's not so much a book of 'spells' as it is a collection of worldly phenomena for which the Catholic clergy had no explanation, many of which remain a mystery to this very day. My guess is that what happened to Constance, and then also to you Dr. Richmond, is outlined on these pages."

"The *mora mortis*," Garrett said, almost to himself.

"Yes," Brooke answered.

"What does that mean in English?" Garrett asked.

"Rather loosely translated, it means: 'The Delay of Death.' "

Garrett turned to look at Constance. She too was mesmerized by what Brooke was telling them.

"Please continue," Garrett said to Brooke. "But first, there's something I don't understand. On hearing our story, how could you possibly go straight to the right book and then turn to the exact page that you needed? Forgive me, but I find that quite unbelievable."

"As would I, if I were in your shoes," Brooke answered. "Put simply, it's because I was born with a photographic memory. Which, by the way, can be more of a curse than a blessing, I assure you. Added to that is the fact that this book was my father's favorite, because everything contained therein remains a mystery. You see, Dr. Richmond, what this book is about to tell us is what has happened to you two, and why. But when we come to the solution, well, that's the puzzling part."

"What do you mean?" Garrett asked.

Brooke again held up one hand.

"Let's not get ahead of ourselves," she said.

"Are all the phenomena described in *The Book of Shadows* so malevolent?" Garrett asked.

Brooke gave him a quizzical look.

"Who said anything about the *mora mortis* being malevolent?"

"It has to be," Garrett countered, "given that it so cruelly traps someone between the worlds of life and death with no chance of salvation."

"Once again you're jumping to conclusions," Brooke answered. "In fact the *mora mortis* is perhaps the most benevolent of all the phenomena in *The Book of Shadows*."

"How can that be?" Garrett asked.

"Because it is based upon love," Brooke answered. "You told me that Brooke fell from her widow's walk the same day that Adam perished at sea. The *mora mortis* is a phenomenon that occurs very rarely throughout history. It states that when two people who love one another unconditionally perish at the same instant, a tear is formed in the fabric of time, causing one to die while the other must live out another existence in between life and death. During this period, only one other person in the entire world will be able to both see that person and communicate with him or her. And if that lover doesn't come along, then the trapped person will live that way throughout all eternity. This is what happened to Constance, and the person who can see her and speak with her is you, Dr. Richmond. Infinitesimal as the odds might be, you two somehow found each other."

Garrett was stunned. He simply stared at Brooke, his jaw slack with amazement. He then turned to look at Constance and saw that her surprise was equally extreme.

"You're claiming that the power behind all this is *love?*" Garrett asked.

"Yes," Brooke answered, "that is exactly what I'm telling you. Love is the most powerful force in the universe. What other dynamism can make us do such things? We strive for it, revel in it, and also suffer because of it. But in the end, who among us can claim to be its master?"

"But if all that's true," Garrett said, "then . . ."

"That's right," Brooke interjected. "Whether you want to admit it or not, you're in love with Constance. Even more than that, your love for her is completely unconditional. You cannot deny it, Dr. Richmond, because you are the one person in the world who can both see and hear her. I'm sorry to speak out of turn here, but I really have no choice. So please tell me— does Constance know that you feel this way about her?"

Out of respect, Garrett looked at Constance before answering. When she nodded, he again turned back toward Brooke.

"Yes," he said. "She knows. She also knows that I have never loved anyone the way that I love her."

"And how does she feel about you?" Brooke asked. "Forgive me, Garrett, but I must know these things if I am to help you."

Garrett again turned and looked at Constance, hoping to hear the answer that he wanted. This would be a moment of truth, he realized, a true crossroads in their relationship. When Constance looked back at him there were tears in her eyes.

"I am confused, Garrett," she said. "I wish to love you, I really do. And now that I have seen Adam die, I know in my heart that I should feel free to do so. But there remains something holding me back that I cannot explain. Please do not be angry with me. This is just how things are."

Although disappointed, Garrett relayed Constance's words to Brooke. When he finished, Brooke nodded.

"I see," she said. "But that is all right. For you to help yourselves, it is not necessary that she love you as deeply as you love her. For when the time comes, the true test will be forced not upon her, but upon you."

"What do you mean?" Garrett asked.

"We will get to that," Brooks answered. "But first I need to ask you something more. This may sound insane, but have either of you experienced flashbacks in time, during which you've experienced something extremely traumatic?"

Yet again, Garrett couldn't believe his ears. Brooke was explaining exactly what had been happening to them. Taking his time, he very carefully described each of their flashbacks to Brooke. When he finished, she nodded thoughtfully.

"Why are they happening?" Garrett asked.

"Simply put, the *mora mortis* is testing you both," Brooke said. "If, while the two of you were experiencing these events, either of you had behaved evilly, the *mora mortis* would have withdrawn its presence, making it quite impossible for the two of you to find a way out. This does not mean that there can't be more such occurrences. This is also why you have been so inexplicably drawn to Seaside, Garrett. Because you are the one person in the world who could love Constance enough to help save her, the *mora mortis* created the need within you to own that house and to restore it. That is not to say that you would not have done so anyway, but the *mora mortis* added abundantly to that desire."

His nervous energy finally overcoming him, Garrett stood and began anxiously pacing the room.

"I simply can't believe all this!" he said. "How do I know that everything you're telling us isn't just some bunch of hocus-pocus?"

"Is your unusual attraction to Seaside not real?" Brooke asked, "or the love for Constance that you carry in your heart, while at the same time freely admitting to never having loved another the way you love her? And what about Constance, who has lived for more than seventeen decades, while quite unable to communicate with anyone other than you? *You* called *me* looking for help, Dr. Richmond. I didn't ask to see you, and I had absolutely no idea what you wanted from me before you arrived here and I saw Constance's aura. So you tell me—do you still really think that all this is just hocus-pocus, as you put it? I am not some crystal ball gazer who does her business down on Essex Street, Dr. Richmond. I am the genuine article, and everything that I've told you is God's honest truth."

Chagrined, Garrett finally returned to the sofa.

"Forgive me," he said quietly. "It's just that Constance and I have been through so much . . ."

"And you will go through much more before it is over," Brooke said. "Before we get to that, let me offer you another bit of proof. It is not definitive, but it is perhaps another valuable bit of information about the *mora mortis*. As I said, this really is all about love. Rather than allow both persons to die, the *mora mortis* helps one of the victims to live and find true love again. That is why I told you it is benevolent, rather than malevolent."

Without answering, Brooke opened the second book and flipped through it.

"Are you both familiar with the name Nostradamus?" she asked.

Garrett turned to look at Constance, and she nodded.

"What of him?" Garrett asked.

"My father studied Nostradamus extensively," Brooke said. "This book is a copy of Nostradamus's collected works of prophecy. Nostradamus wrote in a form called quatrains, one of which my father believed referred to the *mora mortis*, and to two of the people who might eventually become caught up in it. The more I think about it, the more I believe that my father was right."

"What does it say?" Garrett asked.

"I will now read Quatrain four-fourteen to you," Brooke said as she laid the book flat upon her desk.

> *"The sudden death of the first personage*
> *will have caused change,*
> *and put another into sovereignty.*
> *Soon, but late come to so high a position, of young age,*
> *such as by land and sea it will be necessary to fear him."*

"I don't understand," Garrett said.

"No?" Brooke asked. "Then please allow me to explain: '*The sudden death of the first personage will have caused change*' refers to Adam's death, and its subsequent effect on Constance. As lord and master of Seaside, Adam was its sovereign, and his unexpected death enacted the *mora mortis*, thereby trapping Constance between worlds. The next line, '*and put another into sovereignty,*' refers to your eventual purchase of Seaside and thereby becoming its new sovereign. Next, the line that states: *'soon, but late come to so high a position, of young age,'* speaks of you again, Garrett. It means that although you acquired Seaside many years after Constance fell from the widow's walk, the time that passed by in the relative scheme of things was short, and you did so while still at a relatively young age. The last line, that is to say: *'such as by land and sea it will be necessary to fear him,'* speaks of Seaside itself, sitting on dry land yet also situated alongside the sea. The phrase *'it will be necessary to fear him'* speaks of Constance's intense fear when she first realized you could both see and hear her."

Garrett turned and looked at Constance to find her frozen with amazement. At last she said to him, "Can all this really be true, Garrett? My God, did Nostradamus actually predict what would happen to us?"

Garrett turned and looked back at Brooke.

"Do you really believe that?" he asked.

"It doesn't matter," Brooke said. "What matters is that my father believed this quatrain referred to the *mora mortis,* although he of course had no inkling about the two of you, or your situation. Even so, the parallels are difficult to ignore, don't you think?"

As he sat looking at Brooke, Garrett suddenly realized that he was exhausted. Although everything she had told him fit into place perfectly, it was still a great deal to absorb all at once. He needed time to think, and a quiet place where he could decide what to do next. But before that happened, there was more to learn.

"You mentioned a way to end all of this," he said. "Can you please tell us what it is? Is it something that the two of us can carry out on our own?"

With the coming of Garrett's question, Brookes expression turned decidedly grim. Before replying, she closed the two books and set them aside.

"Yes," she answered bluntly, "but you're not going to like what I have to say."

Chapter 26

At first, it was as if Brooke didn't want to explain further. While Garrett and Constance waited, the ticking of the grandfather clock seemed to grow louder, as did the crackling flames in the fireplace hearth. At last Brooke looked Garrett directly in the eyes.

"Simply put," she said, "to save Constance, you yourself may have to die."

Her unexpected words hit Garrett like a thunderbolt.

"What in God's name are you talking about?" he demanded.

"Like the flashbacks that the two of you have been experiencing, what you must do to save her will be another test of your love for her," Brooke answered. "If you survive it, then Constance may survive as well. *The Book of Shadows* does not explain this part in great detail. In fact it makes almost no mention of it all, except for a brief description of what must be done to break the grip of the *mora mortis*."

"And if we refuse?" Garrett asked.

"If you refuse, Constance will die."

"Do you mean that she will *actually* die?" Garrett demanded.

"Yes," Brooke answered. "I'm afraid that I do."

"But why?"

"Not even my father could explain that," Brooke answered. "But he did believe that it was some sort of incentive designed to push the two lovers into action, although he could never be sure."

Brooke then turned and looked in Constance's general direction.

"Tell us, my child," she said, "have you been feeling weaker lately?"

Constance turned and looked at Garrett.

"It is true," she said to him. "I have not been well of late."

Garrett relayed her answer to Brooke.

"I am so sorry to hear that," Brooke said.

"What will happen to her?"

"Anytime now, her presence will literally begin to fade away," Brooke answered. "And once it begins, she will soon be gone altogether, and you will have lost your chance to save her."

"And what would happen to me?"

"You would then be forced to take her place, living somewhere between life and death for all of eternity. Then your only chance for salvation would be for a different person to come along who loves you unconditionally, and is willing to perhaps die for you."

"How much time do we have?" Garrett asked.

"No one knows," Brooke answered.

"This is insane!" Garrett exclaimed.

"Please, Garrett," Constance said to him. "I know that this is difficult to accept, but she has been right about everything so far. Who else in the world could possibly know about these things that have been happening to us? All of which makes me believe that no matter how much we do not wish to accept any of this, it appears to be our fate, just the same. We promised to see this thing through no matter what, and it seems to me that we must accept whatever Brooke has to say."

Garrett stared blankly at her. She was right, of course, but deep down there remained so much about all of this that he simply couldn't accept. He had never been one for the metaphysical, even though he was obviously ensnared by forces he couldn't begin to imagine.

"Yet again, I must apologize," he said to Brooke. "I know that you're only trying to help, but hearing all this is hard for us."

"It's meant to be," Brooke answered. "You wish to accomplish something that has in all likelihood never been done before—that is, to satisfy the *mora mortis.*"

"You said that there might be a way for us to possibly succeed, but that the price would be steep," Garrett said. "Exactly what would we have to do?"

"You must both put yourselves at great risk," Brooke answered. "In short, the person trapped between worlds must re-create his or her death, and the person who loves him or her must do the same. Then and only then will you know whether Constance has been freed from her particular brand of purgatory, or whether she has died, and you took her place. There can be no in between on this, Garrett. If you do this, it will either work or it won't, and I am at a complete loss to tell you which it might be."

"But Constance 'died' when she fell from her widow's walk and crashed onto the rocks," he said. "So to re-create that—"

"Yes," Brooke interjected. "The two of you must go back up to the widow's walk and then throw yourselves from the roof. In the end this is not only a test of how much you love her, but it is also about how much she trusts in your love. A true 'leap of faith' if you will, for each of you."

"And then?" Garrett asked.

"Even I don't know," Brooke answered. "*The Book of Shadows* states possible outcomes, but I can't be sure whether it mentions all of them. One or both of you may live, one or both of you may die, or you may both end up trapped in the *mora mortis* forever. The combinations and permutations could be infinite in number. There is only one way to find out, and that is to go through with it."

Stunned, Garrett leaned back against the sofa then turned to look at Constance. She was trembling noticeably and there were tears in her eyes.

"Do you honestly think we should do this?" he asked her. "It sounds crazy to me."

Constance wiped her eyes.

"What part of all this has ever seemed sane?" she answered. "The only thing that I know for sure is that I believe Brooke. Even so, this is not something that I can ask of you. You should not be forced to risk your life, simply because you and I somehow found each other across time."

"But if I don't do it, then you will die, and I will become as trapped by all this as you are now," he said. "Plus, our episodes are coming faster and faster, and although I can only speak for myself, I simply can't live like this anymore."

"This is a decision the two of you should make in private," Brooke said. "I cannot tell you what to do. I can only state what is in these two books, and how you must proceed if you wish to try breaking free of the *mora mortis.*"

"So that's it?" Garrett asked. "You have told us all that you can?"

"Yes, Garrett," Brooke answered. "I'm afraid so. If you are looking for more, I can't give it to you. All the two of you can do now is to decide whether you want to go through with it. I know the decision is horribly difficult, but you have no more need of me."

When Garrett stood from the couch, Constance followed suit. They were clearly upset, but at least now they had their answers. Garrett turned and looked back into Brooke's eyes.

"Thank you," he said to her. "I have no way of guessing what will happen, but without you, we would never have known how to go forward. I'm afraid that neither Constance nor I are any good at this sort of thing."

Brooke gave them a short smile.

"One should never criticize oneself," she said, "when there are always so many other people willing to do it for you."

Despite the ominous news, Garrett couldn't help but return her smile.

"Before you two go, I have a request of you," Brooke said.

"Anything," Garret answered.

"I would ask that should one or both of you survive, please return here and tell me. In the short time that I have known you, I've come to like you both very much."

"Of course," Garrett answered. "And Constance thanks you, as well."

With that, Brooke escorted them back upstairs. It had begun raining again, each falling drop seeming to impart a sense of fresh gloom over everything. Someone, Garrett noticed, had wisely closed all the French doors. While Constance and Garrett watched, Brooke again situated herself behind her massive desk.

"I have something I want to give to the two of you," she said, "and I will tolerate no argument in this."

She reached for two things and scribbled down a few lines on each with a fountain pen. When she was done she blew the ink dry, inserted them into a vellum envelope, and sealed it. She then handed the envelope to Garrett.

"That is not to be opened until you are off the grounds," she said sternly. "Agreed?"

"Very well," Garrett answered.

Brooke then took up a piece of blank stationery and her fountain pen.

"Take these from me, would you please?" she asked. "I would very much appreciate having your particulars, should I need them later. Your phone number, e-mail address, things like that . . ."

"Certainly," Garrett answered as he stood up from his chair and took the items from her. After completing his task, he handed the items back to Brooke.

"Thank you," Brooke answered.

She then pressed a button mounted to her desktop, and in short order William reappeared.

"Please escort Dr. Richmond back to his car, would you, William?" she asked.

"Of course, madam," he answered.

"Thank you again," Garrett said to Brooke. "Meeting you has been an honor."

"And I feel the same about you," she answered. "*Bonne chance,* Garrett."

About an hour later, Garrett took an opportunity to pull over to the side of the road.

"Why do you stop?" Constance asked him.

Garrett removed Brooke's vellum envelope from his blazer.

"I have to know what this is," he answered. "I can't wait any longer."

"Would you care to hazard a guess?"

"I think it's her last instructions to us, perhaps something that she hadn't the heart to tell us in person. If so, it could be bad."

After staring at the envelope for a few moments, at last Garrett opened it. The first piece of paper read simply: *To help with whatever trials lay up ahead* . . .

The second article was a handwritten check on Brooke's personal account that read: *Payable to Mr. Garrett Richmond in the Amount of: $100,000.*

Chapter 27

Three weeks had passed since the fateful day of their meeting with Brooke Wentworth. Because Garrett knew he would do a poor job of teaching his seminar, he asked the college administration if someone could take over for him, and they agreed. The closing on his condo took place, and he was now living full-time at Seaside with Constance. It was a Spartan existence with him sleeping on the couch in the dining room, and Constance in the master bedroom. Jay's crew had finished renovating Seaside's exterior and had begun working on the inside. Yet hanging over their heads was the decision of trying to free Constance from the *mora mortis*. They had discussed it often over the course of the last three weeks, each time without agreement.

Constance did not want Garrett to risk his life for her, even if it meant her possible freedom. Garrett had countered by saying that if nothing were done and Brooke Wentworth was right, then he would become destined for the same sort of imprisonment that she was now suffering, anyway. But most importantly, if no action were taken, then Constance would literally begin to fade away until there was nothing left of her. And to their great concern that process had already begun.

Ten days prior, while they were sitting on the dining room sofa and talking about their problems, the light from the fireplace danced across Constance's face, and for the first time Garrett noticed a strange sort of translucence there. No difference could be seen in her clothing, but anywhere her skin was exposed he saw the same frightening phenomenon. It seemed that Constance had begun dying for real, and it was happening before his very eyes.

Wanting to be sure, he put off telling her. But to his horror, with each passing day he saw her form grow paler. When at last he broached the subject, Constance erupted into tears. She had been aware but hadn't wished to discuss it because she did not want to upset him further. And now, some three weeks since their fateful meeting with Brooke Wentworth, they were again sitting on the dining room sofa, trying to agree upon the right course of action.

Garrett picked up the bottle of red wine sitting on the cocktail table, and he poured some for himself. After taking a measured sip he put the glass down and looked into Constance's eyes.

"We simply must try and free you," he said gently. "Surely you see that! At first I thought Brooke was crazy. But so far, everything she told us has come true. She knew all about the flashbacks, she realized that you were feeling ill, and she also predicted that if no action was taken to free you from the *mora mortis* that you would begin to fade away. I can't lose you Constance . . . I just can't."

His eyes becoming tearful, Garrett took a moment to dry them. Constance was dying a little more each day, and he could easily see her deterioration. Because he loved her so much, he would do anything to try and save her. But as Brooke had said, neither of them could do this alone. In order to succeed, his love for Constance must be strong enough to survive the ordeal, and her trust in his love for her must be equally resolute, lest they both perish in the attempt. But anything, Garrett reasoned, was better than the alternatives that Brooke had described.

"I simply cannot do it," Constance said. "I know that it means I will soon die," she added. "Even so, I cannot let you risk your life that way, no matter how much you love me."

Garrett stared at her longingly. He respected her emotions, but at the same time he had become utterly convinced that she was wrong. And watching her suffer a slow death for his sake was something that he just could not bear.

As he looked into her eyes, he again felt all his love for her come roiling to the surface, and with it also burgeoned the same overpowering sexual need for her that he had experienced so many times before. But this time, he chose not to fight it. This time he decided to follow his heart and see where it took him. He impetuously took her into his arms, and he kissed her.

To his surprise, she did not ask him to stop. Instead, he felt her body rise and her lips part to meet his, their tongues entwining in a passionate, purposeful kiss. As his ardor for her increased, Garrett ran his hands through her hair and he rather harshly pulled her closer. Breathing heavily, Constance briefly removed her lips from his and whispered the single word: "*More . . .*"

Suddenly both Garrett and Constance began to lose consciousness, their hearts, minds, and souls slipping away to another place and time. Knowing full well what was happening, before passing out fully Garrett did his best to help cushion Constance's fall.

When Garrett awakened, as in one of his previous flashbacks, he again found himself in Seaside's master bedroom. Also like before, the room was completely furnished with Constance's antebellum furniture. Whale oil lamps, again telling Garrett that he had once more gone back in time, supplied the light. Night had fallen, and several of the windows were open, indicating a seasonable time of year. When he looked more carefully about the room, he finally saw Constance. She was sitting up in bed, reading a book.

Moments later, Adam entered the room, carrying a tea tray. There was a pot of tea, two cups, some napkins, and what appeared to be a small selection of fruit. As Adam set the tray down on one of the nightstands, Constance smiled.

"And what have we here?" she asked.

Adam began pouring her a cup of tea.

"A late-night snack," he answered. "Truth be told, this was Eli's idea."

Just as Constance began taking her first sip of tea, there came an urgent pounding on the bedroom door.

"Who's there?" Adam asked.

"It's Emily!" a voice shouted from the other side. "You've just got to open up!"

Adam opened the door to find Emily Jackson standing there. She had a horribly distraught look on her face. She wore a nightgown, and in one trembling hand she held a lit whale oil lantern. Adam cast his gaze up and down the hallway and quickly ascertained that she was alone.

"Emily?" Adam asked. "What's wrong?"

"It's Missy Charleston!" Emily shouted. "Her baby's coming and it's a breech! Miss Constance just has to come, cap'n! She's the only one who knows what to do!"

"Constance!" Adam shouted.

Constance was already out of bed. Still wearing her nightgown, she quickly donned her robe and a pair of slippers. Wasting no time, Adam and Constance left the room and hurriedly followed Emily down the hall. After some initial hesitation, Garrett chased after them.

The moon was full and the grass was laden with cold dew as they rushed toward the barn. At first Garrett couldn't imagine why the barn was dark until he remembered that the cellar was an Underground Railroad station, and lighting the lamps would be far too risky. On entering the barn, Adam swung the trap-door open, and the four of them went down the stairs. During this entire time, neither Adam nor Constance seemed to realize that Garrett was there with them.

The scene belowground was grim. The main chamber, lit with whale oil lamps, was full of slaves crowded around one of the cots. Atop the cot lay a screaming woman, her husband by her side and holding her hand. The woman, covered with perspiration, was naked from the waist down with her legs splayed wide. Blood and embryonic fluid covered the bottom half of the cot and had also soaked part of the ground beneath it. From one of his earliest conversations with Constance, Garrett now remembered her telling him that she had been a midwife, but at the time he had never guessed that he might actually see her talents put to use.

Constance immediately ran to the stricken woman's side and took her hand.

"Missy," she said loudly. "Your time has come, and I am here for you."

Constance reached down and pressed her palms atop the woman's swollen abdomen, trying to confirm whether the child was in fact a breech. As she did, Missy screamed manically again.

Standing back from the stricken woman, Constance wiped her forehead with the back of one hand.

"Is it—?"

"Yes," Constance whispered, answering her husband. "Emily was correct—Missy's child is a breech.

And if the baby is not delivered properly, they both might die."

Constance returned to Missy's side and looked down at her. The terrible pain and fear Missy was experiencing had conspired to produce so tortured an expression on her face that Constance could hardly bear it. Then Missy screamed again, her cries resonating through the subterranean chambers.

"Missy," Constance said to her calmly, "I have to try and turn the baby now. The pain will be terrible but this must be done before I can deliver your child, otherwise it will be born with the cord around its neck, strangling it. Do you understand?"

"Yes, Miss Constance," Missy answered. Her pain was now so all-encompassing that she could barely get the words out. "Just save my baby . . . save my baby . . ."

Bending down, Constance lovingly ran one palm over Missy's forehead.

"I will do my best," she answered.

As Garrett watched, Constance quickly ordered four of the male slaves to hold Missy down by her hands and feet. Once Missy was secure, Constance again placed her palms on Missy's abdomen, but this time with a different intent. While pressing down, and amid Missy's plaintive screams, Constance turned her hands clockwise, trying to reposition the fetus. After trying three times, Constance stood up again and nodded.

"I think that I have done it," she said. She then looked down at Missy's face again. "Very well now, if you want this baby, then your time has come."

Constance went to the end of the cot, where she got down on her knees between Missy's splayed legs.

"Now!" Constance said. "Push now!"

Entranced, Garrett watched the process play itself out as Constance continually egged Missy on while Missy screamed and pushed. About fifteen minutes later, Missy's son was delivered into Constance's arms. At first he did not cry, causing Constance to quickly clear his airway with one finger. At last the infant boy let out a good long scream, and everyone rejoiced. Constance then tied off and cut the umbilical cord, and handed the new baby to his mother. Crying joyfully, Missy held her child close, tears still streaming down her cheeks.

Letting go a tired sigh, Constance, her hands still covered with blood and fluid, finally stood and wiped her forehead with the back of one arm. She then turned and looked at Adam, a radiant smile upon her face. Adam immediately went to her and took her into his arms.

"How fine ye are to me, wife," he said.

Exhausted, Constance laid her head upon her husband's shoulder.

"And how fine ye are to me, husband," she answered.

While Garrett stood watching, he again realized that not a single soul in the subterranean room knew that he was here. And although he could clearly see how much Constance and Adam loved one another, what he had just witnessed caused him to want Constance even more than before. She was an amazing woman and he would do his best to never let her go, neither in this time, nor in the future.

And he now realized something else. Unlike when he had experienced the other flashbacks, this time he understood that this had been a product of the *mora mortis,* and although he had never considered these episodes to be good things, at least some good had come from this one. Constance had saved two lives this night, and seeing her do it was something he would never forget. For some unknown reason, the *mora mortis* had wanted him to witness the birth of this child, and Constance's part in it.

And also because he knew these things now, when he suddenly felt faint again, he realized that it was because he was being returned to his own day and age. Except this time he welcomed the journey.

Chapter 28

The following Saturday Garrett found himself sitting in his college office, nervously waiting. It was nearly two o'clock in the afternoon, and he would soon have a visitor.

Yesterday he had received a very surprising e-mail from Dr. Brooke Wentworth, asking that he please be here at this appointed time, because she had some personal correspondence for Garrett. It was something vitally important that she would not trust to the usual methods, and so William, her butler, would be delivering a note in person. She then apologized for not coming herself, adding that although she still liked traveling, being confined to her wheelchair made it difficult. Her cryptic message also warned that although the decision was of course his alone, he might not choose to share this information with Constance. For that reason she had not mentioned it on the day of their visit, although she wished that she could have done so.

Puzzled, Garrett stood from his chair and went to his office window. It had rained rather heavily all day, the uniformly dark clouds unwilling to part for so much as a moment. He had absolutely no idea why Brooke was contacting him. He would better understand after he read her message, he supposed. Even so, he couldn't imagine any sort of news he might not wish to share with Constance. They had grown so close that he kept nothing from her; especially something so important that it need be personally delivered by Brooke's trusted butler.

Just then there came a knock on the office door, causing Garrett to take a quick look at his watch. It was 2:00 P.M. exactly. Given what Garrett guessed was William's strict sense of punctuality, he wouldn't have expected anything less.

When Garrett opened the office door, William stared back at him placidly. Today he wore a navy suit beneath a rain-splotched, London Fog raincoat. Despite not being in butler's livery, his air of professionalism still shined through.

"William," Garrett said politely, "won't you please come in?"

Before replying, William closed his umbrella then tapped its tip several times against the hallway floor to shake off the rain.

"Thank you, Dr. Richmond," he answered. "It's a pleasure to see you again."

"You too," Garrett answered. He beckoned William toward one of the guest chairs opposite his desk. "Please sit down."

William removed his raincoat and took a seat.

"It's my understanding that you have something for me from Dr. Wentworth," Garrett said.

William nodded as he removed an envelope from his suit jacket. Garrett saw that it was made of the same expensive vellum as the departing note Brooke had given him that day at Fairlawn. Rising briefly from his chair, William handed it over.

"My instructions are quite simple," William said. "First, I deliver that letter to you. Second, I am to make sure that you read it in my presence."

Wondering, Garrett ran his fingertips over the sharply creased envelope. Brooke had written his name on the front in fountain ink, and the back flap was securely sealed with red stationery wax.

"You don't know what this says?" he asked William.

"That's correct."

Garrett used his pocketknife to slit open the envelope. When he removed its contents he saw that

Brooke's note was handwritten, encompassing one full page and half of another. After settling back in his chair, he began to read.

William watched with interest while Garrett perused Brooke's letter. At first Garrett showed no emotion, but as he continued reading, a look of outright astonishment soon overtook his face. By the time Garrett had finished, his breath was coming in ragged gasps and his face was flushed. It was quite clear to William that the note had affected Garrett deeply, perhaps even irrevocably.

Several moments later Garrett read the note again, as if doing so would somehow lessen the terrible tension he was feeling. With trembling fingers he finally replaced it into the envelope. When at last he looked back at William, his eyes were fearful, incredulous.

"I say, Dr. Richmond," William asked. "Is something wrong?"

Before answering, Garrett walked on shaking legs to his office window and again looked out. The rain was coming harder now, the uniform clouds even darker than before. As the drops assailed his window they created tiny rivulets, curiously distorting everything that lay beyond.

Just like this revelation from Brooke has suddenly distorted everything I thought I knew, he thought. *I now understand that my entire life has been . . .*

At last Garrett summoned enough composure to turn and look at William.

"Thank you for coming," he said. "You may tell Dr. Wentworth that I have read her letter in its entirety, and I understand. Please also tell her that I thank her."

William nodded.

"Then my work here is done," he said.

Upon rising from his chair he donned his raincoat and grabbed up his umbrella. When he reached the door he stopped and again looked at Garrett with an expression of concern.

"Forgive me, sir," he said, "but are you quite sure you're all right? Dr. Wentworth will want to know."

Garrett walked back to his desk and sat down. Given everything that he had just learned, it felt good to have a sturdy chair beneath him, rather than his trembling legs.

"Yes, William," he answered. "Please be sure to have a safe trip home, and give my best regards to Dr. Wentworth."

"As you wish, sir," William said. "I bid you good day."

"And to you," Garrett answered.

William left Garrett's office and quietly closed the door behind him.

Still stunned by what he had just read, Garrett suddenly took a little gulp of air. For some reason his office seemed quite unfamiliar to him now, as if he had just stepped into it for the first time. Like some awful beast that had suddenly been released from its lair, a terrible sense of panic gripped his heart. With the coming of Brooke's letter, his plight had suddenly been complicated to such a degree that he could barely make any sense of it.

Even so, he also realized that Brooke had been right to send him this letter in confidence. Would he disclose its contents to Constance? No, he decided. If they succeeded, he could always tell her later. Conversely, if neither of them survived, then what possible difference could it make? He felt deceitful, but it had to be this way.

He now also understood how the information in Brooke's letter fit into all of this. Like the last piece of some gigantic puzzle, it seemed to finally pull all the other pieces into place, but the picture that emerged was far more complex than he could have ever have imagined. Even so, everything Brooke had so far told him had come true, thereby leading him to trust the veracity of this latest revelation as well. As tears began forming in his eyes, he shook his head with frustration.

Could it be possible? he wondered. *I've never believed in such things. But if it is true, then this changes everything. Worse yet, despite its supreme importance I must keep it a secret from the only woman I have ever loved.*

Suddenly feeling the need to move, Garrett returned to the office window and stared out blankly, seeing both everything and nothing. And then, despite how unsettling Brooke's letter had been, one part of it gave him an idea . . .

Chapter 29

Two days later, Constance again stood before the old window in the barn. This was the same window from which she had gazed so many times over the past seventeen decades, wondering if she might ever be released from her terrible purgatory. Yet now that a chance for freedom had come, she hesitated.

She had returned to her corner spot on the barn's second floor to think about what to do. Given that she was now living in the house, it had been some time since she had visited here, and she had missed this little place. Perhaps that was because she had spent some of her most difficult times here, amid the rather sad collection of personal items that had always comforted her. But the only things remaining were the mattress and the full-length mirror, neither of which she wanted.

When she considered looking into the mirror, she hesitated. She had not gazed upon herself for some time now, for fear of what she would see. She knew she was dying, and she felt a little weaker every day. She also knew that she did not have much time left in which to make a decision, and that knowledge haunted her.

At last she gathered up the courage to step before the mirror. Her clothes hung straight down upon her form loosely. Her hair looked brittle and dry, and her skin showed additional lines and wrinkles that had been absent only days before. If one looked hard enough, the beauty that had once been hers could still be seen, but soon even that would be gone. And despite it all, Garrett still professed his undying love for her. Nearly two weeks had passed since their last flashback. At the time she had not known that Garrett shared in the experience, and when he told her she had been surprised.

Turning away from the mirror, Constance again gazed down at the old mattress. How many times had she cried herself to sleep there? she wondered. How many times had she come to lie there, seeking quiet? And how many times had she gone to her knees there, praying to God to set her free? An answer had come at last in the form of a man named Garrett Richmond. But now that he was here, how could she ask him to risk his life for hers?

That question had haunted her since the moment they left Brooke Wentworth's mansion. Neither she nor Garrett had any lingering doubts about the things Brooke told them. That is, the only path to freedom was for the two of them to hurl their bodies from the roof of Seaside, not knowing whether one or both of them might perish, or what might happen to them, even should they live. Time after time her mind returned to that terrible, wonderful, frightening, and reassuring idea. This course of action might actually save her, and also keep Garrett from entering the same sort of purgatory that she had suffered for so long. But should they do it? she wondered. *Could* they do it?

She had no doubt that Garrett would go through with it if she agreed. Yet still she hesitated, because of her highly conflicted feelings regarding him. And so it was that she had decided to return to this familiar spot today, and hopefully make some sense of everything.

She had always done her best thinking here. But before she could do so again, she first needed to understand something that had bewildered her for some time now. As best she could, she needed to ascertain her true feelings for Garrett. For only then would she be able to give him a final answer.

Truth be told, she had been conflicted about Garrett since the moment they met. In many ways he was perfect. He not only understood and appreciated the times from which she came, but he was also intensely dedicated to restoring Seaside. Had the flashbacks not begun, she remained firmly convinced that by now she would be deeply in love with him.

But each of her flashbacks had sent her back in time to Adam, cruelly reminding her of how much she loved him, then only to return her to the present. And each time she returned, there stood Garrett—ready, willing, and able to love her with all his heart, and even to risk his life to help free her. Every time this happened, her confusion grew, and sometimes she felt like she was going mad over it. Was it possible for a woman to love two men at the same time? she again wondered. And if so, did that somehow make her evil?

But most of all, did she truly love Garrett? That was the real question, and she knew it. It had been so long since she had experienced real love, she wasn't sure what it felt like anymore. She already loved him as she might love a brother. And she knew that her romantic and sexual feelings for him roiled just beneath the surface, yearning to be unleashed. Given enough time, would they at last blossom? And would she then have enough closure about Adam to act on them?

Sometimes the more she thought about Adam, the more she truly believed that she did in fact want a romantic and sexual relationship with Garrett. To anyone unfamiliar with her situation, these feelings would probably seem contradictory and selfish, perhaps even adulterous. But her marriage to Adam had been arranged, and love had come later. Garrett was as good a man as Adam had been, and she saw no reason why she couldn't come to love him too. But was that true love? Or was true love something more immediate and visceral, like an unexpected thunderbolt?

Brooke had said that for their attempt to succeed, Garrett's love for Constance must be unconditional and know no bounds. That needn't also be true about Constance's feelings for Garrett, however. According to Brooke, she needed only believe strongly enough in his love for her, and of that she had no doubts. So many times now Garrett had already illustrated his undying devotion. It was like something straight out of a storybook, in which the handsome hero comes to rescue the fair damsel who has been imprisoned in a dark tower. Then again, such storybook lovers never had to overcome a force so powerful as the *mora mortis.*

And if she and Garrett failed in the attempt, what would death be like? she wondered. Could it possibly be any worse than the last seventeen decades through which she had already suffered? Might she be reunited in death with her husband, Adam? And if so, how could that be a bad thing?

Conversely, should they succeed, then what would her new life then be like? Could she continue to live here at Seaside with Garrett, for not only would she wish to stay, but he would want that too. His restoration of Seaside would eventually be complete, and all the furniture from the barn cellar would be returned to the house. Would they perhaps marry and have children? And given the passage of time would she find enough closure regarding Adam, at last allowing her to fully enjoy her new life?

Just then she realized that she had made her decision, and that her answer to Garrett must be yes. When Garrett arrived home tonight she would tell him, and she knew how happy he would be. But most of all, she believed that she had finally made the right choice, no matter the risks that she and Garrett must take. And if their trial succeeded, she no longer had any doubt that she could be happy with Garrett, even if her brotherly love for him never turned into anything more.

When she looked out the window again, this time she saw Garrett's Jeep coming up the dirt road toward the house. And with his arrival, she realized something else.

She had at last found a reason to live.

Chapter 30

Two days later, Garrett sat alone in his business office, thinking. Like Constance, he too had come to a crossroads regarding her imprisonment. When she told him that she wanted to try, he had been overjoyed. But later on, he realized there were some things to be considered.

Standing from his desk, he crossed the room and walked to the large picture window in the opposite wall. He looked out over the restless Atlantic, its wintertime waves now gray, and froth-tipped. They would retain that appearance until next summer, when the weather warmed and they returned to a beautiful dark blue. Would he and Constance live to see that lovely transformation? he wondered. He hoped with all his heart that would be the case, but in truth he had absolutely no way of knowing what might happen to them.

As Garrett had considered all of this during the last two days, he also realized that there were other people to consider besides just him and Constance. His death would have a huge effect upon Trent, his parents, and his sister and her family.

He was not worried about his last will and testament, because it had been drafted only two years ago and he remained very familiar with its language. In the event of his death everything he owned—including Seaside—went to his sister, Christine. Should she wish to have Jay finish the restoration, there would be plenty of money left. Yesterday he informed his attorney about the antique furniture hidden in the barn cellar and ordered him to inform his sister of it, in the event of his death.

Trent would inherit his share of the business, which was only right, because Trent had worked so hard to help make it a success. Save for a few personal items, his parents weren't mentioned. But then again, they didn't need anything from him and they were sure to understand. Not wishing to leave any of his affairs unattended, yesterday Garrett had presented a check to Jay Morgan, which more than paid for any outstanding expenses incurred to date.

He had considered leaving a note, should he die in the attempt. But he soon decided against it, because he didn't want anyone thinking that he had committed suicide. He would, however, take a sledgehammer to the widow's walk front railing, thereby making it appear that it had somehow failed, causing him to fall to his death. Should he die, to spare his family any additional grief, he wanted it to appear as an accident. They would all be beyond consoling, but that was something over which he had no control.

He very much hoped that he had planned for every contingency, but in his heart he knew that was probably impossible. The best he could do was to consider all the resulting consequences, do what he could about them, and then let things take their course. Overall he believed that he had covered things as best he could. Because Constance was growing continually weaker they had agreed to do this thing tonight, when they would be alone at Seaside.

Garrett continued to look out over the ocean, thinking. So as not to arouse suspicion, he would leave work at the usual time. Although he very much wanted to say good night to Trent he knew that he could not, for fear of breaking down and uttering something too revealing. Nor did he dare visit his parents or his sister this night for the same reason.

If he and Constance failed in the attempt, he would then take Constance's place and be imprisoned at Seaside, trapped forever between the worlds of life and death. His only hope for salvation would occur if someone else came along and loved him the way that he loved Constance, and if she were willing to risk her life to try freeing him. But he knew the likelihood of such a thing happening twice was virtually impossible. And so, if he became trapped between worlds he would likely remain that way for all time. He could only stand by and watch, desperately hoping that Christine would finish the restoration of the house as he had intended it to be.

And so it was that around 5:30 P.M. Garrett packed up his briefcase then walked downstairs and happily waved good-bye to the receptionist, just as he did every night. Before getting into his Jeep, for what might well be the last time, he turned and took a long look back at his offices. But before he went to join Constance, he had a job to do.

Four hours later Garrett sat in his Jeep, the vehicle's lights off, the motor purring quietly as he waited where the road to Seaside curved leftward and one first saw the house. He could see Constance sitting on the porch, waiting for him. The sun had fallen some time ago and bright stars filled the heavens, while ever-restless waves washed up against the shoreline. He had an important task to perform, but he could only do it when Constance was inside the house, for he didn't want her to know.

As he waited, the passing minutes seemed like hours. How he longed to go and sit with her, but he could not. He must wait here no matter how long it took, and then go join her only when his work was done. After another twenty minutes or so, he saw her pick up the electric lantern, and she walked into the house.

For ten minutes more he lingered before putting the Jeep into gear and slowly making a wide circle around the house to the left, driving along the edge of the woods that curved around behind the barn. The Jeep's lights still off, he at last came to the place he wanted. An old dirt road, long since covered over with branches and leaves wound its way into the woods, he knew not how far. He had first seen it during one of his trips to the barn and had always meant to walk that road and discover where it led, but hadn't done so. Using only the moonlight to guide his way, he carefully inched the Jeep up the road until both the barn and the lights shining from within Seaside were gone from view.

After traveling another fifty yards or so he found a relatively clear space on the right, shining in the moon-light. He stopped the Jeep, killed the engine, and then went to investigate it. The small, relatively bare area seemed perfect for his needs.

He then returned to the Jeep to grab up the shovel and pickax lying on the passenger-side floor. After carrying the tools to the small clearing, he first loosened a section of ground with the pickax then dug a deep hole with the shovel. When he had finished he went back to the Jeep, started the engine again, and drove the vehicle close to the waiting hole. Little by little he removed the contents of the Jeep, placed them into the hole, and then finally filled the hole with the remaining dirt, followed by enough leaves and branches to ensure that the place looked undisturbed.

Thinking, he glanced around. After a few minutes he found three stones, which he brought back to the clearing. He made a small pile in the center of the clearing—one not so obvious that it would appear staged to some passerby, but enough to mark the spot for someone who knew where to look.

His task complete, Garrett loaded the tools back into the Jeep, started the engine again, and then returned by way of the same route. Once he reached the road, he switched on the lights and drove to the house.

Chapter 31

The house was dark, save for some light coming through the dining room windows, where Constance was waiting for him. As usual, he was about to turn off the engine when he stopped himself. If things did not go well tonight, there was no point in anyone having to hunt for car keys. And so he drove the Jeep around to one side of the house, then he killed the engine and purposely left the keys in the ignition.

Constance was sitting on the sofa. She had not lit a fire in the fireplace tonight, and Garrett silently approved of her precaution, should things go totally awry. He put his briefcase down on the coffee table and smiled at her as best he could. To his great dismay, she looked the worst he had ever seen.

Clearly her deterioration was progressing even more rapidly now, and he found himself doubting that she would survive for more than another two or three days this way.

He sat down beside her and looked into her eyes.

"Hello there," he said to her. "How are you feeling?"

Constance closed her eyes and nodded. The lines on her face were deeply etched now, her hair had become uniformly gray, and she was very thin. Worst yet, her physicality had become so translucent that it was almost as if she wasn't there at all. She had failed so much even since saying good-bye to him this morning that he could scarcely believe it.

"I am here, Garrett," she said weakly. Then she did her best to smile back at him. "I stand ready to do this, but I fear that you must carry me to the roof. As it was, I could hardly make it to the sofa."

Although they were far too large on her now, she was wearing her favorite clothing that he had bought her— the white blouse, the dress jeans, the leather jacket, and the cowboy boots. She clutched her new purse in her hands, causing him to wonder. After pointing at her purse, he smiled mischievously.

"Planning on going somewhere?" he asked.

She smiled back.

"I am hoping so," she answered. "But first, some handsome devil that I know is going to have to lift me up into his strong arms."

He looked at her purse and smiled again.

"Do you think we can take things along where we're going?" he asked.

"I have no idea, but I could see no harm in trying."

With that, Garrett's expression turned more serious. Reaching out, he ran one hand through her hair, then he lovingly stroked her cheek.

"If we don't make it, there's something that I want you to know," he said. "I—"

"I know," Constance answered. "I have always known."

Garrett stood up.

"Then it's time, my love," he said to her.

Garrett helped her to stand, then he picked her up in his arms. To his surprise, she felt light as a feather, as if there was nothing left of her. After taking a last look around he carried her up the stairs, then up the second flight of stairs that led to the roof.

It was a beautiful evening. The dark night sky was filled with lovely stars and a light breeze caressed their faces as Garrett and Constance gazed out at the ocean. The newly refurbished widow's walk glistened beautifully in the moonlight, as if beckoning them to come sit upon one of its benches and languidly take in the view. But they could not do so this night, because time was running out. Still holding Constance in his arms, Garrett looked into her eyes.

"Can you stand?" he asked her.

"I think so."

Garrett set her feet gently down upon the roof and helped to steady her. He then looked back at the widow's walk, and to the sledgehammer he had put there before leaving for work this morning. Its business end sat on the floor, and its strong wooden handle lay propped against the bench.

"I have a bit of work to do," he said to Constance.

"I know," she answered. "It's a shame, but it must be done."

Garrett went back to the widow's walk and picked up the sledgehammer. He then climbed to the second floor, where he began boldly swinging the sledgehammer against the front rail that faced the Atlantic Ocean. After a few stout blows the rail gave way, its many splintered pieces falling down onto Seaside's roof. He then climbed down, walked to the farthest most edge of the roof, and threw the sledgehammer as far away into the night as he could. When he returned to Constance, he saw tears tracing down her cheeks.

"What is it?" he asked.

Constance shook her head and wiped her eyes.

"Silly me," she answered. "Even though that widow's walk was the beginning of all our troubles, I still hated seeing it destroyed like that."

Garrett turned and gazed back at the widow's walk, its beauty again broken and disgraced. He then took a long, final look out across the waves of the Atlantic before gazing back into Constance's eyes. Even during the short time it had taken to come up here, he could see that she had faltered further.

"It's time," he said to her gently.

"I know," she answered. "But you must carry me with you when you do this. I just do not have the strength anymore."

Garrett again picked her up in his arms. She seemed so small and frail lying there, clutching at her purse and hoping for the best. Garrett carried her to the edge of the roof near the front of the widow's walk then he turned and backtracked about twenty paces.

When he again looked down at her, this time there was the slightest trace of a smile on her lips.

"Have I ever told you that you have the most beautiful eyes?" she asked weakly.

When Garrett hadn't the heart to respond, Constance closed her eyes and placed her cheek against his shoulder.

"It is all right, Garrett," she whispered to him. "Please, just carry me away . . ."

With tears in his eyes, Garrett gave her one last kiss on the forehead.

He then took a deep breath, ran as fast as he could toward the edge of the roof, and leapt into the air.

Chapter 32

I can hear other people in the house, Constance thought sleepily. *Jay Morgan's workmen must be here already. And if the workmen are here, then . . .*

With a start, Constance sat up in her bed. If the crew was here, she needed to be up and about. Still not fully awake, she meandered sleepily across the bedroom and opened the armoire. But this time what she saw astonished her.

Rather than finding her usual clothes, she was staring wide-eyed at items she could scarcely recognize. There were chemises, corsets, crinolines, several elaborate dresses, and a collection of slipperlike shoes and button-up boots, to name only some. She quickly pulled a few items out of the armoire and stood looking at them with disbelief, as if they had just been delivered to her from the moon. Very slowly, her memories of them began to return.

When Constance at last turned around and took a good look at the bedroom, she gasped. It was just as she remembered from long ago. All of her original furniture had been returned. The set that Garrett bought for her was gone, and in its place were the bed and armoire from her times with Adam. She quickly looked back into the armoire and selected one of the chemises, which she pulled on over her head. Running across the bedroom as fast as she could, she threw open the French doors and hurried out onto the balcony. As she cast her gaze outward, her jaw literally dropped with astonishment.

As usual, across the bay there lay New Bedford. However this was not the same New Bedford she had just left behind. There were sailing ships in the harbor plying to and fro, but she saw no skyscrapers, modern highways, or automobiles. Completely nonplussed again, she literally staggered backward, trying to understand what had happened. Just then another thought seized her.

She ran pell-mell back into the bedroom to stand before the full-length mirror. To her surprise and delight, she was youthful again, and seemingly no longer a prisoner of the *mora mortis*. For the first time in more than 170 years, she felt totally vibrant and full of life. In her heart she knew that she had somehow been returned to her own time as a fully flesh-and-blood woman.

Clearly at least part of her and Garrett's attempt at freedom had succeeded. But never in her wildest dreams had she imagined that she would be sent back to her original place and time. Nor had this been one of the scenarios suggested by Brooke Wentworth, that day in Salem. Then again, Brooke had also mentioned that any number of differing outcomes might occur. Could this truly be one of them? Constance wondered.

Suddenly, the idea that it had all been a dream seized her imagination. Yes, she realized, that was a possibility, but how could she know for sure? There might be one way. She quickly scanned the bedroom again, searching for something. After a few moments she saw it, and she drew a quick breath.

The purse that Garrett had bought for her—the same one that she had been holding when they made their leap from the roof—sat on her bureau at the other side of the room. She immediately went to it and picked it up gingerly, as if it might not be real or might somehow vanish at her slightest touch.

It's true! she realized. *It all really happened!*

Her mind suddenly awash with questions, her next thoughts turned to Adam and Garrett. *Is Adam really dead?* she wondered. *And is Garrett now trapped here at Seaside between worlds, just as I once was?*

She quickly crossed the room and tore open one of the bureau drawers, where she now remembered keeping her calendar. The crossed-out calendar days indicated that today was September 19, 1840. When she saw the date her heart sang, because no one had to remind her of when the *Intrepid* went down. That had been October 19, 1840, exactly one month from now. Today was therefore also one month before she had plunged from the widow's walk and her and Adam's simultaneous deaths, which thereby stirred the *mora mortis* to life.

If this calendar is correct, Constance quickly realized, *then Adam still lives and he is aboard the* Intrepid*! But what happened to Garrett?*

Desperate to find out, she dressed as quickly as she could, while trying to remember how to wear each of the various items. When at last she was finished, she tore down the circular staircase, then searched the various rooms, looking for Emily and Eli. At last she found Emily in the kitchen, where she was busily working some dough with a rolling pin and humming to herself. Constance embraced her joyously, nearly lifting the startled black woman off her feet.

"Oh, Emily!" she shouted. "How I have missed you!"

Emily gave Constance a curious look before going back to rolling her dough.

"I am not surprised," she said laconically. "Eli and me thought you were going to sleep the whole day away, girl."

Constance looked at her questioningly.

"What time is it?" she asked.

"It's goin' on noon," Emily answered.

Constance took a moment to look around the kitchen. Despite how long it had been for her, everything seemed just as it was before her nightmarish journey had begun. The cupboards, countertops, larders, and the big woodstove all seemed to speak to her like old friends. Then she remembered Garrett again.

"Tell me," she said to Emily, "have there been any gentleman callers lately?"

"Nope," Emily answered, still working diligently on her biscuit dough. "But why would you be asking such a thing anyway, Miss Constance? You've done been here just as much as me, and Eli. If'n anybody had come around, you'd have known it."

Emily was right, of course, given her limited perspective. So far as she and Eli knew, Constance had presumably retired as usual last night, and then simply awakened late this morning. Even so, that still didn't explain what had become of Garrett. Knowing that she had to find out, Constance made for the kitchen door.

"I'm going for a walk, Emily," she said.

Emily raised an eyebrow.

"Where to?" she asked.

"Just around the property," Constance answered. "It is a lovely day, and I want to stretch my legs."

Constance first circled Seaside slowly, looking everywhere, but Garrett did not appear. That was not a surprise, because Brooke Wentworth had said that only one person would be able to see and hear him, should he become resigned to Constance's previous fate. As she passed before the front of the house, she noticed Adam's sailboat bobbing lightly at anchor in the bay, and she smiled as she was reminded of her flashback with him.

She then headed toward the back of the house again and walked the short distance to where Eli and Emily lived. On entering the smaller home she looked everywhere, but again Garrett was not to be found. She then searched the barn thoroughly, lingering for a few moments at the small corner on the second floor where, in a different life and time, she had often come seeking refuge. After still finding no trace of Garrett, she finally returned to the house, where she took a seat on the veranda.

Despite her joyous return here, Constance soon began to weep. She now knew that she would never see

Garrett again, or hear his voice, or feel his gentle touch. The one man who could have helped her had somehow found his way to her, loved her unconditionally, and had then been willing to literally lose his life to set her free. But now, he was no more. In truth, she might never really know whether Garrett had been killed by the fall, or whether he had become trapped for all time by the *mora mortis*. If Brooke had been right that day, then it was the latter, and for that Constance was very sorry.

But what would happen to her now? Constance wondered. Although she was home at last, it would take time for her to fully adjust. Still, she was beyond happy. She had taken an amazing, decades-long trip into the future and returned, an experience that would no doubt prove to be unlike any other in her life. She also realized that she now knew things about this world's future of which no one else on the planet could ever dream. Best of all there was a chance, albeit a slim one, that Adam might still be alive. Despite how much she had cared for Garrett, and how grateful she would forever be for his willingness to help save her, she desperately yearned to be in her husband's arms again.

Was that too much to hope for? she wondered. Perhaps. But for now, it was a chance to which she would cling with all her heart.

Chapter 33

During the next few months, Constance gradually settled into her new life. Truth be told, hers was not a "new" existence, but an old one. Eli and Emily were just as she remembered them, and whether she was experiencing a challenging day or an easy one, she was always thrilled by her surroundings.

Among all the changes, none was greater than the return of her appetite. A few hours after searching for Garrett that first day, she suddenly realized she was ravenous. Like the unexpected return of some old friend, it was a welcome experience. She had immediately asked Emily for something to eat, whereupon Emily rustled up some fried chicken, collard greens, and warm biscuits made from the dough she had prepared that morning.

There were other changes, as well. Although she had Eli and Emily to help her, she had forgotten how rigorous life in this era could be. She helped tend the animals, cleaned and cooked, and for the first week was absolutely exhausted. Even so she didn't mind, because she was doing things that she loved, and it felt wonderful to be useful again.

Compared to the decades-long deterioration of Seaside that she had seen, her home was beautiful. Seaside was exactly how it would have appeared, had Garrett been able to finish his restoration. Constance could only hope that one day someone else might own Seaside who also fully appreciated it.

Despite all her newfound happiness, there remained two great disappointments. The first was that the *Intrepid* had yet to return. She was again climbing to the widow's walk twice daily to search for her husband's ship. There she would sit on the bench and use Adam's old spyglass to carefully scour the bay and horizon, looking for a vessel flying a bright red pennant. Given all the possibilities that Brooke had mentioned, Constance couldn't know whether Adam would ever come home. However she refused to abandon these little rituals, for if her incredible journey had taught her anything, it was the amazing power of perseverance.

It was midmorning of a Tuesday. Eli and Emily were busily working in the house, while Constance sat alone on the veranda. Looking down, she again saw the locket containing Adam's portrait that she still wore. Even after so many years, it meant more to her now than ever. She opened the old locket and again looked at her husband's likeness. How she wished that he would return to her! Her needs for him were both emotional and physical, and despite that Eli and Emily believed only a few months had passed, for Constance it been many long decades.

The second disappointment was that there had been no sign from Garrett. She had hoped that he might display some indication of his presence, as she had done for him, that day with Jay Morgan. However nothing had happened, causing her to finally accept that Garrett was dead.

He died for me, she thought sadly, *and I will never forget him. In the end I could not love him as he loved me, and I believe he knew that. Still, he went to his death saving me. How I wish he could have known that he succeeded, and that I arrived back here safely.*

Constance gathered up her spyglass and began making for the widow's walk. On reaching the roof she took her usual seat on the bench. Before searching the ocean, she paused for a moment to regard this simple structure of wood and nails that had been the catalyst of her amazing journey.

She carefully examined the front rail. Just now it seemed safe, but she also knew that if left to the elements long enough, it would become dangerous. She then smiled as she remembered how Garrett had taken a sledgehammer to it, so that no one would suspect suicide. She still could not grasp that although she had watched him do it only three weeks ago, if that act of destruction were to actually ever happen, it would occur some 170-odd years from today.

I will never understand the workings of all this, she realized. *But now that I am home again, perhaps that doesn't matter.*

Constance stood and raised the glass to one eye. The day was sunny and bright, allowing her to see a good distance. As usual she first examined each sailing vessel plying the harbor, but none carried a red pennant.

She then cast her gaze farther out to sea, where the pickings were always harder to identify. There she saw two more vessels, perched on the horizon. To her experienced eye, the first looked like a small cargo ship, and was therefore too small to be a whaler. The second was a bit more difficult to ascertain. When she finally saw the sun glinting off two rows of menacing cannon along the port hull, Constance put her down for an American naval vessel.

She was about to take the glass from her eye when she heard a voice calling to her. At first she thought it was the ocean breeze wafting through the structure, for when the wind was just right it sometimes tricked one's ears that way. Then she heard it again.

Look again, the unknown voice seemed to whisper. *Look again . . .*

She returned the glass to her eye and scoured the horizon. This time she saw a third ship there, only recently appeared. As Constance examined her, her heart beat faster.

At first she couldn't be sure, but after a time she thought she saw the tiniest bit of red, flying high upon one of the masts. Bright red, she later realized, and perhaps shaped into a triangle. Her mind racing, she hoped against hope that this was real, and not some Cape Horn widow's mirage. She stood that way for another hour, straining to see it until at last she was sure. With tears of joy streaming down her face, she ran back downstairs as quickly as she could.

After more than two full years at sea, the *Intrepid* had finally come home.

Chapter 34

"Hyaaah!" Eli Jackson shouted as he snapped his buggy whip again.

Eli disliked using the whip on the horses. However this was no ordinary day, and so he cracked the whip again, urging the two stallions faster. Constance sat behind Eli in the carriage, holding on to her windblown bonnet as best she could. It had taken her mere seconds to hurry downstairs and order Eli to prepare the carriage. The moment Constance got settled, Eli snapped the reins across the stallions' haunches, and they went charging down the road.

Constance was nervous beyond all reason. The ship she saw was the *Intrepid*, she had been sure of it. In all the time she had spent searching the ocean, no previous vessel had ever flown a bright red pennant.

Even so, she couldn't help worrying about how she might live, if her beloved Adam had indeed been lost at sea. Although she had not seen the *Intrepid* sink, she had seen Adam swept overboard, which in turn breathed fresh life into the *mora mortis* and exiled her to a place between worlds. And because the *Intrepid* was arriving today, nearly a full week before she was supposedly lost, Constance had absolutely no idea what to expect.

Despite that terrible flashback she and Garrett shared, even now Constance couldn't know whether it had been real, or just a dream. What does it all mean? she wondered. Would she and Adam at last share a warm bed this night? Or come the morrow would she have to don widow's garb and begin arranging a memorial?

When at last they reached the piers, the area was already a madhouse. Given all the wagons, sailors, carriages, and townspeople that had arrived ahead of them, Eli was forced to take their carriage three streets over. After tying the horses to a street stanchion, Eli helped Constance down from her seat. As she straightened her bonnet, he could see tears building in her eyes.

"Don't you worry, Miss Constance!" he said. "You look just fine! Cap'n Adam's gonna be mighty glad to see you!"

"Thank you, Eli," she said as she put up her parasol.

She took a few quick steps down the street then stopped and turned around.

"Aren't you coming?" she asked.

Eli smiled and shook his head.

"No, ma'am," he answered. "I can't say exactly why, but somethin' tells me this moment belongs to just you and the cap'n. So you go along now, Miss Constance. Go and collect your man, so that we can take him on home where he belongs."

After giving Eli a warm smile, Constance hurried on down the street. When she finally arrived at the pier, it took some time to wend her way through the crowd, but she eventually found herself standing at the bow gangplank. There was so much noise and bustle that she could hardly hear herself think, but that did not keep her from looking up and reading the name of the ship. Finally, after so much time and heartache, she saw it. To her great delight, the name plaque read: *Intrepid.*

Constance immediately cast her gaze along the gunwale, but the bright midday sun made searching difficult. Men, goods, and seemingly endless barrels of whale product were streaming from the ship now, the entire scene near pandemonium as she desperately tried to find her husband.

She soon noticed someone standing near the top of the gangplank. His back was to the sun, which made seeing his face difficult. He seemed to be searching the crowd below, and as he came down the gangplank she instinctively ran to greet him. Yet when Constance looked into his face she was stunned beyond all reason, for the man standing before her was not Adam.

It was Garrett.

When he found her, his smile was joyous. He immediately took Constance in his arms, lifting her off her feet and literally twirling her around. When at last he set her down again, he stole a moment to look deeply into her eyes.

Bewildered to the point of speechlessness, Constance could scarcely breathe. Garrett was wearing the exact sort of clothing that Adam would've, had it been he who had just walked down the gangplank. She could even see Adam's scrimshaw necklace hanging about Garrett's neck.

"You're here!" he exclaimed. "You made it too!"

"Garrett . . ." she finally whispered. "Is it really you?"

Smiling again, Garrett placed his hands on either side of her face.

"Yes, Constance," he answered. "It's really me."

Her tears starting to come again, Constance asked, "But how can this be? I don't understand . . ."

"I'm sorry, Constance," he answered, "but I wasn't completely honest with you before we leaped from the widow's walk. I couldn't be, if we were to have the slightest chance of finding each other again . . ."

Constance's eyes desperately searched his. "What— what are you talking about?"

Garrett produced an envelope from his captain's jacket and he handed it to her.

"What's this?" she asked.

"That's a letter from Brooke Wentworth," Garrett answered. "She had it delivered to me shortly after our visit to Fairlawn. Please read it, Constance. It will explain everything far better than I ever could."

With trembling fingers Constance unfolded the letter and began to read:

Dearest Garrett,

Please forgive me for writing this letter after the fact but I didn't know how else to approach the issue, given that Constance accompanied you to Fairlawn. Please know that everything I told you is the truth, and I hope that you and Constance have decided to take the leap of faith I described. Yet

*there is more that you need to know, and you will
find it startling. I would have told you all this during
our meeting, but I felt it best to inform you later,
because it may not be something you will wish to
share with Constance. I know of no other way to
explain this, so I will say it as plainly as I can:*

*Simply put, I believe you are the reincarnation
of Adam Canfield.*

*I know this comes as a huge shock, but in retro-
spect it makes perfect sense. The mora mortis de-
scribes this possibility in great detail. That is, the
person who so loves the trapped soul might well be
someone from that person's past reincarnated;
someone whom the other loved very deeply. I know
you will find all of this quite overwhelming, but you
simply must keep an open mind while I explain.*

*By your own admission, ever since you met
Constance, and even before that when you first
dreamed of her, you felt an irresistible pull toward
her unlike anything you had ever experienced.
Moreover, you always had an immense love for
Seaside. You also felt a compulsion to own it, to
renovate it in the classic manner, and to live there
for the rest of your life. In addition you accompanied Constance on several of her flashbacks, the
most important of which was when you both saw*

Adam perish in the sea. The mora mortis wanted the two of you to witness Adam's death, so that you might truly begin understanding the nature of your situation.

This also explains the meaning of the flashback that I expect has always been the most puzzling for you—that is, when you were taken back in time and found yourself making love to Constance. I believe that this was yet again the mora mortis's way of trying to show you who you really are. Will you ever know with certainty whether you were Adam or Garrett at that moment? I doubt it. But if you are truly Adam reincarnated, does it matter?

In hindsight all these things make perfect sense and have convinced me that you are truly the reincarnation of Adam Canfield, reborn seventeen decades later, and ultimately destined to save Constance from her terrible imprisonment. Which of course also means that Adam did actually die in that terrible storm off Cape Horn. As I told you earlier, should the two of you leap from the roof, I have no way of knowing your fates. Yet if, as I fervently hope, you are the reincarnation of Adam, I pray that you and Constance will somehow find each other again. For you see, Garrett, your love for Constance and your purchase of Seaside were not mere coincidences. Instead they were a series of dynamisms caused by the mora mortis so the two of you might have a fighting chance to not only save her, but to also be together as you should. Your past was calling to you. It has been all of your life, and you at last heeded it.

There is one more item of which you should become aware. Again, I did not want to bring this up at the meeting. The Book of Shadows also states that should you and Constance take the leap of faith and succeed, each of you may take along several material things of this day and age. You need only know in your hearts what you wish to keep, and the process will unfold.

In closing, I wish you both all the luck in the world. It is vitally important that you two take the leap of faith from the widow's walk, because if you do not, Constance will truly die, and your soul will likely remain trapped forever. Should I never hear from either of you, my heart will choose to believe that you and Constance did indeed find each other yet again across the infinite expanse of time, for thinking otherwise would be far too painful. Good luck, Garrett, and God bless.

Fondly,
Brooke

Her hands shaking, Constance refolded the letter and handed it back to Garrett.

"My God . . ." she said.

Garrett nodded.

"Yes, Constance," he answered. "Brooke was right. Adam Canfield is now as much a part of me as Garrett Richmond ever was. I can now do everything that Adam once did and I also carry all of his memories, just as I also carry with me all the knowledge and memories I garnered during my time as Garrett Richmond. I didn't tell you because I believed it would keep you from going through with it. If you knew, I feared that you would have done everything in your power to keep me out of harm's way—especially when it came to leaping from the widow's walk. However, because this was our one chance, I believed that we had to take it. I could only pray that we might somehow survive and be together again."

"So you found yourself on the *Intrepid* as Adam," Constance mused. "But what about the crew? Didn't they wonder who you were?"

Garrett shook his head.

"The moment we leaped from the roof I was sent back in time, and I arrived on the *Intrepid* the very instant Adam was swept overboard. I appeared to all the crew as Adam, and for them it was as if Adam never died. And although you still see me as Garrett, the rest of the world recognizes me as Adam. Only you, it seems, can tell the difference. Despite Adam's death, instead of sinking that night, the *Intrepid* miraculously survived the storm and the time line was altered. I was never so scared in all my life."

As she stared at Garrett's face, tears began filling Constance's eyes.

"And despite knowing all the dangers," she asked him, "you were still willing to risk your life for me?"

"Yes," Garrett answered. "A thousand times yes. If I had it to do all again, my decision would be the same."

"So Adam is . . . ?"

Garrett nodded.

"Yes, my love," Garrett answered. "I'm sorry, but he's gone. He really did die that night aboard the *Intrepid*. It was meant to be. There was nothing about that night that either of us could have changed. I'm sorry about Adam, but I'm here now. I've come across time for you, and if you'll have me, I want us to be together."

Although Constance very much wanted to believe him, she hesitated. She looked at him with beseeching eyes, remembering those days not so long ago when she was desperately trying to convince him of her own bizarre story. Now he was trying to prove his equally strange tale to her, and like Garrett had been, she needed something more to become a believer.

Garrett sensed her hesitation. After thinking for a few moments, he removed his captain's coat and handed it to her. Then he rolled up the left-hand sleeve of his shirt to a place between his elbow and shoulder. When he turned his arm toward Constance, he saw her gasp.

To her amazement, there was a mark on Garrett's arm that was an exact twin to the harpoon scar Adam had carried for so many years. The same one that Constance had claimed to find so endearing, the night of their wedding. The likeness was absolutely identical, and Constance now knew she had no choice but to believe Garrett's story. Yet again, her eyes searched his face incredulously.

"I've carried it all my life," Garrett said. "My parents told me it was a birthmark, and I had always accepted that explanation. However now I know differently, Constance. I even bear Adam's bullet wound scar from his duel with Jack Rackham. I am truly part Adam and part Garrett."

After rolling down his sleeve, he took her into his arms again.

"So please tell me," he said. "Can you find it in your heart to love both of us at once? Because that is who I am now, and from this day forward I always will be."

At that moment everything became clear for her at last, and her imprisoned love for Garrett finally broke through its bonds. It was a great and all-encompassing ardor that she had once done her very best to suppress because of the love she had felt for Adam. She could now also accept that although Adam was really gone, much of him had survived in Garrett, the one man in the world who loved her enough to free her from her many decades of torment. Without a scintilla of hesitation, she pulled him to her and gave him a passionate kiss. At last all of her inhibitions about Garrett had vanished, and her sudden liberation felt joyous, invigorating.

"Yes, my darling," she answered him. "Of course I can love you now. I have waited so long . . ."

Garrett then turned back toward the *Intrepid* and watched the many barrels of oil and bone continuing to be unloaded. This voyage had been highly successful but had also caused him to make a fateful decision. After letting go a long sigh, he looked back into Constance's eyes.

"Although part of me is now a whaling captain," he said, "I am done with all of this. I've already seen enough of it to know. Instead, I want to stay home with you at Seaside and begin my new life. And if you'll have me, to start a family."

His news was like music to her ears.

"Of course, my darling!" she answered joyously. "There is nothing that could make me happier!"

Relieved, Garrett cast his gaze past the *Intrepid* out to where the horizon of the Atlantic met the sky. He was finally home. This was where he belonged, and he had at last found the one woman he was meant to love. Even so, he still carried regrets. He would desperately miss his friends and family whom he had left behind when he and Constance made their leap of faith. They would be desolate, of course, all the while assuming he had fallen from the widow's walk to his death on the rocky shore below, his body having apparently washed out to sea. But it did him no good to wonder about such things anymore, and he knew it.

Brooke Wentworth had been right. This had all been a test of love designed to ascertain whether he and Constance deserved the chance to free her. He now also understood that in the end, the *mora mortis* had put him and Constance together because it was with her that he rightfully belonged. Moreover, the experience had changed him. His amazing love for Constance had made him more reflective and more tolerant. He was no longer one to laugh at the eternal verities, or to scoff at the possibility of forces in the universe that were far greater than mankind, for he had now experienced the true power of such wondrous things.

Then he finally smiled a bit as he remembered something his father recently said to him—the same father he still loved so much, but would never see again: *"If you want to hear God laugh, just try telling him your plans . . ."*

As for Constance, like Garrett she still didn't fully understand how or why all this had happened, nor did she believe that she ever would. Even so she was content because in the end, the fates had been kind. She was finally happy, and that was what truly mattered. Constance now fully realized that of all the men in the world, Garrett was her one true soul mate, and she was at last free to be with him in every way that true love demanded.

Before escorting Constance from the pier, Garrett took a moment to look up at the bright red pennant still attached to the *Intrepid's* mainmast. Constance also raised her face to admire it.

"Do you want to take the pennant home with us?" he asked. "If so, I will order one of the crew to fetch it."

Constance shook her head.

"No, my love," she answered. "It has done its job, and we shan't be needing it anymore."

Garrett smiled at her.

"Then at last it's time to go home," he said.

However, as they began walking to the waiting carriage, a growing look of concern crossed Constance's face. The change in her expression was not lost on him.

"What is it?" he asked.

"If you no longer go to sea," she said, "then how will we live?"

To her surprise, Garrett let go a little laugh.

"Do you remember the hundred-thousand-dollar check Brooke gave us, that day out at Fairlawn?" he asked.

"Certainly."

When Garrett again looked into Constance's eyes, he smiled mischievously.

"Well," he said, "before we took the leap of faith I cashed her check and converted all those funds into gold bars. Then I loaded them into the back of my Jeep and buried them in the woods behind Seaside. When I finished, I made the wish that those gold bars and Brooke's letter were what I wanted to accompany me, should our leap of faith succeed."

Constance gasped.

"My God, Garrett!" she said. "Do you really think that the gold came back with you?"

Garrett stopped walking and took her hands into his.

"I do indeed," he answered.

"Then that means . . ."

"Yes," Garrett said. "Before we took the leap, I did a little research. In today's currency those gold bars are worth about three million dollars. We're filthy rich!"

Pausing for a moment, he looked deeply into her eyes.

"How fine ye are to me, wife," he said.

As she realized that at last all the promises had been made and all the pacts had been sealed, Constance smiled.

"And how fine ye are to me, husband," she answered.

Just as the happy couple rounded the next corner, Eli spotted them and began happily running their way. Thinking, Garrett pursed his lips.

"You know," he said to Constance, "there's something that you must begin doing right now, or people like Eli will start to wonder about us."

Constance gave him a quizzical look.

"And what might that be, my love?" she asked

Laughing a little, he put one arm through hers.

"You must start calling me Adam."

HarperLUXE

THE NEW LUXURY IN READING

We hope you enjoyed reading
our new, comfortable print size and found it
an experience you would like to repeat.

Well – you're in luck!

HarperLuxe offers the finest in fiction and
nonfiction books in this same larger print size and
paperback format. Light and easy to read, HarperLuxe
paperbacks are for book lovers who want to see
what they are reading without the strain.

For a full listing of titles and
new releases to come, please visit our website:
www.HarperLuxe.com